D0786860

ODYSSEY'S
END

ODYSSEY'S END

A RICK CAHILL NOVEL

MATT COYLE

OCEANVIEW(C)PUBLISHING
SARASOTA, FLORIDA

ISBN 978-1-60809-481-3

Published in the United States of America by Oceanview Publishing

Sarasota, Florida

www.oceanviewpub.com

10 9 8 7 6 5 4 3 2 1

PRINTED IN THE UNITED STATES OF AMERICA

For Angus

The best four-legged writing partner a writer could ever have. You were at my side in the office for the writing of all ten Rick Cahill novels. You are missed, but always remembered, and your spirit lives on in Midnight.

ACKNOWLEDGMENTS

My sincerest thanks go to the following people for helping to make this book the best it could be:

My agent, Kimberley Cameron, for her friendship, expertise, advocacy, and an important confidence-building read.

Bob and Pat Gussin, Lee Randall, Faith Matson, and Tracy Sheehan from Oceanview Publishing for doing a great job of publishing and marketing this book and for putting up with me for all these years.

Lisa Daily for finding new, innovative ways to market this book and for an important late read.

Pam Stack and Jane Ubell-Meyer for additional marketing expertise.

Nancy Denton for the vital and ever-expanding paper-clip read.

Allison Davis and Dsu-Wei Yuen for information on cryptocurrency exchanges.

Dan Williams for hooking me up with a military special operator who prefers to remain anonymous and who educated me on automatic weapons and suppressors.

George Fong for information on FBI Special Agents.

David Truett for information on the underside of a 2019 Honda Civic.

Amanya Wasserman whose question to me in 2021 led to an important location in this book and to a number of new friendships.

Juliet Grossman for creating book club discussion questions and for being an important part of the team.

Lisa Daily, Joan Brown, and Kim Bowser for invaluable support when it was most needed.

Any errors regarding weapons, the FBI, Honda Civics, or cryptocurrency exchanges are strictly the author's.

ODYSSEY'S
END

CHAPTER 1

I HADN'T SEEN Peter Stone in five years. Not since the night he saved my life. When he'd wielded a shotgun with deadly efficiency. Five years before that, he'd tried to kill me with a handgun. Maybe I wouldn't have been so lucky the first time if he'd had a shotgun.

Stone had changed a lot since the night he'd blown away two assassins in his lair up in the hills above La Jolla.

His gray hair still spiked to a widow's peak dagger point on his long forehead, but now the dagger started farther up. His eyes still beamed menace, but they'd lost their soulless shark void. Still a predator, even with his Parkinson palsy, but less dangerous. His once lean, athletic frame, now thin and slumped and leaning on an ivory-handled cane. As if the sum of a lifetime of malicious machinations finally weighed him down. Pulled at him.

Like everyone who's ever walked the earth but one, Stone couldn't escape the degradations of time. It doesn't matter how much money you have or how narcissistic your behavior. Time erodes us all.

Could the ravages of life have possibly made Peter Stone human?

Maybe, but I doubted it. Yet, there he stood on my porch at 7:30 a.m. in early November. Slightly stooped, a shudder to his left hand and his head. Looking very much human. Even vulnerable.

But like wild animals, former casino owners and real estate moguls are at their most dangerous when injured.

Even those who no longer exist.

That's why I grabbed a Colt Python off the top shelf in my hall closet after I checked the peephole in the front door. I had guns hidden all over the house. One of the reasons my estranged wife took our child to live with her parents. She thought I was paranoid. Maybe I was, but when Peter Stone is standing on your porch, there is no such thing as paranoia. I opened the door.

"Stone." It wasn't an invitation, a greeting, or a question. Just a statement. A bad memory that had suddenly returned. Unexpectedly. Like cancer after decades of remission.

"Rick, you've aged. And the glasses are new since our last encounter." His voice had lost some of its melodious command. The hot tar on asphalt viscosity that used to make each verbal barb sink deep beneath the skin was gone. Now a slight creak thinned out the timbre. Still, a fresh gleam shined the menace in Stone's pale gray eyes. He was happy with himself. Always was when he could stick a knife in. And twist it.

Visually, his dig had no merit. I looked much the same as I had that night on the hill above the ocean when he saved my life. I had a sampling of gray hairs that hid among the brown. My back, still straight. My chest and chin, still high. I did have scars. More than when Stone last saw me. But my collared shirt covered most of them, and my glasses hid the remaining hollow under my eye.

The real damage from my life of violence was invisible. Hiding in the whirls of my brain. CTE. Chronic Traumatic Encephalopathy. Prognosis: diminishing cognitive capabilities, dementia, and early death. One of its symptoms, irrational rage, had been the final slice through my marriage that now hung together by a single thread stretched from San Diego to Santa Barbara. Where my wife and twenty-month-old daughter now lived. Only two-hundred-ten miles away, but a lifetime when I was apart from my family.

CTE. The hidden truth. Locked up in a back room like the portrait of Dorian Gray. Disfigured. But Stone couldn't know anything about my disease. Only my doctor, a couple of nurses, my wife, and my best friend knew what no one else could see.

"What do you want, Stone? Is there an FBI minder in a dark sedan parked on the curb?" I stretched my neck to look around him through the front door. "Shouldn't you be off playing dominoes in a clubhouse in Sun City, Arizona, under an assumed name?"

Stone had gone into witness protection shortly after testifying against a Russian Mob boss months after he saved my life.

"You don't have many friends in San Diego, but there must still be plenty of enemies. At best, I'm somewhere in between." No vengeance in my voice. Maybe a trace of sarcasm to cover the anxiety I always felt when Peter Stone barged back into my life.

And he *had* tried to kill me. But saving my life once with a gun and brokering for it another time on the phone evened that out. The other stuff was gone, if not forgotten.

Still, Peter Stone was not a man you wanted to see standing on your front porch at any time of the day. Really, not a man you wanted to see anywhere.

"Well, aren't you going to invite me in?" He smiled a predator's grin.

"You haven't told me what you want. If it's breakfast, you're too late."

"I want to hire you."

CHAPTER 2

"I'VE NEVER WORKED for someone who doesn't exist." I looked at the menacing eyes. "And I don't think I want to."

"Very few people are lucky enough to maneuver through life guided solely by their wants, Rick." He made a big show of looking over my shoulder into my house. "Most are forced to chase after their needs."

As usual, Stone's barb pierced the truth. My house was not as modest as his neck wrenching made out, but it wasn't a home I'd want over others, say, in La Jolla where Stone used to live before he vanished into his new life as somebody else. Every month was a scramble to pay the mortgage on the house I needed. Particularly with Leah living in Santa Barbara with our daughter, Krista. Leah was working again, but up there. My nut was my nut alone down here.

I still had hopes that we'd all be together as a family again in San Diego. But that had gone from an unlikely possibility to a pipe dream.

Leah and I worked out an arrangement where I had Krista roughly two weeks out of the month. The time away from her was agony. So was the time away from Leah. I grabbed every private investigative job I could on my off weeks to try to put away money for Krista's future. A kickstart or a small cushion to land on when life knocked her down. And life would. It always did. And, more than likely, I wouldn't be around to catch her.

I'd last seen Krista a week ago and I already ached for her. When I pulled her out of her car seat once we'd arrived home from Santa Barbara, she folded down the two inside fingers of her right hand so just her index and little finger were sticking up and said, "Dada." She repeated it over and over, looking expectantly at me. Then she started crying. I called Leah and found out she'd been teaching Krista baby sign language so she could communicate what she needed to when she couldn't pronounce, or didn't know, the correct words.

Krista was telling me in sign language that she loved me.

And I didn't respond. Didn't tell her that I loved her too. I tried to make up for it the whole two weeks we were together.

Leah and Krista were moving forward, and I was standing still. Krista's present was divided between Santa Barbara and San Diego. I couldn't change that. Not yet. But a brighter future for her was within reach if I could land a case that could lay her a golden nest egg.

And that case might be standing on my porch, staring me in the face. Glaring, really. A double-edged sword. More like a stiletto. Quick and deadly.

I stepped back from the door and let Stone in.

"You've got ten minutes." The truth, but I'd never tell him why my time was short. That I had my weekly Zoom call with a therapist to work on my intermittent explosive disorder. Or more politely, anger management. Compliments of my CTE. Stone would use any of that information to gain the upper hand. Or just for his own amusement.

"The time needed is up to you, Rick." Stone walked past me, a slight wobble to his gait, magnified by the Parkinson's tremor of his cane hand as it kept him from toppling over on his journey to my couch.

Stone, a man used to plowing through life guided by his wants, was now relying on aids to fulfill his needs. It wasn't an ah-ha moment for me. Rather one of sympathy. Tinged with caution. The wounded animal.

Stone sat down with a muffled grunt onto the couch. He rested his cane against his leg and smiled a mirthless smile. I noticed the cane had a heavy silver handle in the shape of a wolf's head.

I sat diagonal to him in my recliner. Fully upright. I wanted to be able to move quickly if the wolf head suddenly came loose from the cane and a blade appeared in Stone's hand.

"Why do you want to hire me?"

"Shouldn't there be a wife and daughter here somewhere?" He looked at Krista's pink toy bin in the corner of the living room. "A belated congratulations on both, by the way."

His usual smug tone. Was he sticking the knife in—or was he just stuck in his default persona? Could he possibly know that Leah and I were estranged? How did he even know that I was married? Had he been keeping track of me from his witness protected life in who knows where?

Why?

The better question was why I even let Stone pass over the threshold into my home. My sanctuary. He could give Krista that jump-start on her future with an envelope full of cash. And he could ruin my life or end it with a phone call or a nod of his head.

Stone was my past. Leah and Krista were my future. I hoped. Right now, they were barely my present.

Midnight, my black Labrador retriever, growled from the other side of the sliding glass door in the backyard. Teeth clenched under his gray snout. I'd put him out back after Stone rang my doorbell. They'd never met, but Midnight was an excellent judge of character. His growl, maybe a conjunction between his read of my unease and his sense of Stone's danger.

"They're not home and they're not your concern." I stood up. Midnight's growl flipped the switch on my self-defense radar. Working for Stone would be a bad decision. "And you're not mine. Sorry I wasted your time. I'm sure you can find another private investigator or . . . someone else who is well-practiced at doing the kind of work that you need. And who is better at it than me."

"Don't sell yourself short, Rick." The death grin. "You and I both know you're quite adept at doing the kind of job you *think* I want you to do. When it suits your needs and, perhaps, wants, you've been known to make life and death decisions."

That was true. I'd killed people in self-defense and in defense of others. Those killings had been in the news and deemed righteous by law enforcement. But there were others. Deaths the police knew about, but that were unsolved. Deaths I considered to be future self-defense or in defense of others, but the police would consider them differently.

Murder.

There's no get-out-of-jail-free-card for future self-defense.

But Stone couldn't know about those. Only one person other than me did.

"Time to go, Stone." I took a step toward the front door. "Your FBI minder is going to start worrying about you. Or whoever knows you're out of your witness protection cubbyhole."

Stone stayed seated. I stopped my exodus and turned toward him.

"Sergei Volkov is getting out of prison in four days." Stone's voice, a blunt object.

"What?" My stomach folded in on itself, and I went back to my chair and sat down. "I thought he got fifteen years. He's only been in five years, max."

"Four and a half."

That wasn't good news for either one of us. Sergei Volkov was a Russian Mob kingpin and a former associate of Stone's. Stone turned state's evidence on Volkov then went into witness protection hiding. I'd tangled with Sergei's daughter and her henchmen a couple times. Stone probably figured that's why I was concerned about Volkov getting out.

But that wasn't the real reason. The real reason was much worse and potentially deadly. For me.

"How is that possible?"

"All things are possible when dealing with the Federal Bureau of Investigation and the Department of Justice." He smirked. "The Department of Justice. There's never been a more ironic name of a governmental agency. Sergei, no doubt, worked out a deal with the square chins at the DOJ. Told them something they wanted to know and was rewarded with an early release."

"Then wouldn't it be better for you to stay hidden in WITSEC instead of sticking your head up now?"

"You mean rely on the enforcement branch of the DOJ who just made a deal with Sergei to get him out of prison? You're not buying into the righteousness of the FBI, are you? They're as corrupt as any large, powerful, governmental entity. More corrupt."

I didn't have to be convinced about the FBI by Stone. I'd had my own encounters with the Feds. And one very bad seed who'd worked for them. I'm sure there were other bad seeds, but that didn't mean they had a mole working for a jailed Russian Mafia boss. If they did, Stone would probably already be dead.

"It doesn't matter what I think. What matters is why you're in San Diego when you should be anywhere but. San Diego or La Jolla would be the first place Volkov would look."

"I'm not worried about my safety. Not yet. I'm worried about Angela." No smirk or dead-eyed glare now. Vulnerability brought life to those normally lifeless eyes.

Angela Albright was Stone's daughter. Although only a couple people still alive knew that. I was one of them. Angela was not. And Stone had good reason, an awful reason actually, to keep it that way. She was the wife of the former mayor of San Diego who made an unsuccessful run for governor of California a decade back. The two of them used to come into Muldoon's Steak House, the restaurant I managed at the time. I hadn't seen or thought about Angela Albright in ten years.

"Why?" I asked.

"I haven't been able to contact her for a month." Stone's eyes flickered humanity. "She's the only family I have left."

Stone's son hadn't followed him into witness protection. He was on the periphery of Stone's illegal enterprises. A tatted-up, pierced dullard who had none of Stone's cunning. They had nothing in common but blood. About a year after Stone disappeared, I heard on the news that his son had died of a drug overdose. Fentanyl.

"I was sorry to hear about your son, and I'm sorry about Angela." My voice dropped. "But I can't help you."

"You may want to rethink that." His eyes morphed back to hollow predator. "I haven't figured out what to do about Sergei yet, but you're going to need *my* help when he comes after *you*."

"Why would he do that?" A tremor roiled my stomach.

"You know why, Rick."

"I don't know what you're talking about." He couldn't know. Only one person did, and she'd never tell anyone. I stood up again. A bravado bluff. Like I had command of my life. "Time to go."

"I'm referring to Tatiana. If I can put the pieces together, Sergei can too."

My heartbeat hit redline.

CHAPTER 3

"No judgment here, Rick." Stone remained seated. "We all have to make tough decisions and take bold action from time to time. Tatiana was a nasty piece of work. A chip off Sergei's block, with his viciousness but without his finesse or intelligence. She was a threat. She had to be put down like the rabid dog she was. I commend you on your ruthless sense of self-preservation. I would have done the same thing."

"Are you trying to tell me in your not-so-subtle way that you think that I killed Tatiana Volkov, and Sergei does too?" I played it off with an exhaled laugh and willed my heartbeat to get back into rhythm. "There are no pieces to put together. I didn't kill Tatiana, and I don't know who did. And if Sergei really thought I'd killed his daughter he would have already tried to have me killed. I'm sure he's still calling the shots. Even in Fed lockup in Victorville."

"He doesn't have all the pieces of the puzzle that I do." A malevolent smile.

"What pieces are those?" I racked my brain about the actions I'd taken late one night five years ago. I'd been careful. Meticulous. No witnesses.

That I knew of.

"I know Tatiana threatened you."

"She threatened a lot of people. She also stabbed me in the leg a long time ago, and I didn't take revenge on her right then when I could have."

"She also threatened your friend Moira MacFarlane." A deadpan stare. "And I know what you'll do to protect those you love."

The blood drained from my face and pooled in my stomach. That threat had come over the phone when I was alone and presumed Tatiana was too. Stone couldn't have had my cell phone bugged. Tatiana's? No. She used burners. He couldn't have been with her at the time of the call. Stone had as bad a relationship with Tatiana as I did.

Could Stone have had a mole in her camp?

Whatever the case, he did have more pieces than I thought were out there. What if he wasn't the only one?

"She did? That's news to me."

"Today, Rick, just today. You're a bad liar." Stone looked at me under raised eyebrows. "I know the truth, and sooner or later Sergei will too."

"Is that a threat?" How far would Stone go to try to force me to his will? I knew how far I'd go to stop him from telling Sergei Volkov what he thought he knew.

"Of course not." Icy smooth. Like black ice on a mountain pass. And just as dangerous. "Just letting you know that you're on a clock. Sergei's clock. One that you don't want to reach midnight."

"So *you* say. You're wasting my time. Tell me your whole piece and leave or just leave."

"Your secret is safe with me, Rick." The mellifluous baritone. The aging squeak now smoothed out of his voice. Confident. Arrogant. At ease in my sanctuary. Where I no longer was.

Another growl from Midnight outside. I looked at him, then back at Stone.

"My dog comes in and you go out. With or without teeth marks. Sixty seconds to spit out the specific reason you're here."

"I want to hire you to find Angela and be her bodyguard until I figure out what to do about Sergei."

"This doesn't make sense. Why would Volkov go after Angela if he doesn't know she's your daughter? Hell, *she* doesn't even know she's your daughter, right?"

"No, Angela doesn't know. And the fact that you didn't tell her is the main reason I'm here today." Stone's voice dropped. "But Sergei knows that Angela is important to me. That's enough reason for him to harm her."

I wondered how Sergei Volkov came to know something so intimate about Stone, who was so concerned about keeping it hidden that he tried to kill me after I found out ten years ago.

"Angela is already in hiding. Wouldn't it be safer to let her stay that way instead of having me go around shaking bushes?" I needed the money, but I couldn't square that with putting an innocent in danger. Not anymore. "Word would get around that I was looking for her."

Stone sat quietly for a moment and stared at the floor. His face a granite slate.

The impenetrable façade fell away to reveal the concerned face of an aging man in his seventies. A con? Maybe. But it was something I'd never seen before in Stone. Eyes alive. With fear.

"My kidneys are failing." He looked down at his left hand, which tremored slightly. "Some researchers think Parkinson's and kidney failure are related. True or not, the fact is that I need a kidney transplant. Angela can give that to me."

"Sorry." I still didn't know if I could believe him. I might never. But if true, it was sad. Even for Peter Stone. But that opened up a new question. "Does this mean that Sergei is not getting out of prison?"

"No. Sadly, it does not mean that. Sergei is, indeed, getting out of prison at the end of the week, and I do fear for Angela's life. But she can also save my own."

"But you don't necessarily need a relative to get a kidney transplant. Are you on a list?"

"An aging Parkinson's patient in WITSEC would be at the very end of any list." He gave me a flat grin. "But I have a doctor, staff, and a facility ready to go, and I've started my own donor list. Would you like to be on it?"

"I'll pass. Thanks." I matched his grin. "Does Angela know about any of this?"

"No, she doesn't know about Sergei or the kidney . . ." He looked away from me. "Or that I'm her father."

I felt sorry for Stone. In the part of me that was still God-fearing, decent, and kind. And I felt sorry for Angela for what she would soon learn if I was able to find her.

"Why didn't you just tell me that up front?"

Stone stared at me for a solid ten seconds before he spoke.

"I'm a proud man, Rick. You know that." A faint smile. "I abhor showing weakness."

The first thing he'd said today that I knew to be 100 percent true.

"How do you even know if she's compatible? Just because she's a relative doesn't mean she's a match, does it?"

"Not necessarily, but we have the same blood type. That's one marker."

"What if she doesn't want to do it?" Giving up a kidney was a lot to ask of anyone. Especially for someone you barely knew, secret father or not.

"Angela will be well compensated for the operation. And will be seen to after in my will." The smirk. "But, of course, she'll be paid more to keep me alive. A lot more."

"Of course." Everything was a business transaction to Stone. Even when it came to blood. His or someone else's. Sometimes spilled.

"Are you going to help me or not?" He gave me a flat, neutral expression. Nothing menacing, like the decision was really up to me.

"You said you had to figure out what to do about Sergei." I squinted my eyes down on him. I didn't want Stone or Sergei Volkov in my life again. For the same and different reasons. "I'm guessing you already figured it out, and I don't want to have anything to do with it."

At the end, only one of them would end up aboveground. The odds favored Sergei, but I'd never count out Peter Stone. I'd seen what his puppets could do when he pulled their strings. And I'd seen him wield a shotgun in close quarters. Even leaning on a cane, Stone was dangerous. But I didn't know how many puppets were still available to him.

However, I was sure he had access to a shotgun. And a full arsenal of other weapons.

"I just want you to find Angela and protect her. It won't be for very long."

"If you want to find Angela, why not talk to Steven Albright? He's a politician. They're easy to find. Just look for a TV camera or a deep-pocketed donor. I'm sure you can find him. He probably still lives in La Jolla."

"Angela and Steven have been divorced for three years. He won majority custody of Casandra. He and Angela barely communicate now. She's not home and hasn't been seen or heard from in a month."

"How do you know all of this? You're supposed to have been holed up somewhere out of touch under an alias."

"I have my sources."

I took a beat to mull over whether I should ask the obvious questions. "Have your sources checked with the police? Hospitals?" The final question that had to be asked. "The morgue?"

"She'd not dead or in jail. She's on a sabbatical somewhere. And I need you to find her."

"What makes you think that she'd allow me to be her bodyguard? I haven't seen her in a decade, and I'm just supposed to show up and tell her I'm there to protect her?"

"Tell her that I sent you and tell her about Sergei." Stone's face pinched tight. "But don't tell her about the kidney...or about the rest."

Stone, Angela. DNA could get complicated. And I had my own to think about.

"I've got my own family to take care of." When I had the chance to see them. "Besides, missing persons is not my specialty. There are plenty of private investigators in San Diego who are better at it than me. You should hire one of them. Or one of your sources."

"You're the only person who knows I'm in San Diego. My sources know how to wag their tails and offer their heads for a scratch behind the ear when it benefits them, but they're mercenaries. They'd sell me out to the first person who offered them a Milk-Bone. You're exactly the man I need for the job. The only person I can trust now."

Trust. Between Peter Stone and me. We'd had an almost decade-long armistice. But I wouldn't call it trust. Only fools and dead men ever trusted Peter Stone.

"We're not friends. Never were. We weren't before you tried to kill me, or even after you saved my life."

"We don't have to be friends. Or even associates." Stone leaned forward on the sofa and stared at me intently. No menace. Sincerity? "I'm asking for help from someone who stood next to me when we lived and our adversaries died. I know you're a man of honor, Rick. You won't sell me out to set yourself up for life." He stood up and put out his hand. "And I'll pay you $50,000."

CHAPTER 4

ANGELA ALBRIGHT'S LAST listed residence was a condo in Carmel Valley, a nice community inland from Del Mar that gets some of the ocean breezes its neighbor does but not the views. Her ex-husband, Steven, was paying the mortgage on the residence, but it wasn't the home where they'd raised their daughter together before the divorce. That was a $3,000,000 house in La Jolla above La Jolla Shores. With a view of the ocean. This was a modest 800 square feet in a complex with thirty-one other similar units.

A bank of key-locked metal mailboxes sat next to the walkway of the complex. The one marked with Angela Albright's address looked like all the rest. No bulging door from too much mail or note left on it requesting she empty the box.

If Angela was on an extended vacation or on the run, she'd had her mail delivery stopped, or someone else was picking it up for her.

Her unit was on the second floor of a two-story block of four condos. I knocked on the front door that was fronted by a wooden deck it shared with the next-door unit. Nothing. I did three rounds of knocks with no response. The shades were drawn, and the only plants on the deck were potted succulents. They could live unattended for years. No sign of how long Angela had been gone. The condos didn't have garages, and her 2020 Tesla Model S wasn't in the parking space with her unit number painted on the asphalt in front of the complex.

Coastal haze pressed down over the morning as I got out of my car. The November sun was a late riser.

I sensed the bulk of the Glock 19 holstered under my left arm beneath my bomber jacket. The sensation felt awkward after not wearing a gun for a while. I'd lost the right to have a concealed carry license after I made a deal with a prosecuting attorney to stay out of jail a couple years ago. That didn't mean I hadn't broken the law since then. I had. But it had been infrequent and only when I felt I could be in danger.

With Peter Stone, and possibly Sergei Volkov, back in my life, danger was an everyday possibility. I couldn't depend on remembering to grab the Glock and stick it in my coat pocket every time I left the house. It had to be a piece of clothing that I felt naked without. Again. I'd hang the holster off the back of my chair in my bedroom every night before I went to bed while I was working for Stone, there to be put on with all the other clothes I'd wear each day.

I knocked on Angela's deck-mate's door. Ten seconds later a woman answered. She looked to be in her seventies with the crinkly leather skin of someone who'd spent a lifetime worshipping the sun.

"How can I help you?" There was the honey hint of a southern drawl, like she'd started life in the Southeast and followed the sun west decades ago.

"I'm trying to locate Angela Albright." I gave her my warmest nice guy smile. *Locate* sounded less aggressive than *find*. "Do you know where she went?"

"Why are you looking for Angela?" A little tart to go with the honey, but not confrontational. I got the sense she was only looking out for her younger neighbor. Good. I might be able to use that concern.

"One of her relatives asked me to contact her." The only phone number I could find for Angela was out of service, and I'd gotten no response to a message I'd sent to the only email address I found for her. I was hoping her neighbor could fill in the blanks.

"Who are you?"

"My name's Rick Cahill. I'm a private investigator." Seventy percent of the time people clam up when they hear "private investigator." I felt optimistic today and was betting on the thirty percent side. Besides, I figured I'd have to tell the woman the truth sooner or later.

"Who hired you?"

"That's confidential, but I can tell you that it's a relative who's quite anxious to locate Angela." Hangdog smile. "Can you help me?"

She studied my face through pale blue eyes. Finally, "I don't know where she is."

I thought she was telling the truth, but not all she knew.

"How long has she been gone?"

"I don't know. She doesn't confide in me. We've only had a few conversations since she moved in here two years ago."

"How long has her car been gone?"

"I don't know."

My weathered southern belle didn't like giving up information on neighbors. The kind of neighbor I'd like if I were living next to her. But not when I was fishing for information on a case.

"Really?" I twisted my head and shoulders toward the parking lot and looked at the old Prius I'd noticed parked next to Angela's space when I arrived. "Your Prius is parked right next to Angela's empty parking space. I'm sure you've noticed her car hasn't been there for a while. I'm just asking you how long it's been gone."

"What did you say your name was again?" She squinted one eye and twisted her head.

"Rick Cahill." I took out a business card and handed it to her.

She read the card then looked back at me. Her eyes caught a spark.

"You ever been on the news?"

Shit. A local news watcher. Didn't come across one of them very often. Although, her age fit the demographic.

"Yeah." Been down this road before. The shine that had already worn off. In fact, it had never been there in the first place. More tedious than anything else. I didn't yearn for the spotlight. I'd never even taken a selfie. I wasn't of my generation.

"I think I saw a story about you shooting some people but not being tried for it." More sparkle. No fear.

"Self-defense." Not precisely, but close enough to be released from jail.

"The news made it sound like the people you killed had it coming to them." A natural born vigilante. Or, at least someone who admired one.

My fifth or sixth fifteen minutes of fame. One where the press only got it partly correct.

"Circumstances out of my control." Mostly. I tried not to sound as weary as I felt after the "this is your life" flashback. "Do you remember how long it's been since you last saw Angela, ma'am?"

"Well." She tilted her head at me and lifted the corner of her mouth. "I think it's been about a month."

"Would you mind telling me your name?" I asked.

"Not at all. It's Alaina. Alaina McCreery."

"Do you know if Angela has a boyfriend?"

"Well." Her sun-bleached eyebrows rose up her forehead. "She's had a few."

A former southern belle's way of saying Angela was promiscuous?

"How many and how often?"

"Five or six in the last year."

"Any repeaters?"

"One. A hunk in a Maserati. Bobby or Billy. Something like that. He was the last one, and he probably came by four or five times."

"Do you remember the last time he was here?" I asked.

"Not exactly, but it was probably a few days to a week before Angela disappeared."

"Do you have Angela's phone number?" Maybe Angela had gotten a number that I hadn't found.

"No."

"Can you call me if you see or hear from Angela, Alaina?"

"You bet." She looked at my business card again, smiled, and put it in her jeans pocket. "Wait here a sec, darling." She went inside and came back out fifteen seconds later with a piece of paper from a small notepad that had a phone number written on it. "You can call me anytime if you have any questions."

I took the piece of paper, folded it, and put it in my wallet.

Alaina McCreery had joined team Cahill. Maybe it was my history of perceived righteous violence. Maybe it was just because I'd been on TV. Either way, a rare benefit to my multiple fifteen minutes of fame.

I checked with all of Angela's neighbors who were home that morning. None of them gave me any information that was different from what I got from Alaina McCreery. And none mentioned that they'd seen me on the news.

CHAPTER 5

STEVEN ALBRIGHT HAD an office in the La Jolla Financial Building on Prospect Street in La Jolla. An old-fashioned cement rectangle that was built in 1973, six years before I was born. My "office," Muldoon's Steak House, was just a few hundred feet up the street. The owner there, Turk Muldoon, let me meet clients in a booth before the dinner rush.

Albright was now a consultant for the biotech industry in San Diego. Biotech was one of the county's biggest and most profitable industries. Possibly a pit stop while Albright decided which ring to throw his hat into next. I never knew a politician to get out of the game when there were still more steps up the ladder. Only when they were forced to or got too old to be able to fake it anymore.

I didn't know what a biotech industry consultant did, but it must have been a profitable endeavor by the looks of Albright's office. The view out the window to the west made up for the blocky look of the front of the building facing the street. A crisp view of the ocean stretching out in deep Pacific blue to the horizon, fronted by Ellen Browning Scripps Park.

A gorgeous vista to get lost in on those slow consulting days.

Albright was seated behind a sleek modern desk facing a wall with a map of San Diego County on it. He swiveled his Ergolux leather executive chair to face me as I stood in front of his desk. The ocean view would always only be one twist away.

"Rick!" Albright smiled, stood up, and stuck out a hand. Not the usual greeting I got when working a case. I could get used to it. "It's been a long time. I miss seeing you at the restaurant."

Muldoon's. A simpler time. Three or four concussions and a few less scars ago. Albright was a natural glad-hander, but the believable warmth of his greeting surprised me.

"Mr. Mayor." I shook his hand. Politicians and soldiers were always given the lifetime honor of being addressed by the highest rank they'd reached while on duty. Must have had something to do with going to war. Either on battlefields in faraway lands or on television screens in people's homes.

Albright was in his early fifties but looked ten years younger. Blond hair without a hint of gray, square chin that could hammer nails, and blue eyes a shade lighter than the ocean behind him. His year-round tan hadn't yet wrinkled his skin, and his prototypical Caucasian good looks were cast in bronze for eternity. Steven Albright, All American.

The only blemish was his divorce from Angela, but that was under the skin, not on it.

"Have a seat and, please, call me Steven." The smile still big and vote-attracting as he sat down. "We go way back. I started having dinner at Muldoon's long before I was Mayor. All the way back to when I was on the La Jolla Town Council."

"Well,"—I sat down in a leather office chair and looked around his office—"you've come a long way since then."

"So have you." Albright sat back down. "Seems like I'm reading about you in the newspaper or seeing you on television every few months. Looks like you made the right move becoming a private eye. Although I know Turk misses you."

Turk and I were still friends, but I doubted he missed me much. He'd always seemed happy running the joint on his own when I stopped by to meet a client.

"The press seems to find me on my busy days and their slow ones." I crossed my leg over my knee. Keeping it friendly. The difficult part was up next. "I'm hoping you can help me with a case I'm working right now."

"I can try." Albright's face went jut-chinned concerned. "What do you need?"

"A relative of your ex-wife has hired me to find her." True. Stone was indeed a relative of Angela. A secret one. Albright and Stone had crossed paths before Stone went under Fed protection. Politicians always know where the wealth is in any city. And Stone had amassed quite a fortune. First as a casino owner in Vegas with Mob connections, then as a real estate mogul-slash-philanthropist in La Jolla and San Diego.

Publicly supporting charities for needy children has a way of whitewashing anyone's soiled background. I didn't know if Stone ever contributed to any of Albright's campaigns, but I wouldn't have been surprised. He would have ulterior motives beyond owning a piece of a politician who could enhance his business interests. He'd be looking out for his daughter's interests, too. Even if the daughter didn't know she had a father looking out for her.

"What's the name of the relative?" Albright's eyebrows rose. "I wonder why they didn't call me on their own."

"The person prefers to remain anonymous. It's an investigator–client privilege thing. I'm sure you understand." Always put the responsibility for propriety on the interviewee. "Do you know where Angela is?"

"No, I don't." Albright's eyebrows furrowed down toward the bridge of his nose. Angela was a sore subject.

"Could you tell me the last time you saw her?" I wanted to know if Albright's timeline matched up with Alaina McCreery's.

"I can't tell you exactly, but it's been at least a month."

"And she hasn't seen Cassandra in all that time?" Their daughter, who had to be high school age now. I remember Angela as an attentive mother. I hadn't seen her in ten years, but for her not to see her daughter for a month seemed out of character.

"No." A quick snap.

"Has she contacted her?"

"Has who contacted who?" Anger tightened his mouth. The next time we met, Albright's greeting wouldn't be so warm.

"Well, either. A month is a long time to go without seeing or speaking to your daughter." Two weeks without seeing Krista was a life sentence, and I at least got weekly Skype calls. "Doesn't Angela have some form of custody?"

"The specifics of custody are none of your business, but Angela is allowed to see Cassie." He shifted in his $1,500 executive desk chair. "I've told you what I know. Angela is not a part of my life anymore. I'm not responsible for her whereabouts or what she does."

"What *does* Angela do? I mean for work?" I hadn't found much on Angela through online searches on pay investigative websites. Just her residence. No social media presence since she and Steven divorced. No job history. She'd been involved in numerous charities when she and Albright were married, but another zero over the last three years.

I imagined she was collecting a nice alimony from Albright. But I also knew she'd sold her body for money years before she met her ex-husband. I didn't know whether or not Albright knew that. The last time I saw her ten years ago, she was being blackmailed by a scumbag who'd pimped her back in her prostitution days.

Things didn't end well for him. It looked like things hadn't turned out well for her either. Now.

"She's been well compensated for her fifteen years of marriage to me." His voice an icy cool. Sounded like a business arrangement, but every time I'd seen them together in the restaurant, they were affectionate. Clearly in love. Was Albright's dismissive attitude toward his ex-wife a defense mechanism to hide the pain? Marriages gone wrong hurt a lot. I knew that from experience. "She's living a celebrity lifestyle and doesn't want for anything, I can assure you. I don't want to be rude, but I have to get back to work."

Angela's place in Carmel Valley was nice in an attached condo sort of way, but it wasn't the kind of place you'd find a Kardashian film crew. I let it go.

"Just a couple more questions, then I'll leave you alone." I didn't wait for an objection. "Has Angela ever gone this long without seeing Cassandra or communicating with her?"

Albright let go an exasperated breath that signaled he was going to tolerate me a bit longer.

"No. The longest she'd gone without seeing Cassie before this was probably a couple weeks."

"Do you have any idea where she is?"

"Nope. I told you she's no longer a part of my life." The defensive dismissal again.

"Does she still use any credit cards that you pay the bills for?" I was walking the edge with this one. I didn't have a legal way, or even an illegal way, to get a look at Angela Albright's personal credit card statements. I hoped that Steven was still footing the bill for at least one of them.

"This is getting pretty personal, Rick. I'm trying to help, but you're crossing a line."

"It's only to find a location on her." I opened my hands in front of me. "It would be helpful for me to see the latest statement, but I don't have to. You could just tell me when and where the charges were made."

"She hasn't used any credit cards that I'm responsible for." He folded his arms in front of him. "Is that it?"

"Almost. What about friends? Anyone you can direct me to?" I took a stab. "A boyfriend?"

"I have no idea if she's seeing anyone." He stood up. "I really have to get back to work."

"What about other friends?" I stood up but didn't move for the door. "Surely you know who her best friend is."

"Lyndsey Breck. They used to play tennis together at the club. I assume they still do. On Lyndsey's membership."

"The club?"

"The Beach and Tennis Club."

The La Jolla Beach and Tennis Club. The oldest of old money clubs in La Jolla. A relic from a bygone era. But one that would always be real estate on the beach.

"Do you have her phone number?" I could find her contact info on online people search sites, but why make it harder than it had to be.

"Yep." He pulled out his phone and gave me Lyndsey Breck's number.

CHAPTER 6

LYNDSEY BRECK LIVED in a sleek modern home up the hill from La Jolla Shores Drive. She was wearing a white tennis skirt and visor like she'd just gotten off the court. The Beach and Tennis Club was less than a mile away. When I'd called to ask about Angela a couple hours ago, Lyndsey invited me to meet her at her house at 12:30 p.m.

The brown hair that peeked through the cutout of the visor was matted down, and her face glistened with sweat.

"Sorry. I didn't get a chance to get cleaned up. Second set tiebreaker." She blotted her neck with a towel and invited me in.

Lyndsey led me into a living room with a massive bay window that looked out over the ocean and La Jolla Shores Beach. She sat down on a slate-colored chenille sofa, crossing tan, fit legs. I took the oversized velvet straight-back chair next to the sofa.

The November sun shone through gray clouds, casting the ocean in blue iron. A hazy piece of paradise.

"Where are my manners? Can I get you something to drink? Iced tea, water, beer?" Breck's voice had a throaty purr. "Or something a little stronger?"

"I'm good. Thanks." I'd done my homework after our brief phone call. Lyndsey was forty-six, a onetime flight attendant who'd been married to Franklin Reynolds Breck for twelve years. No children. Her husband was sixty-eight and was a founding partner in the La Jolla law firm Breck, Howe, and Daily. Her first marriage. His third.

"So, are you going to tell me who's looking for Angie?" Lyndsey's dark eyes peered at me from under the bill of her visor.

She withheld any information on Angela over the phone when I wouldn't identify who hired me to find her. I wondered if she'd called Angela as soon as we hung up. I hoped so. At least that would mean someone knew where she was.

"All I'm at liberty to say is that it's a relative." I gave a poor man's smile and opened my hands in my lap. "It's like an attorney-client privilege, but the person is looking out for Angela's best interests."

I hoped that was true. Angela was Stone's daughter, after all. One thing I knew was that Stone was looking out for his own best interests. I just didn't know what all those interests were, yet.

"Except it's not really." She smiled a rich woman's smile. "It wouldn't hold up in court."

"I've given my word."

"A stronger bond than enacted law, Mr. Cahill?" A flat smile. "Are you the last honorable man?"

She was enjoying the conversation more than I was.

"I'm getting paid to keep my word. So, probably not. And you can call me Rick."

"I think you're selling yourself short, Rick." The smile turned up the corners of her mouth and flashed in her eyes. "I know who you are. I've seen the news stories and Angela has mentioned you. I think you *are* a man of honor. And violence."

After trying to live a quiet life in anonymity of late, I'd stumbled across two vigilante junkies in one day. I wondered why Angela mentioned me after not having seen each other in ten years.

"Did she bring me up out of the blue, or was it after I'd made the local news?"

"We were having drinks over here one night a few months ago and had the news on in the background. The story about someone trying to kill you came on, and your picture popped up on the screen. She told me she used to know you."

"Oh." The last night Krista and Leah and I were all together in my house, our house, as a family.

"That was awful. You could have died."

"Yeah." I survived, but my family unit didn't.

"Anyway, Angela told me that you used to manage Muldoon's Steak House when she and Steven had dinner there back when they were happy together."

"Good to know. Let's talk about Angela." Enough about me. Way too much about me. "When was the last time you saw or talked to her?"

"That's between me and her."

"This doesn't have to be so hard, Lyndsey. I don't even have to know where she is. Her current phone number would be enough. When was the last time you talked to her?"

Lyndsey studied me, probably debating how much she wanted to tell me or thought Angela would be okay with her telling me. Finally, "It's been a couple weeks."

"Is it unusual for you two not to talk for that long? I got the impression from Steven Albright that you were Angela's best friend."

"I am." Defensive. "When did you talk to that asshole?"

The comment about Steven Albright cemented Lyndsey's claim that she was Angela's best friend. Only a good friend could take that kind of ownership of her hatred for her friend's ex-husband.

"Today. He said Angela hasn't seen her daughter for a month. Is that true?"

"How is that some ancient relative's business? Or yours?"

"It's probably not either of ours. It's just that I remember Angela being a devoted mother to Cassandra when she used to come into

Muldoon's. It surprised me that she'd go that long without seeing her daughter. I have a daughter and . . ."

I let some of my personal life slip out in an unguarded moment. Something I rarely did while working a case—unless I thought doing so could help me get the information I wanted. That wasn't the situation today. I'd let my ache for Krista bubble up to the surface.

"And what?" Gentle. She must have read something in my face.

"And I can't stand to go a week without seeing her or at least talking to her." The truth. But, now that I'd opened up, I *was* using it in hopes of learning what I needed to know. "Being away from her daughter must be eating Angela up inside."

"You're right about that." Lyndsey's whole face had softened up now. "She misses Cassie dearly. They're very close."

"Then why doesn't she visit her?"

"I honestly don't know." Sadness in her voice and in her eyes.

"Do you know where Angie is, Lyndsey? Do you think she's in trouble? In danger?"

"No, I don't know where she is, and I don't know why she left. She won't tell me either." Her brow furrowed. "I don't think she's in trouble. She doesn't sound upset or worried on the phone, but I don't even have her phone number. She won't give it to me, and there's no caller ID when she calls."

"Can you think of anyone that she might be hiding from? Her husband?"

"No. Steven's a jerk, but I don't think he'd ever do anything violent to Angie. I think they're both happy to be free of each other." Her eyes went round. "Do you think she's in danger?"

Peter Stone was trying to find Angela. That almost by definition put her in danger. And I was his vessel. But this wasn't the Peter Stone of five years ago, and I wasn't a Stone enforcer. Angela was Stone's blood. His last remaining child. And heir. His days aboveground were counting down. Just as mine were. That gives a man a new perspective. Make amends? *Amends* probably wasn't in Stone's vocabulary.

Like everyone Stone encountered, he used Angela as a chess piece in his game of life. And worse than most. But that was before he knew Angela was his daughter. Once he found out, he helped her turn her life around. Took her off a self-destructive path and put her on one that led to the affluent and happier life she now lived. Or did at least until she and her husband divorced.

Maybe Stone *had* made amends. The danger he now claimed Angela could be facing was from Sergei Volkov. When he got out of prison. In four short days.

"She could be. I hope not. The person who hired me wants to make sure she isn't."

"This is all very cryptic." Breck's face turned sour. "Why should I trust you or Angie's mysterious relative?"

"Because Angela trusted me. I helped her once a long time ago. Ask her about me when you talk to her. Tell her to contact me."

"I don't know if or when she'll call me again."

"She'll call. You're her best friend. Did she tell you why she won't give you her number?"

"No. And I didn't press her about it." The sour expression on her face smoothed into concern. "We may be best friends, but everyone has the right to keep a few secrets."

Preaching to the choir. But secrets made working a case more difficult. They hadn't always worked out well in my personal life, either.

"When is she supposed to call you next?" I asked.

"Like I said, we don't have a set time. It could be soon, though. It's been almost two weeks."

"Do you remember her mentioning anything new happening in her life before she disappeared? Sudden changes?"

"No. Nothing like that. I left a couple messages on her voicemail and some unanswered texts about a month ago and she called me on the phone with the blocked number and said she was out of town, and she couldn't tell me why then but would later. Everything seemed fine."

"Is Angela dating someone right now?" The hunk in the Maserati?

Breck eyeballed me some more. Obviously debating what she should tell me. Finally, "Yes, but she won't tell me his name or what he does. I think whatever he does, though, he does it well."

"Why do you think that?"

"She sent me a photo of her on the beach in the Bahamas about two months ago. No picture of him, though. Whoever he is."

Must be the guy in the Maserati.

"Is it unusual for her to keep a boyfriend's identity secret?"

"Yes. I'm guessing it's coming from him. Probably married."

Lyndsey Breck had given me more information than I expected she would upon first greeting her. But not nearly enough to help me find Angela, unless I flew to the Bahamas and scoured every beach. And her limited cooperation didn't mean she was on my side. I needed to know if Angela had contacted her daughter, Cassandra, without her ex-husband knowing. If I asked Lyndsey, she might tell Angela the next time they talked, and that might disrupt my next move.

I stood up and handed her my card. "Please ask Angela to call me. It's only a phone call. Nothing more, but it's important."

CHAPTER 7

I CAUGHT THE tail in my rearview mirror heading south on Torrey Pines Road. A late model black Chevy Tahoe. Tinted windows. It ran the yellow to red traffic light behind me at Prospect Street.

The second tell was when I turned right on Hershel Avenue, then a quick left on Kline and a right on Girard Avenue. The Tahoe made all the turns behind me. The first was a near slide onto Herschel. Going too fast. Afraid they'd lose me. I caught the Chevy's license plate number in the rearview mirror and committed it to memory by saying it over and over again.

I stayed on Girard for a block, then whipped a left across the street and grabbed a rare open parking space in front of Warwick's, La Jolla's iconic independent bookstore. The Tahoe passed behind me. The tint of its driver-side window gave up a faint shadowed outline of the driver. I couldn't tell if it was male or female.

I got out of my car, walked toward the bookstore, and tried to catch the Tahoe in my peripheral vison. No luck, but that was fine. I knew whoever was in it would either wait for me, come inside the store, or hover around the entrance on the sidewalk.

Difficult to identify without seeing them get out of the SUV, but I knew where to get help. I stood behind the current events table pretending to peruse the latest nonfiction while I eyed the doorway and pulled out my phone to make a call.

"What now." The sharp, machine gun voice. Moira MacFarlane. The best private investigator I knew. My sometime partner. And my best friend.

"Want to have some fun?" I kept my voice low so as not to draw attention from any of the other customers. The closest person was about ten feet away in front of the mystery table.

"Don't be coy, Rick. What kind of trouble are you are in now?"

"I'm waiting out a tail in Warwick's. Picked them up coming down Torrey Pines Road." I scanned the room to make sure no one was listening in. "They passed behind me as I came into the store about a minute ago. Hoping you can help me identify them."

"Is it about a case you're working, or do you think this is someone from your past?"

"Don't know." A new customer walked through the entrance of the store. Late-middle-aged woman wearing yoga pants and a gold leopard print jacket. Her face was stretched and plumped in all the right places. Forever young. Or, forever frozen in time. I didn't see her driving a Chevy Tahoe. More likely a late model Tesla or Mercedes. "But I have a plate number. Can you run it with your pal at LJPD and head over here? I want to tail the tail, if you have time."

A puffed exhale. "Give me the tag number."

I gave her the license plate number and a description of the Tahoe. "Text what you find out. I have a feeling I might have company soon and won't be able to talk."

She hung up without a goodbye. Or even a grunt. Not for the first time. I put my phone back in my pocket and picked up a new release about the war in Ukraine. Light reading. I pulled the brim of my Padres baseball cap down low and eyed the front door through the narrow opening between the top row of the book table and the bill of my hat.

A couple customers exited over the next few minutes, but no new ones entered. I flipped a page in the book I wasn't reading and kept my eyes on the entrance. Then I saw him. Late thirties. Six feet. Lean. Short, coiffed blond hair. Blue eyes. Navy blue slacks. White dress shirt, no tie, open at the collar. That was the giveaway as much as anything else. Even more than the perfect hair and the darting eyes. He should have just kept the coat and tie on. The attempt to disguise who he was by stripping off half the plainclothes uniform was more telling than wearing the full suit.

Fed. FBI. Ninety percent certain. Either that or an employee on a break from the Ascot Shop, the old-school men's clothing store down the block. Not many men wore suits in La Jolla in the middle of the day anymore. Or even half suits.

I spotted him before he did me, so when his eyes came across me my own were reading the book in my hands. I kept him in my peripheral vision as he walked by to my left. The Fed moved his head around like he was looking for something. But he overdid it. High school drama club stuff. He'd never be a lead.

I put my prop book back on the table and headed for the front door. Just for fun. I wasn't going anywhere until I knew Moira was in place to tail the Tahoe. Which, I suspected, was parked on the street with someone else behind the wheel. White shirt was a scout, sent to make sure I hadn't slipped out the back of the store. Whoever was driving the Tahoe would have eyes on my Accord.

I stopped three feet short of the door and grabbed one of the books from the stack behind the new releases posed in the front window. Reed Farrel Coleman's latest. I cracked the book and turned toward the center of the store and caught the Fed in mid-stride coming toward me.

He made an awkward move to his right and stopped in front of the new mystery table. Busted. I now had a tail on foot and probably one on four wheels. I drifted away from the door and stopped next to the locals section, still fake reading.

Moira lived less than five minutes away via car, and it had only been about that long since she ended our phone call. I didn't expect her to drop everything and jump in her car immediately. Plus, she had to call her contact at the La Jolla Police Department and ask him to run a trace on the Tahoe's license plate number. Moira had contacts with police departments all over San Diego that I could never make. Even though I'd once been a cop. Because I'd once been a cop. No friends left on the other side of the thin blue line.

I flipped a page in my book and shot a glance at the Fed. He was fake reading Robert Crais's latest. Our eyes met and we both poker-faced it. But he might have figured out that I made him. I walked over to the mystery table, now with Reed Farrel Coleman's book at my side, and picked up a copy of the Crais book. Selling that I'd been interested in the book the Fed was reading, not the Fed.

We were only a few feet apart, and I could feel his eyes on the side of my face. Instinct from my cop days. Years of watching people without looking as a private investigator. Paranoia. Whichever the case, I had a sixth sense about being watched. Most of the time. Maybe that's why I checked the rearview mirror when I did and caught the Tahoe running the red light.

That sixth sense had served me well over the last twenty years. Saving my life more than once. It was a nice safety net, but I couldn't always rely on it to keep myself and others safe. It wasn't turned on 100 percent of the time. The Tahoe must have been tailing me for a while. Before or after I went to Lyndsey Breck's house? It didn't come from the ether. There had to be a starting point. And I'd missed it. I was rusty. I'd only been out from behind my computer and back out on the street for a few months, working cases with shoe leather and instinct instead of fingers on a keyboard. Since I got out of the hospital and Leah took Krista up to Santa Barbara.

I had to be hyper alert when I was on a case with high stakes. Stakes where someone would do almost anything to protect their secret. But I'd made enough enemies over the years as a P. I. that someone with a grudge could be out there anytime. Watching. Lurking. Planning. Someone like Sergei Volkov. Waiting for the right moment to strike violently. At me. Or my family.

Leah understood danger. Her sister had been a cop. And had been murdered. She'd almost been killed herself, more than once. Because of cases I'd worked. But even while comprehending that the world was dangerous, she didn't understand evil like I did. Couldn't comprehend the dark merciless pit that metastasized in men's souls. And in some women's. Remorseless. Malevolent. Determined.

As much as I tried to protect my family from evil, I sought it out, too. Fought it on its turf and on my own. Tried to understand it in order to defend against it. Got too close to it. Let it brush up against my soul. And leave a mark.

My phone vibrated in my pocket.

I took it out. A text from Moira.

Moira: *I'm parked on Girard. A block east of warwicks in front of the bank. I have binos on the Tahoe. Its parked across from the candy store west of W.*

Me: *What about the plate?*

Moira: *A rental from Avis.*

What were the Feds doing in a rental SUV? And why were they following me in it?

Me: *Roger. Im going to leave in a couple minutes and head home via torrey pines.*

Moira: *On it.*

She'd tail the Tahoe after I left. It would more than likely still be tailing me.

Me: *Thanks.*

Moira: *Yup.*

A woman of few words. Except when she needed to explain my shortcomings to me. Happened at least once a month. More often if we worked a case together. But she was the person who moved into my house for a couple weeks to take care of me while I was convalescing after I got out of the hospital with stitches in my chest and a cast on my hand.

After Leah left our home and took Krista up to Santa Barbara. This time probably for good.

Moira didn't know me better than Leah, but she knew things about me that no one else did. Not even Leah. Things that no one else could. She knew about Tatiana. And other things that could put me in jail.

I put my phone back in my pocket and took my two books up to the counter. Needed to continue to sell the con to the Fed all the way. I was in Warwick's to buy books or stationery like all the other customers in there. Paying for the books should seal the deal. Plus, sometimes when life settled down and it was just Midnight and me in my empty house, I needed a good book to get lost in. Now I had two.

CHAPTER 8

I CHECKED THE rearview mirror and caught the Fed coming out of Warwick's, watching me drive away. No sign of the Tahoe. Yet. I connected my phone to my car and called Moira on the entertainment system. "I'm heading down Girard to Torrey Pines. Has the Tahoe moved yet?"

"Just did. I'm two cars behind it."

"Let me know if—"

"A guy in blue pants and a white shirt just jumped into the Tahoe in front of Warwick's. The Tahoe barely stopped."

"That answers my question." The Fed team was back together, and they were still on my tail. I checked the rearview mirror again and now caught a glimpse of the Tahoe pulling away from the stop sign at Girard and Silverado. "I think white shirt and whoever is driving the Tahoe are Feds."

"He had the look," Moira said.

We were thinking the same thing. We often did. We'd worked thirty to forty cases together over the last ten years. Enough to get into a rhythm and read things the same way. Not always, but much more often than not. We were a good team. Moira was like a sister to me. A judgmental older sister who loved me in spite of my shortcomings. I loved her in spite of my shortcomings, too. She didn't have any.

"Yup," I said.

"What do the Feds want with you, Rick? What did you do now?" The judgmental sister.

"I don't know. I haven't done anything." Except agree to look for the daughter, by DNA only, of a formerly mobbed-up ex-casino owner turned real estate developer who was supposed to be in witness protection under a new identity. But I hadn't broken any laws. The Feds were after me to find Stone. They must have figured out that he was on the run.

But why would they know he'd come to me? Hell, I never could have imagined he'd look me up when he stepped away from his new life and came back to his old. Maybe they'd had a tail on him his whole trek back to San Diego from wherever he'd been living and had followed him to my house. But if that were true, they'd know where he was right now and wouldn't need to tail me to find him. What did the Feds really want from me? And why?

"I don't believe you," Moira said. "What have you gotten yourself into? Something has caught the FBI's attention."

Of course, Moira was right, but her saying the FBI out loud made me realize something was slightly off. The FBI. They arranged for Stone's new life through the WITSEC program with the Department of Justice, but the United State Marshal Service runs the program. The marshals protect the witnesses during trials, relocate them, and monitor their new lives. At least for a time. After Stone disappeared from his new life, the marshals should be the ones looking for him. And they would probably be much harder to spot than the FBI who might as well have had their name in neon lights on top of the Tahoe where a police cruiser lightbar would go.

The FBI wasn't tailing me to find Stone so they could protect him or usher him back to his new life. They wanted him for some other reason.

Moira's question rang in my ears: What had I gotten myself into? The Feds didn't like me any more than the local police did. But they didn't dislike me as much either. Still, if they thought I was tangled up in something illegal with Stone, they could make my life miserable. And, possibly, no longer under my own control.

First things first. I turned left on Torrey Pines Road and took it to La Jolla Parkway then onto I-5 South. The Chevy Tahoe with the tinted windows stayed two or three cars behind me the whole way. I didn't spot Moira's white Honda Accord behind them but had no doubt she was there somewhere. Just much better at tailing someone than the Feds in the Tahoe were.

They followed me off the freeway and all the way up Balboa, Moraga, and even onto Cadden Way, my home street. Unless they were going to walk me to my front door, they were really bad at a concealed tail. I pulled into my driveway, and the Tahoe drove past behind me. I walked up to my front door like I had no idea I'd been followed home.

Midnight nuzzled me with his graying snout as I entered the house. The comforts of home. I pulled out my phone and called Moira as I led Midnight through the kitchen and into the backyard. Now recovered from an injury sustained trying to protect my family, his family, Midnight was left with a permanent limp. Thankfully, not bad enough to keep him from going upstairs to sleep in my bedroom every night. If it had been, I would have carried him upstairs or slept on the couch the remaining years of his life.

Moira picked up on the first ring.

"Looks like they're putting me to bed. And they are really bad at not being noticed."

"Roger. I've got 'em. They're parked two houses down from you on your side of the street."

"Where are you?"

"On Moraga at the beginning of your street. Got my binos on them."

"How many in the Tahoe?"

"Just two. White shirt, and the driver is a white female. She's doing most of the talking. I'm texting you a picture."

My phone pinged, and I opened the picture she sent. It was a shot through the windshield with a telephoto lens. The blond man was in the passenger seat and a dark-haired woman sat behind the steering wheel. She looked to be in her early to mid-thirties. Attractive. Strong chin.

"Got it. Thanks. What are they doing other than talking?"

The sun had finally pierced the morning haze, casting a golden glow on the morning. Midnight's ears were at alert and his body tense with anticipation. I grabbed a tennis ball off the picnic table on the deck in the backyard and tossed it about thirty feet in front of Midnight along the tightly mowed lawn. He lumbered after it. There was more want-to than athleticism left in his battered thirteen-year-old body. But his spirit was still that of a young, active dog. And his heart and inherent protectiveness were still strong. He'd give his life to save Krista or Leah or me. Almost did more than once.

"Nothing. Just watching your house. Amateurs. I have the feeling they haven't tailed a lot of targets, if they are the FBI. They don't even have binoculars." She clucked her tongue. "It feels like tailing you wasn't a pre-planned event. More like it was done on the fly."

"Agree."

"I think it's time you tell me what's going on." A steel spine in her voice.

"I'm working a case for someone who it looks like the FBI is interested in, and they're either hoping I'll lead them to that person or are trying to figure out where I fit in." As much as I trusted Moira, and I trusted her with my life, I had a responsibility to my client, even if he was Peter Stone, to keep his identity and why he hired me confidential.

"If those two in the Tahoe are, indeed, FBI, they can turn your life inside out like no one ever has. I know you've escaped death more than once, but the FBI can kill the rest of your life while you're still trying to live it. Do you really want to deal with that during the limited . . ."

She didn't finish her sentence because she realized how bad it would sound. The limited time I had left. To live. To be fully cognizant. Either or both. They were the same to me. And she was right, I didn't want my time left to be spent under the FBI's thumb.

Their tail had something to do with Stone, and I needed to find out what that was before I became collateral damage. But I had to wait for him to contact me first.

"My client has a bit of a history with the FBI, but none of it can roll over onto me. I'm doing a simple missing persons check for the client. That's all. And there's no reason for the Feds to be interested in that person."

"Well, they're definitely interested in something, and you have no idea if the FBI can make whatever it is roll over onto you. They don't have to have proof of anything to investigate you and make your life miserable."

"You're right. So it's time for you to head back home. I really only wanted to see where they were going, and since they followed me home, I now know. Thanks. I owe you."

"You're damn right you owe me, Cahill." She only used Cahill when she was upset with me. More so than the usual irritation. "For too many things to count. You can pay down the debt by telling me what's really going on. Who is this person that the FBI is interested in?"

"You know I can't tell you that. You understand client confidentiality better than I do."

"I don't care about confidentiality when the FBI is on your tail. You know whatever you tell me will go no farther than my ears. Tell me what you're up to so I can help you. Or at least give you better advice than whatever thoughts are swirling around up in that dense, dark brain of yours."

Moira was the last best friend I had and, aside from Leah, the only person I truly trusted. And she trusted me just as much. I needed friendship and trust in my life. Now more than ever.

"Peter Stone showed up on my doorstep this morning."

"What?" The volume over the speakerphone snapped Midnight's head to attention. "I thought he was stashed in WITSEC somewhere far away."

"So did I, until seven thirty this morning. He did the most dangerous thing you can do in WITSEC. He came home."

"Why, and why did he come to you? You two don't have a great history."

"He trusts me. He thinks we're blood brothers because of that night in his house five years ago."

"Can you trust him?"

A question I'd been going over in my head since he hired me this morning.

"You can never completely trust Stone, but . . ."

"But what?"

"There was something about the shoot-out at his house. He saved my life. And his own, I know, but I was the one under fire when he took the guy out." I couldn't explain exactly how I felt because I wasn't exactly sure what I felt. But there was something between Stone and me now. A bond that couldn't be easily stripped away. A bond I didn't welcome but couldn't ignore. "Things could have gone a different way."

"I don't buy this male bonding bullshit, Rick. He's Peter Stone. He's using whatever connection you're feeling to get you to do something for him. What is it?"

She had a point, and it was something I'd considered myself. But there was also fifty thousand dollars at stake. Half of which I already had in cash stored in my gun safe. The money had been more persuasive than the bond.

"I told you. He wants me to find someone."

"Who?"

"Angela Albright."

"Why the hell would Stone show his face out of WITSEC to try to find Angela Albright?"

There it was. My answer would be one step closer to fully betraying Peter Stone. Bond or no bond. A dangerous man.

"Because Angela is his daughter."

CHAPTER 9

"WHAT?" MOIRA'S VOICE roused Midnight again. "How is that even possible?"

Biologically, a simple question to answer. Family tree–wise, a question way too complicated and too dangerous to answer.

"It's possible, but it's a secret. You are now one of only three or four people alive who knows it." Emphasis on *alive*. "And Angela is not one of them. And you cannot tell her. It's up to Stone and Stone alone to tell her. If he ever decides to. Understand?"

"Don't talk to me like a child." Rattle gun snaps. "Everything you tell me is in confidence. Have I ever betrayed your trust?"

"Of course not. I apologize." I knew saying *understand* was a mistake as soon as the word left my mouth. "Shouldn't have said it. But it's Peter Stone. I have to admit that he's got me a bit on edge."

"Then why the hell are you working for him?"

"Money. He's paying me enough to start a nice nest egg toward Krista's future."

"I get it now." Moira was Krista's godmother, part-time babysitter, and full-time aunt as much as if she were blood. The absence of Krista full-time in my life hurt Moira, too. I always invited her for dinner one of the nights I had Krista and she'd babysat her a couple times when I had to work a case, but it wasn't like before. She'd babysit for Leah and me at least once a week when we were together and had us to dinner at her house just as often. She loved Krista as if she were her own. "But you just proved my point."

"What are you talking about?"

"Stone made you an offer you couldn't turn down. He figured out your weakness in five seconds without having seen you in five years."

"Money's not my weakness. Stone knows he can't buy me." Another post-verbal recognition too late to silence. An absurd statement considering he'd done just that.

"Money means something different to you now than it did five years ago. Back then, money meant paying your bills and doing whatever it is you do for fun. I've known you for ten years and still haven't figured that one out. Anyway, now money means improving Krista's future. Five years ago, you could say no to extra money. Now, you can't. Stone figured that out. He knew money means more to you now than it ever has. Or ever will."

She was right, of course. She usually was. But it was maddening that I was so easy to read. By her. And by Stone.

"Whatever the case, he needs a kidney transplant, and he thinks Angela Albright could be a donor."

"The Feds got out of the car and are walking toward your house." Moira's voice, sharp.

Shit.

CHAPTER 10

I HUNG UP with Moira, went back inside the house, and left Midnight outside. Like me, he had a problem with authority, and I didn't trust the Feds to keep their guns holstered if he growled at them—that's if the two people in the Chevy Tahoe really were Feds. I went to the front door and looked through the peephole.

The man I'd seen in Warwick's wearing a dress shirt and slacks stepped onto my porch. He'd now added a tie and blazer to the wardrobe, seemingly confirming my suspicions that he'd left them in the Chevy Tahoe in an attempt to look casual before he entered Warwick's. He was now joined by the short, dark-haired woman wearing a blue pinstriped suit I'd seen in the picture Moira sent me. They both wore aviator sunglasses. Midnight growled from the backyard. The man gave the door a couple hard knocks. I waited a few seconds until he raised his hand to knock again, then opened the door.

"Rick Cahill?" The man's voice had a flat command presence. He flipped open a leather badge holder in front of me that held a gold FBI shield. Suspicion number two confirmed.

"Yes?" I tried to look innocent.

"I'm FBI Special Agent Dennis Sorensen and this is Special Agent Charlene Bowden." He nodded to the woman then looked back at me.

They took off their sunglasses in perfect synchronization like they'd practiced together in front of a mirror.

"Do you mind if we come in and speak with you?" Bowden's voice had more life in it than her partner's. Everything about her demeanor was more pleasant than Sorensen. Bowden was attractive in a handsome kind of way, athletic physique and had a nice smile.

"How about you tell me what you'd like to talk about?" I knew they wanted to ask me about Stone, but I felt like asking the questions since I was standing in my own house.

"About an associate of yours." Sorensen's face stayed deadpan.

When someone in law enforcement mentions an "associate" of yours, they don't mean friend. Or pal. Or upright citizen. Not that anyone would ever think of Stone in those terms now anyway.

"I don't have associates. I have friends. Which one do you want to talk about?"

"Peter Stone." Sorensen.

"Peter Stone? He's not a friend or an associate."

"Are you going to invite us in, or do you want to make this difficult, Mr. Cahill?" Sorensen put his hands on his hips, opening his jacket and exposing a pancake holster with a Glock 19 in it. A macho move with a kicker.

I didn't have to talk to the FBI—and probably shouldn't without a lawyer sitting next to me, telling me not to say anything. Lying to the FBI, if charged, was a felony. Even in your own home. But maybe the Special Agents would slip up and I'd learn something that Stone didn't tell me. I knew there was a missing piece to the puzzle. I also knew how much I needed an extra $50,000.

"Come on in." I opened the door all the way and butlered an arm toward the living room. The two Feds walked over to the sofa and sat down. Bowden was wearing a wedding ring. Sorensen was not. I sat in my decade-old La-Z-Boy recliner at an angle to them.

They stared at me without saying anything. I stared back. If this was going to be a game of blink, they had no idea who they were dealing with.

Finally, Sorensen spoke. "When was the last time you saw Peter Stone?"

"I thought he was stashed away somewhere under WITSEC," I said.

"I need to inform you, Mr. Cahill, that lying to the FBI is a felony." Sorensen scowled at me. "Would you like to rephrase your answer?"

"I didn't give you an answer." I smiled. No one smiled back. "I made a statement. I have a question for you. Why do you think I've seen Peter Stone? Like I said, I thought he was under witness protection."

"Is this really the way you want to play it?" Sorensen stood up, reached behind his back, and came out with a pair of handcuffs. "Do you want to do five years in a federal penitentiary, or do you want to tell us the truth?"

My heart did a double tap despite the fact that I knew he was bluffing. Or, most likely bluffing. Sorensen couldn't arrest me on suspicion that I was lying to him, which I hadn't done. Yet. He needed some sort of verification that I'd seen Stone recently. Did he have him bugged? As intrusive as the FBI was becoming, I doubted they'd somehow bugged my house in anticipation that Stone might drop by sometime.

"It sounds like you think you have proof I've seen Stone recently." I looked at Sorensen; he took a step toward me. "Hold on, I'm getting to the good part. Stone came by here this morning. Out of the blue."

"What did he want?" Sorensen returned the handcuffs to their case behind his back and sat down.

Now came the tricky part.

"He wanted to hire me."

"To do what?" Sorensen leaned forward.

I thought of the envelope full of two hundred and fifty one-hundred-dollar bills in my gun safe. And of another envelope with the same waiting for me if I found Angela Albright for Stone. I hadn't lied to the special agents yet, and they'd need a warrant to force me to tell them everything they wanted me to. But I still wanted to know what they knew. I needed to know what Peter Stone was really up to.

"Find someone."

"Find who?" Sorensen.

"For that you'll need a warrant. Private detective–client privilege."

"No such thing between a private detective and a client." Sorensen snapped off the words, offended.

"Nonetheless, I don't have to tell you. I don't even have to talk to you without a warrant. I'm just trying to help." I moved forward on my recliner, linked my fingers together, and rested my forearms on my knees. "Maybe we can help each other out."

Sorensen and Bowden rolled their eyes at each other.

"What did you have in mind?" Sorensen frowned at me.

"How about you tell me why Stone came out of hiding."

"To hire you to find someone, smart-ass," Bowden jumped in. Not so pleasant anymore. "Now you tell us who that person is, and you can enjoy the rest of your day."

"Let's try this instead." I smiled, the only one of the three of us who seemed capable of moving their mouth that way. "I heard Sergei Volkov was getting out of prison this week. Is that true?"

Sorensen and Bowden looked at each other again. This time no eye rolls. Concern instead.

"Did Peter Stone tell you that?" Bowden.

"I shall not lie to the FBI. Yes." I held up a three-finger salute like the Boy Scout I never was. "Why is he getting out early? He's only done four and a half years on a fifteen-year leash. What kind of deal did he make?"

"I don't know what you're talking about." Sorensen made a big effort to stare me in the eyes. A tell. Volkov was getting out early.

"Does the fact that you two are asking me about Stone have anything to do with Volkov getting out? He did help the FBI put Sergei behind bars." I blew out a laugh. "For four and a half years."

"Cut the bullshit, Cahill." Sorensen reached into his pocket and pulled out a cellphone. He fiddled with it and then pushed it toward my face. "Is this the man who Peter Stone hired you to find?"

The man?

I reached for the phone and Sorensen pulled it back out of my reach. "Don't touch. Just look."

The man in the photo looked to be about forty to forty-five years old. Brown and brown. Good-looking in a spray tan kind of way. Aging model or someone with money. Sculpted for display.

"What's his name?"

"Is it the man or not?"

"He didn't show me a picture. What's his name? You give me the right name, and I'll confirm."

Sorensen and Bowden traded another look.

"Theodore Raskin." Sorensen put his phone back in his pocket and eyeballed me.

Who the hell was Theodore Raskin?

"Never heard of him. Who is he?"

"Are you stating that Theodore Raskin is not the person who Peter Stone hired you to locate?" Sorensen's flat voice caught an edge.

"Stating, saying, telling. Whatever you want to call it. Stone did not hire me to find a Theodore Raskin."

"We've already explained what can happen to you if you're lying, Mr. Cahill." Bowden, calmer.

"I've never heard of this Raskin person, and Stone didn't hire me to find him." I did the Boy Scout salute again. "Who is he, and why would Stone be looking for him?"

"Who *did* Stone hire you to find?"

"Special Agent Sorensen, as much as I'd like to tell you, I can't." I smiled like I meant it. "But I don't really think there's a connection to this Theodore Raskin. As I'm sure you know, Stone's a man who has a lot of irons in the fire. When did he leave WITSEC?"

"How would you know if the person Stone hired you to find had any connection to Raskin?"

"Because the name never came up when I was investigating." I leaned forward toward Sorensen. "Who is Theodore Raskin?"

"If you're lying to us, you're going to feel the full weight of the federal government coming down on you like a bunker buster bomb." Sorensen shot up from the couch and leaned over me. Midnight's snarl from outside echoed inside the house. "Last chance, Cahill. Did Peter Stone hire you to find Theodore Raskin, and do you know where he is?"

Not lying to the FBI was easy when I didn't have to.

"No."

Sorensen's mouth tightened into a fist. He snapped a look at Bowden, and she sprang up from the couch. The two of them strode out of my house without another word, leaving the front door wide open.

CHAPTER 11

I WENT TO the door, closed it, and called Moira.

"They're headed back to their car, and they are real Feds. Even threatened me."

"What was the threat?" Concern in her voice.

"The usual. Jail. Just trying to intimidate me. Empty threat. Nothing to worry about. But something seems a little off about them. They played that card pretty early. Almost desperately." I put my phone on speaker and searched the internet. "You ever hear the name Theodore Raskin?"

"No. Why?"

"The Feds asked me if Stone hired me to find him. Hold on for a sec . . ." I found the name online and did a quick scan. "Apparently, he started some cryptocurrency exchange called BitChange a couple years ago. Not much more about him online."

A couple photos of Raskin showed a man in his mid-forties. The same man Sorensen showed me a photo of on his phone.

"Peter Stone and some crypto exchange guy?" Moira whistled. "That sounds like a combination fraught with illegal possibilities."

"Sure does." I'd see what Stone had to say when he contacted me again. "Anyway, come on in after the Feds drive away and I'll pay you $500 for today's work."

"Later. I have something to do first." A lilt to her normal machine gun voice.

"What?"

"I'm going to see where these Feds go next."

"Your work's done. Following federal agents is not a good business or personal practice. Come get your money."

"First of all, I'm not going to take your money. Jerk." A rumble in the background. Probably the ignition of Moira's car. "They're not driving a normal Fed-mobile. Something is off about them. You said it yourself. So, why not check them out?"

"Because they're Feds and can make your life miserable."

"They turned right at the bottom of Moraga onto Balboa. Wonder if they're going to FBI headquarters up in Sorrento Valley or somewhere else."

"It's not your concern."

"It wasn't before I learned that the FBI was following you. And that you were working for Peter Stone. It's my concern now." Car noise, like Moira had pulled away from the curb.

"You don't know all of it."

"What do you mean?"

If Moira was going to jump in—and I didn't think I could stop her now—she needed to know everything. Especially the dangerous part.

"Stone told me Sergei Volkov was getting out of prison at the end of the week."

"What?" The hint of fear in her voice? Maybe it was just in my head. Either way, it was warranted. "I thought he got twenty years for racketeering."

"Fifteen, but according to Stone he must have a get-out-of-jail-free-card."

"Why did Stone tell you this? Does he want you to protect him *and* find Angela?" Higher pitched anger. Or worry.

I didn't want to further agitate her, but I couldn't hold anything back. Except how Stone and Angela met. I'd given Stone my word on that years ago. It felt like a blood oath now.

"He told me as a warning. He's afraid Sergei knows about Angela, and he not only wants me to find her but protect her. And..." I searched for an easy way to explain further. There wasn't one. "And Stone thinks that Sergei will find out that I'm responsible for Tatiana's death."

"What! How does Stone know about Tatiana?" Her voice boiled over. "You didn't tell him, did you? Some stupid, macho bonding confession."

"Of course not." An edge to my own voice. More from the situation I was in than in annoyance at Moira. "Stone somehow put the pieces together. I didn't admit to anything, but he knows. And he thinks Sergei will figure it out too, if he hasn't already."

"What if Stone told Sergei about his own suspicions?"

The thought had crossed my mind that Stone might somehow get word to Sergei that I killed his daughter. But it wouldn't make any sense. Not now.

"The two of them aren't exactly pals." I punched the "P" in pals hard. "Sergei wants Stone dead, and I'm sure Stone sees killing Sergei as his only chance to stay alive."

"You really put yourself in the middle of one now, Rick."

"Maybe, but you don't have to join me there."

"Yes, I do." She hung up. I called back and got her voicemail. I didn't leave a message. I knew it would be fruitless.

Moira was in now. In what, I didn't fully know yet. Whatever it was, I was better off with her on my side. But she was my responsibility now, too. And any mistake could cost us both everything.

CHAPTER 12

MOIRA WAS RIGHT. Something was off about Sorensen and Bowden. The Chevy Tahoe. The lack of the usual Fed cool. The quick threat to put me in jail. I needed to find out more about them, and I knew someone who could help me do that. If I could convince him to.

I searched the contacts in my phone and found a number I hadn't called in five years. I tapped the CALL button. The person on the other end wouldn't be happy to hear from me. He never was.

"Rick." My name sounded like a swear word. FBI Special Agent John Mallon's mood regarding me hadn't changed in the last five years. "I don't have a lot of time."

But he picked up when he didn't have to. As much I annoyed Mallon, he took my calls. Maybe because, despite how things might seem at first, he knew I wasn't a crank. A couple things I'd asked for help on turned federal, and I once helped him with something in his personal life.

But I think the main reason he took my calls was because he genuinely wanted to help people who needed it. Something we had in common, although, even as he broke a few rules, he didn't follow the code I did, handed down to me by my late father decades ago: sometimes you have to do what's right even when the law says it's wrong.

FBI Special Agent John Mallon stayed on the bright side of the law. Sometimes I crossed over into the dark.

"Hi, John. Thanks for picking up." I tried light and breezy. "I want to know if you can sneak away from headquarters for a coffee in the next hour. Won't take long. Starbucks. I'm buying."

Straitlaced John Mallon liked the sweet, frothy caffeine that Starbucks produced by the metric ton.

"Unless you have some intel on a homegrown extreme fringe group, I don't think I can help you."

Mallon had been a young accountant when he joined the FBI after his big brother was killed overseas fighting terrorists. Homegrown fringe groups seemed like a million miles away from that.

"Is that where the command structure is putting all their resources now?"

"What do you need help with today, Rick?"

"I'm sure you remember Sergei Volkov. Russian Mob kingpin?" My way in. Maybe. "You helped put him away four and a half years ago for racketeering."

"Of course. Please get to the point."

"Rumor has it he's getting out of prison by the end of the week."

"What?" Genuine surprise. "Where did you hear that?"

I wasn't under oath.

"Rumor mill. Thirdhand. It's pretty clear that you know nothing about this. How about you either verify or debunk it and call me back."

"I can't make any promises. I'll call you back if I get a chance." He hung up.

I checked the time on my phone. 2:37 p.m. High schools were probably already done for the day or just letting out. I needed to talk to Cassandra Albright. Delicately. I didn't believe that Angela hadn't talked to her daughter in a month. If she was as crazy about her daughter as Lindsey Breck said she was, she had to be in some kind of contact with Cassandra. Too late to go by the high school today, and I wouldn't be able to talk to her at home. Her father wouldn't allow that. But I felt certain she was the key to finding Angela.

I pulled up Instagram on my phone. I didn't know what the favorite social media apps for sixteen-year-olds were these days, but I'd had clients with high school–aged kids, and a couple of them had at least a mild presence on Instagram. I looked up Cassandra Albright and found four people listed under that name. None of them were sixteen-year-old girls. I tried Cassie Albright and saw a photo of a young woman who could have been the grown-up version of the six-year-old little girl whose parents brought her to Muldoon's Steak House and always ordered her a burger, which she ate half of and took home the rest in a doggie bag every time.

She had blue eyes and blond hair like Angela but a squarer chin. Like Steven Albright? Maybe. Or maybe my imagination was filling in the blanks I wanted to see. I looked through a few of her posts, many of which showed her playing tennis. The backdrop from one of the photos looked a lot like the tennis courts at La Jolla High School. In most of the shots she was wearing a red top with LJHS across the chest and a black tennis skirt.

I got on the La Jolla High website, looked up Girls Tennis, and found a photo of Cassie Albright with her name listed right below it. Bingo. Their schedule said they had a match at Torrey Pines High School on Friday. It was only Monday. La Jolla High had a long tradition of good tennis teams going back to even before my time there twenty-five years ago. I figured they practiced every day. We did for football all those years ago.

*　*　*

La Jolla High School was only a ten-minute drive from my house on Nautilus Street and Fay Avenue.

I found a parking spot on Fern Glen a little after three o'clock. An hour earlier, the street and surrounding areas would have still been clogged with high schoolers' rides. Most of the cars probably went for twice what I paid for my 2019 Honda Accord. La Jollans, like the rich mentioned by F. Scott Fitzgerald, were different than the rest of us.

I'd grown up there in a tract home section on a cop's lower-middle-class salary in a house that had since been torn down and rebuilt up to two stories to take advantage of a view out of my childhood reach. After my dad was kicked off the La Jolla Police Force and spent the last years of his life in a whiskey bottle, I got a job at fourteen working in a restaurant. My "income" had to plug the holes left by my dad as he moved from one low-wage job to another. A once great man that life picked away at. Finding cracks that eroded away into gouges until all that was left was dust.

Somehow, I'd managed to fit in with the kids driving late model Mercedes, BMWs, and Volvos with my twelve-year-old 1985 leaky oil Mustang. One of the years when Ford decided to make the Mustang ugly. But my friends accepted me as one of their own. Being a star jock helped in the cliquish world of high school life.

Most of my friends' parents weren't as welcoming. My father's reputation had still traveled through La Jolla estates in hushed whispers almost a decade after he'd lost his job as a cop.

I was accepted, but never felt completely at home in La Jolla.

Now a lot of people who lived in those estates hired me to fix their problems. I didn't feel any more welcomed by them now than I did as a high schooler, but cashing their checks made up for it.

La Jolla High's six tennis courts were located below the football stadium at the end of Fern Glen along the alley that ran parallel to Draper Ave. I got out of my car and heard the thwocks of tennis balls being hit back and forth. A gate that led to a walkway above the courts was surprisingly open. These days, public schools were locked up as tight as the Central Jail downtown. I understood the need for security but wouldn't have when I attended the same high school decades ago. Columbine happened two years after I graduated.

Student life had changed a lot since then. Many times over.

I stood at the beginning of the walkway near the gate and searched the tennis courts. I wore my Padres cap down low above my prescription sunglasses. It had been ten years since Cassandra Albright saw me in person. I didn't know if she'd ever watched the news with her mom, but either way, I figured the hat and sunglasses were enough to conceal my identity.

All six courts were being used by young women, girls really, each dressed in black skirts and red tops with LJHS in black letters across the chest. Four courts held two girls each playing singles, and the other two courts had four each playing doubles. I saw Cassie Albright trading strokes with another lone player across the net on the third court. Her blond hair was pulled back in a ponytail, blue eyes in squinted intensity. She was taller than I remembered her mother being, by at least three or four inches. I put her at five nine or ten. Lean and broad-shouldered like her father. Quick on the court with a powerful two-handed backhand.

A man in his fifties and a woman much younger, both wearing LJHS black and red windbreakers and tennis visors, sat on a bench in front of the courts, occasionally shouting instruction.

Another man, around my age, leaned against the railing above the courts and watched. Tanned, leathery forearms. A dad who'd played tennis for decades watching his daughter maintain the family recreation.

I thought of Krista, still four months shy of two years old, and wondered what she'd be like in high school. Would she be an athlete like her mother and me? She was already exhibiting athletic traits. Quick to walk and now scooted around the house like a two-foot tall scatback. Ambidextrous when tossing the tennis ball in the backyard for Midnight to chase.

Yes, she definitely had her mommy and daddy's genes. If she was interested in sports, I'd do all I could to help her succeed and enjoy them as she grew. But would I be cognitive enough to watch her practices and games like the man with the leathery arms fifteen years from now?

Would I even be alive?

My phone vibrated a call in my pocket. I put in a pair of earbuds and answered. Moira. I stepped off the tennis walkway back out onto the sidewalk beyond the gate.

"Your FBI friends went to a motel in P.B. instead of Headquarters up in Sorrento Valley."

P.B. was short for Pacific Beach. La Jolla's neighbor to the south. Higher zip code, but lower rent.

"So. They're probably from out of town. From wherever Stone was in WITSEC. They tracked him here and need a place to stay."

"Sharing the same room?" Moira put an emphasis on *room*.

"Maybe the Feds are finally on a budget," I said.

"Remember, this is a man and a woman team."

"A tight budget."

"I sat on them for an hour and was about to leave when the blond guy came out of the room with an ice bucket, unkempt hair, and wearing loafers without socks."

"You think they fooled around and were having a post-coital drink?" Something was off. An ice bucket at three in the afternoon. If you're a Fed working a case, do you check out for the day at three and start happy hour early? In your motel room with a female agent? Why else get ice at that time in the afternoon?

"That's my read. He looked pretty loose and content."

"You got all that watching him walk to the ice machine?"

"I had him in my binos. He was happy about something." Her voice flirty at the end of the sentence.

"Did they bring luggage into the motel room?"

"No, but they didn't go to the front desk either. They already had a room key."

"She was wearing a wedding ring when they came inside my house. He wasn't."

"So they're having an affair along with whatever else they're up to." Moira, sour.

"Sounds like it. What are you going to do now?"

"Sit on them for a while longer."

"What's the name of the motel?"

"Mission Bay Motel."

"They are on a budget." I glanced back up the walkway. The leathery man was walking along it toward me. I realized the sound from pounding tennis balls had lessened. Practice was coming to a close.

"Yes and, FBI or not, they're up to something."

Moira was dug in. She wouldn't walk away from the case unless I did. And maybe not even then. She was the best private investigator I knew and had always been pragmatic about the work. You don't take it personally. It's a job, not your life. But things changed a couple years ago when her son went missing and we teamed up to find him. Ever since, she'd adopted my philosophy. Some cases do become personal. Find the truth no matter what. I hadn't decided yet if the change was to her benefit or detriment. The philosophy hadn't worked out great for me. I didn't have a choice. The need was in my blood.

But now, we didn't have a braking system when we were cannon-balling down the train tracks. Blind curves could be disastrous.

"Be very careful." I tried my best to be the brakeman, even if I had no experience at it. "And you have to be paid."

"No, I don't. But I do have to write up a final report tonight on a case I just completed, and then I can work this full-time. But I'm not taking any money from Krista's future fund. Keep it."

"You're getting paid or you're not working this with me. Half." I needed Stone's money, but even half of the $50,000 would leave a nice chunk to go to Krista's future.

"I'll take a two-thousand-dollar retainer and refund you the difference if we find Angela Albright before the end of the week. If it goes longer than that, we can talk about it then. I'm giving you the friends and family discount. No arguments. That's the deal."

"Okay." It felt like a victory to get her to take anything. She was never hesitant to take her fair cut on cases we worked together that she had asked for my help with. I guess it was different for her when she helped me. Like she was taking money away from Krista that had already been placed in her piggy bank. "Call me if anything happens in the next hour and a half, then let's meet at your house around five thirty and talk about where to go from here."

"Are you going to tell Stone that you have a partner looking for his dau . . . looking for Angela Albright?"

"I haven't decided yet."

"Do you believe he's really looking for Angela because he needs a kidney transplant?"

"I haven't decided that yet, either. I'll make that decision when we find her."

CHAPTER 13

THE LA JOLLA High Girls tennis team headed to their locker room after a team huddle. More than likely, Cassie Albright would go home once she left the locker room. When she was home, I wouldn't have access to her for the rest of the day and night. I had to decide whether to try to intercept her on her way to her car or on her way to a friend's car, or on her way to wait for her father to pick her up, or not talk to her at all.

I doubted Cassie would tell me where her mother was if Angela wanted to stay hidden. And it certainly seemed that way.

My gut kept telling me that Cassie was in contact with her mom. If I staked her out for a few days she might lead me to Angela. But what if Angela was out of town? That seemed more than likely if her best friend, Lindsey Breck, hadn't seen her in a month. If so, she and Cassie were probably communicating via phone.

Tapping someone's cell phone was difficult and against the law, but not impossible. However, monitoring calls to and from an innocent sixteen-year-old girl who was secretly communicating with her mother so her father or, maybe, someone else didn't know about it was creepy. And when it came to children, creepy was where I drew the line.

Would it be any less creepy to tail her around town, hoping she'd meet her mother? Yes, just less creepy enough to stay behind the line.

It was invasive, but there was nothing illegal about it unless the police thought I was stalking her. But for that to happen, Cassie would have to know I was following her, and I wouldn't let that happen. That's where Moira would come in. We'd do a two-car tail.

First, I needed to find out if Cassandra Albright had her own car. She was only sixteen, but La Jollans buying their children cars on their sixteenth birthday was a rite of passage. Kind of like Latina girls and quinceañeras. I wondered if La Jolla Latina girls got the huge celebration on their fifteenth birthday and a car the next year. Double dipping.

I logged onto an insurance company website on my phone and started the process for a quote on car insurance. I typed in Steven Albright's name and his home address. When I hit the button for a quote, the make, model, and year of three cars for the residence came up, and I was asked if I wanted insurance for them or a different car.

A nice hack to find what someone drove that I found by accident when I was thinking of changing insurance companies last year.

The cars listed at the Albright residence were a 2020 Tesla Model S, a 2019 Lexus RX, and a 2023 Kia Soul. No license plate numbers, but I got what I needed. The Tesla was Angela's. Maybe a divorce parting gift. I didn't see Steven Albright driving around in a Kia Soul, unless he was campaigning again and targeting a younger demographic.

I jogged back to my car and drove around the school looking for a Kia Soul. I found four of them. Two on the street and two in the high school parking lot. I looked up the 2023 model and saw only one that matched. Parked in the parking lot. I went all in that the yellow-green Soul belonged to Cassie Albright.

Ten minutes after I began my stakeout from my car parked on the street a half a block down, my bet was confirmed. Cassandra Albright got into the yellow-green Soul and pulled out of the lot. I waited until she turned right onto Draper, then slowly followed after her.

She took Draper to Pearl Street then left onto Girard. When she got onto Torrey Pines Road, I was 90 percent certain she was heading to her family home. Sure enough, she turned onto La Jolla Shores Drive and finally left onto Spindrift Drive. I passed behind her after she turned into the driveway of her father's mansion across from the La Jolla Beach and Tennis Club. That consulting gig must have paid much better than being a politician. Then again, he probably wouldn't have been offered the consulting job if he hadn't been, and still could be, a politician.

The skids the public never sees that have to be greased.

My phone rang on my car speakers. Special Agent John Mallon. I answered through the car.

"Who told you about Sergei Volkov?"

"Like I said, I heard it through the grapevine. About to lose my mind."

"What?" Gen Y had no sense of musical history. My dad raised me on old-school R&B. "What are you talking about?"

"Never mind. So, I take it it's true. Sergei is getting out? Soon?"

"You need to tell me where this information came from."

Legally, I didn't. But to learn what I needed to, I had to tell him something.

"How about we meet at the Starbucks in UTC in a half hour and I'll tell you what I know?" I wanted to be face-to-face when I asked Mallon about Special Agents Dennis Sorensen and Charlene Bowden.

A long stretch of silence, then Mallon finally spoke.

"Okay, but you better not be wasting my time."

"I'm not." At least not yet.

* * *

University Towne Center was buzzing. The Starbucks at UTC, the massive shopping mall northeast of La Jolla, was like Starbucks everywhere. Impersonal in a faux personal way, filled with twenty- and thirty-somethings with their eyes pinned to individual social media devices.

Mallon was already seated at a two top in the back by the time I came through the door. He sipped something drenched in whipped cream. Looked like a caffeinated milkshake. The golden boy's one vice. Well, that and sometimes helping me without his Special Agent in Charge's consent. Or knowledge.

Mallon had golden boy looks without the gold. Dark hair. Strong jaw. Fit in an accountant racquetball kind of way. Looked younger than his mid-thirties age.

"John." I smiled and sat down opposite him. "Thanks for meeting me. What do I owe you for the coffee froth?"

He frowned. "I'm paying for it."

"I guess, as a taxpayer, I sort of am already paying for it." I smiled, but he didn't like the joke. Feds didn't have much of a sense of humor these days. If they ever did. "Kidding."

"Who told you about Sergei Volkov?" The frown tightened. Mallon leaned forward and spoke in almost a whisper. "Peter Stone?"

The name not to be spoken out loud. Even by a special agent from the FBI. The same organization that gave Stone a get-out-of-jail-free-card. After he ratted out Volkov and his syndicate. And the same organization that Dennis Sorensen and Charlene Bowden worked for when they threatened me with prison if I didn't tell them the truth about talking to Stone

The less people who knew about my connection to Stone the better. For my health. But I didn't think John Mallon, who was almost a friend, or at least an acquaintance, would want to send me to prison.

"I have the feeling the information came from Stone." Some truth and some lie. My usual for law enforcement.

"Do you know where Stone is?"

"No." The truth. Right now. "How would I know where he is? He's stashed away in some small town under a new name via WITSEC, right?"

Mallon looked around the coffee shop at all the froth sippers, most of whom were near his age. And all of whom seemed fully absorbed in their "smart" devices. The machines we kept within an arm's length of our bodies twenty-four hours a day that made us dumb and docile. When Mallon was sure no zombies were listening, he leaned forward and spoke again in a low tone.

"Stone disappeared three days ago."

"Wow." Emmy-worthy. "You think his disappearance had something to do with Volkov's early exit from prison?"

"I don't know." He blinked rapidly a couple times. His conscience rebelling against his lie. A tell. "Have you talked to him?"

"What? Why would Peter Stone want to talk to me?"

"You forget that I know about what happened at his house in La Jolla before he testified against Volkov." He tried to read my expression, which was feigned bewilderment. "I know about the gun battle."

Gun battle. Spoken like someone who'd never pulled a trigger except on a range. I thought about the lives lost and the ones I'd taken and wished I'd never pulled a trigger anywhere else, either. For the thousandth time. But the past was my destiny and there was nothing I could do about it now.

"Stone saved my life while saving his own. It was happenstance. It doesn't make us confidants. Or even friends." This time I leaned forward and lowered my voice. "This is in confidence, friend to friend. Stone tried to kill me in that same house many years before. He and I are not pals, Special Agent Mallon. He's a bad memory."

Mallon blinked. Stone trying to shoot me was news to him. But it would be news to anyone except Moira. She was the only person I ever told.

"That doesn't change anything." Mallon recovered his composure. "You two obviously set aside your differences by the time he saved your life."

"I didn't set aside anything. You can believe me or not." I took my phone out of my jeans pocket, found the photo Moira sent me this morning, and put it down in front of Mallon. "These are Special Agents Dennis Sorensen and Charlene Bowden. They came to my house this morning looking for Peter Stone. Are they from your office up in Solana Beach?"

"I can't comment on Bureau personnel even to confirm or deny." Mallon's eyes micro-blinked. Wouldn't have noticed it if I hadn't been looking. He gave away nothing else. He was getting better at the game. When I first encountered him a few years ago, his face was a lie detector. But he gave me enough to know that he recognized someone in the photo.

"Well, would it surprise you that these two followed me through La Jolla to my home today in a non-FBI company car?"

"What cars people drive is their own business." No tell this time.

"Are they married? To each other?"

"I just told you I can't comment on Bureau personnel."

"I guess shacking up together in a run-down motel room is okay now, too. Especially since she was wearing a wedding ring and he wasn't." I leaned over the table toward Mallon who was sipping from his paper Starbucks cup. "And Special Agent Sorensen looked pretty satisfied and a little ruffled on a post-coital ice run."

"What are you getting at, Cahill?"

"You ever hear of a Theodore Raskin who created the cryptocurrency exchange BitChange?" I studied him again. Nothing.

"No." He snapped off the word and narrowed his eyes on me. "What is this all about? You promised not to waste my time, but you're playing games about whether you spoke with Peter Stone and now you're asking me about cryptocurrency exchanges."

"I didn't waste your time when I told you that Sergei Volkov was getting out of prison this Friday." I folded my arms across my chest and leaned back on my stool. "You didn't know about it. And you're probably wondering why you didn't know about it. So am I. That's worth a piece of your time."

"Go on." He threw his hands up.

"Bowden and Sorensen asked me if Stone hired me to find this Theodore Raskin. I thought you might know who he is and why special agents want to know if Stone is looking for him."

"What are you getting at?"

"I've got FBI agents threatening to put me in jail if I don't tell them things that I don't even know about Peter Stone. I want to know if they're on a legit assignment or working something on their own."

"I already told you I can't—"

"Are you going to make me pull out the favor card, John?"

"You've already used that up."

"This is my life, dammit." The words tumbled hard out of my mouth. Ever since I'd learned about the CTE, I felt my life clock ticking in the background. My time was running out at a faster pace than before. That had a way of focusing me on the important things. Quickly. "And all the favors I asked for ended up benefiting you in some way."

Mostly.

Mallon frowned at me, then gazed at nothing over my shoulder. Thinking.

"They're both out of the Seattle Office. I'm not privy to what assignment they're working on."

"Did they check in with anyone at San Diego headquarters about working a case down here?"

"I don't know." His eyebrows went up. He was telling the truth.

"Wouldn't that be standard procedure?"

"Yes." Mallon took one last sip of his coffee, then stood up.

"Where are you going?"

"To find some answers."

"Remember who asked the questions first," I said.

Mallon left Starbucks with his coffee froth.

CHAPTER 14

I MET MOIRA at her house on Fay Ave., a block down from the high school, at 5:35 p.m. The forest green California Craftsman Cottage had been in her late husband's family for years. Tiny lot without a garage or even a driveway that would probably go for two million for someone to tear down if she ever wanted to sell. She didn't.

Moira wasn't alone when she met me at the door. She never was anymore. She'd found the new love of her life after living alone since her son left for college eight years ago. Bandit, her one-eye rescue pug mix, jumped up on my leg as soon as she opened the door. He didn't even bark at my knock anymore. He either smelled my scent through the door or recognized the cadence of my knocks.

"Hey, buddy." I leaned over and scratched him behind the ears.

"I guess you passed the security check." Moira stood holding the door, then stepped back. "Come in."

I went over and sat down on the sofa that represented the living room area in the modern open floor plan that was in stark juxtaposition to the classic exterior of the cottage. Bandit jumped up and sat next to me and put his head on my thigh.

"Anything happen with the Feds after our call?" I laid an envelope of cash down onto the coffee table between the sofa and armchair Moira sat in. Her $2,000 retainer.

"I would have called you." A frown. Needless small talk. She picked up the envelope, walked over to the dinner table, and set it down in the middle. She came back and sat across from me. "Bandit likes to chew up paper. Anything paper."

I looked down at the little munchkin and got a pop-eyed look of innocence.

"Good to know." I told her about my time watching tennis at La Jolla High and following Cassie Albright to her home.

"You're really certain that she's talking to her mother?" Moira asked when I was done.

"You're not? Put yourself in Angela's shoes. Wouldn't you be in contact with Luke if you were in some sort of hiding and he was still in high school?"

"Not all mothers are created equal," she deadpanned. "Or fathers."

"What do you mean by that?" My face flashed hot, and I felt a rage I'd kept at bay for months crawl up my spine. Irrational anger triggered by my CTE. I closed my eyes and pushed my right index finger against my left palm and slowly counted to three inside my head, visualizing the numbers changing colors with each slow breath. The rage slid back into the darkness, but I could still feel its muted presence.

When I opened my eyes, Moira was staring at me. Concern in her big brown eyes. I ignored the look and continued. "If I moved to Santa Barbara now, I still wouldn't see Krista more than two weeks a month. And if Leah and I aren't back together by the time Krista's in school, I'm going to move up there so I don't miss any of her life's milestones."

"Whoa! Whoa!" Moira threw up her hands. "I wasn't talking about you. You're a good father. I meant both Angela and Steven Albright. I'd never let myself be in Angela's position. No way would I take off and leave my sixteen-year-old child behind. And it sounds to me like

Steven Albright was more concerned about winning the divorce than thinking about what was best for his daughter by fighting for majority custody. That's what I meant. None of this had anything to do with you, Rick. I know you're a good dad."

I exhaled long and slowly and felt the heat dissipate along my skin. "Sorry."

"Don't worry about it." She shrugged her shoulders but couldn't hide her concern.

But I did worry about it. All of it. My reawakened rage, Krista dealing with living in two houses in two different cities, my broken marriage. The weight of it all pressed down on me. Pressure building inside me. Moira across from me, fading into the background. The background itself fading into nothingness.

Images of Leah and Krista swirled in my head. Leah, the night in Santa Barbara when I fell in love with her. Then the night we both almost died. Her morning fresh-faced bedhead smile at her most beautiful. Krista, red-faced and crying at birth. Saying "Dadda" for the first time and every time. Tossing the tennis ball to Midnight in the backyard. The memories of my life. More memories yet to be made while I could still experience them.

And still remember them.

Then it hit me like a taser. Carbon pressurized into diamond. I sprang off the couch. Bandit's ears and one eye popping. Moira squinting.

"What are you doing?"

"I need a favor."

"What?" Her head pushed back and tilted to the right?

"Can you go to my house, feed Midnight, and bring him over here for the night?" I hurried to the front door.

"Of course. Where are you going to be?"

"Santa Barbara."

CHAPTER 15

EVENING RUSH HOUR. I couldn't have picked a worse time to drive to Santa Barbara. Well, maybe morning rush hour. It took me forty-five minutes to get past Oceanside and two and a half hours to get past Los Angeles. I finally pulled up the Landingham driveway at 9:55 p.m. Leah wasn't expecting me. I didn't call her on the way up. What I had to say needed to be said in person. Face-to-face.

Her Ford Escape SUV sat in the darkened driveway of her parents' home. Parents who could barely stomach me when Leah, Krista, and I were an intact family. Their contempt was up front now that we permanently lived apart. The fact that I got into an altercation with Leah's father, Spence, the last time I was inside the house didn't help. I was now the enemy.

Tonight, I didn't care.

I was too late to see Krista, unless I wanted to watch her sleep. Something I'd done manically when she lived in my home. And one of the things that led to the situation I was in now. Estranged from the family I loved. From the one human being on the planet who loved me unconditionally. And from the other one who used to.

I got out of my car, pulled out my phone, and texted Leah.

Me: *I'm outside on the driveway. We need to talk. It won't take long. I don't have to come inside.*

I waited thirty seconds. A minute. Two. I doubted Leah was asleep. She stayed up late. Possibly in the shower or in front of the TV with her mom and dad.

I leaned against my car and waited. I wasn't going to knock on the door and disrupt the whole family's life. I didn't even really want to disrupt Leah's life. My goal was clarity. For both of us. As clear as things could be at the present time.

I could wait. Until morning when she went to work, if needed. I'd sleep in my car.

Finally, a couple minutes later, the porch light went on. I didn't move. The door opened a foot, and Leah's head popped outside.

She spotted me from forty feet away. The expression on her face was hard to discern. A frown or just a flat expression? She slipped out onto the porch and eased the door closed. It didn't make a sound. She didn't want her parents to know that she'd gone outside. And that I was at their home. I understood and didn't care.

She stepped off the porch. Sweatpants and a white T-shirt. Barefoot. Her normal attire for a quiet night at home. The nights I missed more than I let anyone know. Sometimes, even myself.

We met at the hood of her SUV. Her arms wrapped tightly around her chest. A grim expression on her face.

"We have an agreement, Rick." Her voice low and stern. "We each have her for two weeks without interruption. I've been more than fair."

The "more than fair" comment could be interpreted a number of ways. None to my benefit. One being that Leah was being generous by letting me see my own child. I let it pass. I hadn't driven four hours to argue.

"I'm not here to usurp any of your time with our daughter. I'm not even asking to see her."

"Then why are you here?" She gripped herself tighter.

"I've decided to sell the house." No need for a preamble after the long drive. The porch light illuminated her eyes. A shade of blue that always made me think of the ocean just after sunrise. Eyes that up until five or six months ago reflected love and filled me with warmth. Eyes that now kept me at arm's length and were clouded with suspicion. "And move up here."

I didn't tell her that I'd only made the decision four hours ago, more on a gut feeling than after deep consideration. Or that I hadn't even considered how I'd make a living as a private investigator starting from scratch in a city with a population of less than 90,000 after drawing from a client base of one and a half million. But maybe it was time to find something else to do. Something that wouldn't compel me to make decisions that drove a wedge between my wife and me.

All that mattered was being close to Krista. Even if I couldn't see her every day or even every week. Being near her was enough. Knowing I could get to her in minutes if I was needed.

And being close to Leah. And maybe getting one last chance to be a family again. Whole. Intact. Content.

"Wow." She squeezed herself still tighter. "When did you decide to do this?"

"Today, but it's been on my mind for a while." True, but always as something in the future. Three or four years down the road. But my quality of life wasn't guaranteed four years from now. Life only offered one guarantee. An end.

"Things have changed over the last few months, Rick. You know that." She looked down at the driveway and let out a long exhale then looked back at me. "Krista has gotten used to the routine we have. I don't want to confuse her right now. And I feel like you and I have grown farther apart."

"I'm not asking to change the routine we have right now. I'm not asking anything. I just don't want Krista to live two hundred miles away from her father. And I wanted to tell you right away. Face-to-face."

"I understand. I appreciate that." She looked at the ground again. "But then you should know that I've talked to a lawyer."

The air left my body. Somehow, I kept from doubling over. It wasn't a huge surprise, but it still stunned me. Divorce was always a possibility. But in the back of my mind, and sometimes foremost, I always imagined Leah and me getting back together. I didn't think it would be easy, and I didn't have a timetable, but I thought it would happen. It still could, but now it would take a Hail Mary.

As bad as that news was, it didn't change my decision to move up to Santa Barbara. I was moving for Krista. And, selfishly, for myself. Getting back together with Leah would be, to me, the logical conclusion to reuniting with Krista. But not getting back together, or even having a chance, wouldn't stop me from being close to my daughter.

"Should I expect divorce papers in the mail soon?" The pride in me, that foolish pride, forced me to maintain my composure.

"No. Nothing's finalized. I'm not that far along. I'm only looking at my options." Tears welled in Leah's eyes and her voice wobbled. "But do you think that things will miraculously get better with us if you move up here? Nothing's changed between us."

"Maybe nothing's changed between us, but I'm making a big change. I'm moving from my hometown, the city I love, to be near my daughter." My voice caught in my throat. "And you."

"That could just make everything worse." The tears now rolled down her cheeks. She dropped her arms and started pacing back and forth. "You'd still be a private investigator. And—"

"I'm—"

"Let me finish." Her voice rose. "You'd be bringing danger back into Krista's life again. You have no idea how much I worry every time she stays with you in San Diego. I don't sleep for two solid weeks because I can't stop wondering if you're working some case that you won't let go of that will put you and Krista in danger. That you've awakened some killer who's now targeting you and our family. You know I'm right. That's why you have loaded guns all over your house. I can't have that in my life for three hundred sixty-five days a year. Half the time is bad enough."

"I can quit. I'll find something else to do." The words stung as I said them out loud. Made them real. My life's mission, found late and through tragedy but one that gave me a purpose, had to be abandoned. For my family. A greater purpose. The frenetic drive inside me would have to be redirected.

"I don't think you *can* quit." She stopped pacing, turned toward me, and wiped her cheeks, but the tears kept coming. "It's who you are. I've come to terms with that. Your drive to right a wrong is one of the reasons I fell in love with you. But I see now what it has done to you. It's made you reckless when your family needs you safe more than a client needs you solving their problems. Righting wrongs has become more important than living a good life. It scares me, and I can't have it in Krista's life."

Leah knew me as well as I knew myself. Even though I kept some of the darkness inside me from her, she knew me from my soul out.

I didn't see the world in black and white. Hadn't since I was a ten-year-old kid and found out that my father, a hero to me, faultless, could do wrong. The beginning of the gray I saw in life. I lived it. But I also knew that there was true evil in this world. And when confronted by it, I had to fight it. I could run, and maybe hide. But I'd leave a vacuum for it to exist and grow stronger.

If I ran, would I still be the father Krista could be proud of?

The police were supposed to be civil society's protection against evil. And it worked much of the time. Sometimes when I needed it to. At its best, law enforcement was a force for good and held civilization together. But I'd been a cop. I'd seen the internal politics that could skew justice. Slow it down.

Evil didn't wait. Didn't follow rules or laws. It followed its immediate wants without the restraints of conscience.

Could I ignore it for the rest of my cognitive time left on earth?

"I'll quit. As soon as I sell the house."

I forced myself to believe my own words even as I knew Leah didn't.

CHAPTER 16

I PULLED INTO my driveway around 2:15 a.m. The drive home from Santa Barbara had been extended by a stop at a Denny's in Torrance. The first thing I'd eaten since lunch yesterday. Midnight breakfast for dinner. The pancakes had dropped a drowsy carbo bomb in my gut, and I couldn't get into bed quickly enough.

The right side of my garage had a home gym in it; the left side was empty. The spot where Leah used to park her Ford Escape. She hadn't been home, at our home, for six months.

I left my car in the driveway and walked to the front door. The left side of the garage would remain vacant for the 174th day in a row. The house was completely dark. I'd left Moira's for Santa Barbara on a whim that turned into a mission. No time to stop by my house beforehand. Moira picked Midnight up, so I didn't hear him snuffling on the other side of the door when I put the key in the lock.

The first thing I noticed when I went inside the house was that there was no blinking light on the alarm panel next to the hall closet.

Too late.

"Hands up." The voice hit my ears at the same time as cold cylindrical steel pressed against the back of my neck. My heartbeat turboed, but I stood stock-still. A wrong move, a twitch, a quick breath, anything could get me killed.

I slowly raised my hands and waited for the next command. And hoped there was one coming and not the vibration from the click of a trigger and a boom I'd never hear. I said a quick prayer in my head asking God to watch over Krista and Leah and thanked Moira for picking up Midnight. If he'd been home, he would have died protecting the house. Even without me in it.

A hand reached around my chest and searched both sides and under my arms. It stopped when it pressed against the shoulder holster under my left arm through the leather of my bomber jacket.

"Don't move." In my ear. Slavic accent? The barrel of the gun pressed harder against my neck, and the hand slipped inside my jacket, undid the snap on the holster, and pulled out the Glock 19. It disappeared behind me. The unseen man removed my gun so deftly that it was clear he'd disarmed someone from behind before. Probably many times.

The hand, empty again, slid up and down the inside and outside of my legs. The Glock was the only gun I had. On me. There were more in the gun safe upstairs and a few scattered in hidden places throughout the house. One in the hall closet directly in front of me. But if I played hero now, I'd end up dead. If killing me was his initial plan, I'd already be dead. I needed to play along and find out what he wanted. His hand went into my jeans pocket and came out with my phone.

"Walk." The voice behind me and then pressure from the gun against my neck. I walked into the living room, which was dark, but I could just make out the outline of someone sitting in my recliner and two other bodies standing around it.

I had a brief flashback to another time when a gunman invaded my house.

I made it out alive that night. So did my family.

One of the standing outlines moved, and the lamp on the end table next to the recliner lit up the living room.

And revealed Sergei Volkov sitting in my chair. In my house. I'd seen him on the TV news before, but never in person. He dwarfed my La-Z-Boy in his blue and gray Adidas sweats. He was a flesh-colored brick. Thick, rectangular, and hard. Bald head the size of a pony keg, a fist for a nose, and coal black eyes devoid of emotion. Thick slashes of eyebrows matched the color of his eyes.

Everything about him read merciless. Final.

It was true. Somehow, the cutthroat leader of the Southern California Russian Mob had gotten out of prison. What kind of deal had he made with the Department of Justice? Whatever it was, the high-up official cocooned in his or her generously appointed office in Washington, D.C., may have just signed my death warrant. Collateral damage in favor of the greater good. Whatever that was this month.

Sergei aimed a glare over my shoulder and nodded his chin a sixteenth of an inch. The gun barrel left the back of my neck. I slowly brought my arms down to my sides.

"Where is Stone?" The deep-chested wolf snarl I'd heard on the phone when Peter Stone brokered a deal to save my life, and again a year later when I had to pay the back end of the agreement. A hard-edged Russian accent that sliced through my living room.

No mention of his daughter, Tatiana. Volkov wanted Stone, just like everybody else. He hadn't put together the supposed pieces of Tatiana's murder as Stone claimed to have. Yet.

I didn't have to lie, just like when the Feds asked the same question about Stone. But I doubted Volkov would walk away as gently as the FBI agents did after I gave them the answer.

"I don't know. He came by here this morning, but I haven't seen or heard from him since." I didn't try to look sincere. I didn't have to. I was telling the truth. But I knew it wouldn't be that easy. The next question would be more difficult to answer.

"Why did he come here?"

The moment of truth. "He wanted to hire me, but I told him I didn't want the job."

"What job?"

An image of Krista popped up into my mind. When she was here with me in San Diego. Tossing a tennis ball with Midnight in the backyard. An underhand flick that sent the ball fifteen or twenty feet. A giggle accompanied every toss, and again when Midnight returned the ball to her. Then Cassandra Albright took her place, pounding tennis balls over a net. Children who needed both their parents.

"He wanted me to find someone, but I turned him down."

"Find who?"

"Some long-lost relative. He needs a kidney transplant, but missing persons isn't my specialty. I'm not very good at it, and my caseload is heavy right now." The most convincing lies always contain kernels of truth. The more kernels the better. I threw the lie off as convincingly as I could. A true statement that I didn't have to think about even though I was mostly lying. A discard.

"What's the name?"

I had to give him someone. Someone real. I'd give him Angela Albright, but he'd never find her.

"Louise Abigail Delano." The name on Angela's birth certificate but not on any driver's license she'd ever owned. The trail to find her would lead to a dead end. Angela would be safe, unless she was already unsafe or someone other than Stone was after her.

"You take me for a patient man because I let you live five years ago." Matter of fact. No menace. A man used to getting his way. Couldn't imagine a world in which he didn't. Probably even when he was in prison. "That was a mistake. You had very little value to me then. Now you have none. Where is Stone?"

Cold steel pressed against the back of my neck again. Right on cue. My body fisted and I waited for the threat and the punishment.

"If I knew, I'd tell you." The truth. I might not have told the Feds the whole truth, but they didn't stick a gun in my neck. "I have no reason to lie and a lot of reasons not to. Peter Stone isn't worth it."

"Who is this Delano woman?"

"Some relative Stone hopes will be a match as a kidney donor."

Sergei looked over my shoulder at the gunman behind me. "Phone."

The man tossed my phone to the bodyguard on Sergei's left.

"Check texts and calls over the last week," Sergei said to the man now holding my phone.

"1215," I said.

"What?" Sergei.

"The passcode to open the phone."

The man tapped my phone a few times and then used his thumb. Scrolling. We all waited in silence while the bodyguard searched for something he'd never find—contact between Stone and me.

Sergei stared at me the whole time. Dead eyes that had seen more death than Stone's and mine together.

"Nothing." Heavy Russian accent from the bodyguard.

"Like I said." Volkov grunted and rose up out of the recliner to his full six-foot-four-inch height. "You have no value to me."

Another slight nod to the man holding death against my neck, then Volkov stepped around me. The gun barrel pressed harder into me. Sweat squeezed out of my pores. The time left on my life's clock was only the few seconds it would take Volkov to exit my house.

"Move." The killer behind me, pushing me farther into the living room.

"What about Theodore Raskin?" The words sped out of my mouth, a high-pitched prayer to live. I hoped God heard me. But I hoped Volkov heard me more.

The man behind me kept pushing me deeper into the living room.

"Vlad." Volkov.

The pushing stopped and the gun barrel against my neck was replaced by a hand around it. The hand directed me to turn and face the Russian Mob boss.

"What about him?" The snarl returned to Volkov's voice.

"The FBI was here this morning asking about Stone, too. Special Agents Sorensen and Bowden. I told them exactly what I told you. That Stone had come by here and I didn't know where he was. Then they asked me if Stone hired me to find Theodore Raskin."

"But you said Stone hired you to find some relative named Louise Delana."

"Delano." I reflexively corrected him for some odd reason, though it did add veracity to my half lie. "He did, but the Feds think he's looking for Raskin, the cryptocurrency exchange guy."

"What do you know about Raskin?" He barked the question like an accusation.

Volkov knew who Raskin was. He knew more about him than I'd gotten from a Google search. His agitation seemed personal. I had the feeling that Theodore Raskin, who the Feds and Sergei Volkov both knew about, was the centerpiece to the whole Stone puzzle. Yet, Stone didn't mention him.

"I'd never heard of him until the Feds asked about him. After they left, I googled him and found out he was some kind of computer genius who started his own cryptocurrency exchange. I don't know anything more than that."

"No value." Volkov turned and headed for the front door.

The hand on the back of my neck twisted again, directing me into the darkened part of the living room, next to Krista's pink toybox. Best-case scenario was that I'd die quickly unless I could make it into the kitchen over to the butcherblock island. There was a knife block on top of it with very sharp knives. But my aim was for the drawer underneath. And the Sig Sauer P320 inside it.

Seconds left. I couldn't make my move into the kitchen until Volkov and his other two killers were out the front door. A move that would probably end my life, but the only one I had.

"The Feds are looking for Raskin and wanted to know if Stone was, too. Maybe he is. Maybe he hired someone else to find him. I can find out."

No response. Just the click of the front door opening. I took a deep breath waiting for the sound of the door closing. But I heard a voice instead.

"Vlad." Volkov again.

The hand turned me back to face the front door. Volkov handed something to the man on his left. Tall and thin, all in black with a leather jacket, a wedge of jet-black hair. The man walked over to me, a smirk on his face. He handed me a blank business card with a phone number written on it in black ink and my phone.

"Set up a meet with Stone." Volkov, his voice as flat as the blade of a boning knife. "Make it for here at your home. Give him whatever reason you can think of to get him here. Then call that number."

"I don't have a number or an address for him. He contacts me."

"Well, I hope he contacts you very soon."

"What if he won't come?" I didn't like Stone, and I didn't trust him. But I wasn't going to set him up to be murdered.

Volkov thrust his chin out and looked behind me. Where Krista's toy crate stood.

"It's a shame that you are separated from your family. Protecting his family is the most important thing a man can do in his life." His voice caught an edge that could cut diamond. "I know what it's like to lose a child. I wouldn't want someone to do something stupid like talk to the police or warn Stone and have to worry about his own little girl."

My hands balled into fists and my neck flexed into a tight cord.

"Hun, uh." The voice behind me. The hand dropped away from my neck and was replaced by the gun again.

Volkov turned slowly and went out the front door. His two bodyguards followed. The gun dropped away from my neck and I got my first look at the man who'd been behind me for the last ten minutes. The black jeans and leather coat uniform of his compatriots. Hair and eyes that matched his coat. A nine-inch suppressor was screwed into the barrel of his Sig Sauer. A suppressor to quiet the shot that Volkov had intended for my head.

The assassin grinned at me, then headed for the door.

"Give me back my gun," I said to his back.

He laughed and went out the door. I ran to the hall closet, grabbed the Colt Python from the top shelf, and sped to the door. I checked the peephole. No sign of the Russians. I spied and waited. The rumble of an engine, then its sound dissipating, then silence.

I pulled out my phone. 2:23 in the morning. The time of night when a phone call can only be bad news. I had to make it anyway.

I went into my phone's contact list and tapped a number. The person picked up on the fourth ring.

"Hello?" Gruff, foggy. Spence Landingham, Leah's father and Krista's grandfather. And someone who drifted between disliking and despising me. Tonight, I'd give him more ammunition for the despise side.

"Spence, it's Rick. I need you to listen very carefully."

"What the hell is this all about? It's two thirty in the morning!"

"Spence? What is it?" Myriam Landingham's voice in the background.

"Just listen to me. This is important. You need to take Leah and Krista away from the house as soon as they get up. For at least a week or two. Maybe to your friend's place up in the mountains. Leave Krista's car in the driveway and go someplace that you don't own, and don't use a credit card for gas or anything you buy."

"What the hell's going on, Rick?"

"I'm just taking precautions. I don't think we'll need them, but you need to take care of your family."

Spence had been a cop for thirty years. He knew when to ask questions and when to take action.

"Okay." Spence Landingham hung up and prepared to protect his family.

My family. Who I should have been protecting myself.

CHAPTER 17

My phone woke me out of a coffin fog later that morning at 7:00 a.m.

"We have work to do. I'm sitting on your FBI friends at the motel. Might want to tag team them when they leave. When are you going to be home? I don't hear car noise. You're not on the road yet?" Moira's rat-a-tat-tat voice immediately shook the lingering slumber out of me. I was used to operating on minimal sleep. I'd done it most of my life. But not usually from having killers surprise me in my own home. That *had* happened before, but it's not something you get used to. Especially when one of the killers threatens to kill your daughter. My night of sleep shrank down to a two-hour sweat nap.

"I'm home. How's Midnight?"

"He's fine. He's such a sweetheart. I'm hoping he can teach Bandit how to behave."

"Thanks for taking care of him." Moira had saved Midnight's life by picking him up before Sergei Volkov and his goons arrived.

"Anytime, of course. Anything you want to tell me about the trip?" A hint of softness in her voice. She knew Santa Barbara meant Leah and Krista. My family. My heart. Disassembled.

"No." I wasn't ready to tell Moira I was moving. And I wasn't ready to tell her about Leah's divorce lawyer. Hell, I wasn't ready to deal with any of it myself. And a more pressing matter had shown up in my house last night. "Not yet, but I did have a welcome party waiting for me when I got home at two fifteen this morning."

"What? Who?" Agitated.

I told her about Sergei Volkov and his men. And his threat.

"Oh my god!" Her voice pitched high. "What are you going to do? Go to the police? The FBI?"

"You know I can't do that after what Sergei said. Besides, the FBI have to be behind his early release from prison."

"Then what are you going to do?"

"Work the case." It was either that, set up Peter Stone for assassination, or kill Sergei Volkov and all his men. Something I'd do without a second thought to save my family. Though unlikely that I'd be able to kill them all without being arrested or killed by one of them I didn't account for. But if it came to that, I'd plan well. I'd done it before. Right now, things weren't that dire. Not yet. When they were, I'd do what I had to. And live or die with the consequences.

"What about Leah and Krista?" I could feel the vibration of her worry through the phone.

"I called Spence Landingham last night and warned him. He's going to move Leah and Krista to a hideaway. They'll be safe." For now. "I'll get a rental and meet you at Mission Bay Motel in about forty-five minutes."

The Feds knew my car. As incompetent as they appeared to be at surveillance, they'd probably catch on seeing Moira's car in their rear-view mirror all day, and I couldn't tag team in my own vehicle.

I still planned to tail Cassandra Albright in hopes that she would clandestinely meet her mom somewhere after school in the next few days. But she had school and tennis practice. I'd get to La Jolla High School by 11:30 a.m. in case she slipped away for a meet with her mother at lunch. Until then, I planned to try to stake out the Feds with Moira.

I took a quick shower, dressed, then scarfed down a bowl of Cheerios. I wasn't particularly hungry after the late dinner / early breakfast last night but didn't know when I'd get another chance to eat today. Cheerios were quicker than eggs and fairly harmless.

My phone rang as I sat down to eat.

Leah. Shit. I answered.

"Eight hours after you told me you were quitting your investigative work, Dad is rushing us out of the house to his friend's cabin up in the mountains?" Her voice a tight wire of anger. "What did you do? Who's after you, and why didn't you tell me that you put us in danger again when you were here last night?"

"I . . ." I didn't know how to answer that without alarming Leah more than she already was. "I received new information when I got home. There's really not much to worry about. Your father and I are just being cautious."

"Don't bring my dad into this, Rick." She hit the hard "C" in my name with a jackhammer. "This is all you. What is going on? And I thought you were quitting."

"I am. As soon as I sell the house. This has to do with an existing client."

"What is the *this*, Rick? You have to tell me!"

"Someone with a vendetta against one of my clients is out of prison and looking for him. That's all." And threatened Krista's life. "I just want you guys out of reach until this blows over."

"Who's the client, and who's looking for him?"

"You know I can't talk about clients." My voice, an apology.

"You're putting my family in danger." Each word a stab. "I need to know who the client is."

Peter Stone and Sergei Volkov were before Leah and I got together, but she was a cop's daughter who followed the news. She'd know the names. And I had to tell her them.

"Peter Stone is my client." I tried not to make the words sound as ominous as they were.

"The casino guy?" Her voice lost its edge. "Isn't he supposed to be in witness protection somewhere?"

"He is, but he's not right now."

"What does he want you to do?"

"Find his daughter." Maybe the familial aspect of the case would lessen Leah's worries.

"Who is looking for him?"

Shit. No lessening those worries now.

"Sergei Volkov." I tried to make his name sound nonthreatening. Impossible.

"The Russian Mafia boss?" Fear pitched her voice high. "I thought he was in prison."

"He was. He's out now."

"Do the police know about this? What about the FBI?" Frantic. "Have you talked to them?"

"He's out on a reduced sentence. Pretty sure it's compliments of the FBI via the Justice Department."

"What? Why?"

"I don't know." The truth. "He probably gave the Feds information on someone or something they wanted pretty badly?"

"Didn't Stone testify against him and help get him convicted?"

"Yes."

"You need to go to the police."

I didn't say anything. I didn't want to lie, and I didn't want to tell her the truth.

"Volkov threatened you if you go to the police, didn't he?"

I didn't answer.

"Oh my God!" Terror in her voice. "He threatened us, didn't he?"

"Stay in the cabin. Don't use any credit cards." I tried to sound calm, under control. As if I had control of anything in my life. "Your dad knows what to do."

"Dammit, Rick!" She hung up.

I stared at the phone and remembered for the thousandth time in my life that every decision, good or bad, had repercussions. Then I went upstairs and opened my gun safe and grabbed my Ruger SP 101 and its shoulder holster to replace the gun the Russian took off me last night.

I needed to be ready. For the next repercussion.

CHAPTER 18

THE NEAREST ENTERPRISE Rent-A-Car was only a mile from my house down on Garnet Avenue, off the I-5 freeway. I decided to walk and leave my car in the driveway so Volkov's men or the Feds would think I was home. No unfamiliar cars on the street, but the Russians or the Feds could be on higher ground with binoculars. I'd take my chances on foot.

Morning haze pushed down, leaving just a kiss of mist in the air. I figured I'd be moist but not drenched by the time I finished my twenty-minute walk to Enterprise. Not wet enough to Uber a mile or move my car from the driveway. My Padres hat kept the mist off my glasses.

Braving fall weather in Southern California wasn't easy.

Half a block down Moraga, I heard a car moving slowly behind me. My senses were still on high alert. They would be until Peter Stone and Sergei Volkov were again out of my life.

The hair on the back of my neck spiked. I spun around to face the car and thrust my hand under my coat and grabbed the grip of the Ruger in my shoulder holster.

Then let it drop.

Peter Stone stared at me through the windshield of a dark blue Mercedes Benz GLS. A slightly conspicuous car in my neighborhood, but run of the mill in Stone's old haunts of La Jolla. He pulled alongside me and stopped. The passenger window rolled down. His ivory-handled cane leaned against the passenger seat. An image of dead tuskless elephants invaded my mind.

"Out for a walk? Not ideal conditions for the morning constitutional."

I couldn't tell Stone what I was really up to. He'd want all my attention directed toward finding Angela Albright.

"We need to talk." I grabbed the door handle of the Mercedes, but the door was locked.

Stone gave me a Grinch grin, then slowly picked up his cane, put it in the back seat, and pushed a button on the control panel of his door unlocking the passenger side. I whipped the door open and jumped in.

"Drive." My family and I couldn't afford for me to be seen in a car with Stone in my neighborhood. Or anywhere. But, if I set up a later meet with him and told Sergei about it, my family would be out of danger. And maybe I would be, too.

"Where to, Miss Daisy?" Stone smiled like he thought he was being clever mentioning a movie that came out when I was ten years old.

"Make a left at the bottom of Moraga and head up the hill on Balboa."

"Certainly." The smile again. "Sorry I don't have a lukewarm bottled water to offer you."

Stone playing Uber driver surprised me. I couldn't imagine him ever using a ride-sharing service. Maybe he had gone really deep cover in his new life. Slumming it like the rest of us 99 percenters. Doubted it.

I let his stupid comment clank to the ground and didn't say anything until after we turned left on Balboa and were halfway up the hill.

"Pull into the Del Taco parking lot on the right at the top of the hill."

"Greasy fast food. The breakfast of champions."

I ignored him again and waited to speak until he turned into the parking lot.

"Park in the back." The back of the lot looked down over Balboa. I peered through the windshield looking for black Chevy Tahoes or black Hummers, which I'd seen Sergei Volkov's men drive years ago.

Stone parked and killed the engine of the hundred-thousand-dollar car. "No drive-through?"

"Why'd you come back today?"

"To learn about the progress you've made." His voice sharpened. "So tell me, Rick. What progress have you made?"

"Why not just call me?" I turned and looked at him. Blank expression. Dead eyes. "I'm sure you have my number, and if not, it's easy to find. I'm listed online like all the other P.I.'s in San Diego."

"I like to look a man in the face when I talk to him." He did just that.

"Maybe. Or maybe you don't want to take a chance that the Feds could be listening in on my phone. Are they listening to my calls?" Feds first. I needed to learn all I could about why the FBI was looking for him before I dropped the Sergei bomb.

"Why would the Feds, as you say, be listening to your phone calls? Is there something you're not telling me, Rick?"

"Same question. What aren't you telling me?"

"I don't know what you're talking about or what kind of game you're playing." Flat affect. To the uninitiated, Stone's response could pass for the truth. It wasn't.

"Two Feds in a black Chevy Tahoe followed me home from La Jolla yesterday then knocked on my door. Male-female team. Special Agents Sorensen and Bowden." I watched his eyes. They gave nothing. "You know them?"

"Hmm, I don't think so."

"Really?" I snapped the word off. Stone playing dumb was irritating. I preferred his normal menace. At least it was honest. "They knew *you*."

"I don't really deal with the FBI. The U.S. Marshals operate the WITSEC program. The FBI has nothing to do with it. They're involved on the front end, not the back. And I'm free to come and go as I please at my own risk."

"You're not supposed to go back to your hometown and contact former associates." He was hiding something. More than usual. He routinely held back information to wield later or withhold forever, whichever enhanced his power and control. This felt like something else. More a show of weakness than strength.

"I don't think anyone would consider you a former associate, Rick. Although I'm flattered that you do." The Stone smirk.

"You know what I mean." I spat the words at him. Stone had wedged his way under my skin. His method of keeping the upper hand. A mistake by me. I needed to keep it business. Not personal. "The agents asked about someone named Theodore Raskin. Wanted to know if you'd hired me to find him. Who is he?"

I studied Stone's eyes. They usually told me nothing or only what he wanted them to tell me. Or conveyed menace. Now they were cyphers. Blank. Not even malice.

"Raskin used to work for me. He was a computer whiz kid. I have no idea what the Feds want with him. What did they tell you?"

"Nothing. But I did my own homework. Raskin started a crypto-currency exchange a couple years ago." I gave Stone my best cop stare. It was like peering into obsidian. "So why don't you tell me what's really going on?"

He didn't say anything right away.

I watched the traffic flow up and down Balboa. The beginning of Clairemont's suburban rush hour. A steady pulse heading west down the hill toward the Interstate 5 commute. A trickle heading east. Nine-to-fivers starting their day. A rote routine that paid the bills and filled in the backbone of civilized society.

My job was different. For at least a few more weeks, I'd try to help people on the outskirts of civilized society or those desperately trying to stay inside it.

Stone finally spoke up. "Raskin works for Sergei's syndicate. Or, at least, he used to. I've been out of the game for a while."

Stone could claim to have been out of the game for a while, but I'd bet everything I owned that he still had mobbed-up connections who kept him informed about all things Sergei. Just as he had Fed connections in order to know that Sergei was getting out of prison. Or rather, was out of prison.

"What does he do for the syndicate and what did he do for you?"

"He made sure that the odds were fair for all the electronic gaming in my casino." A raised eyebrow.

"So, he made sure the odds were in your favor, more so than how the odds are always in the house's favor."

"I'll just say we were never cheated."

"Okay, that's what Raskin did for you. What does he do for Sergei?"

"I don't know. I told you. I've been out of the picture for a few years."

Stone lying to me, unaware that I held his life in my hands.

"You need to tell me the truth." More exasperation than anger in my voice. "I need to know everything you do in order to find Angela. If you don't tell me what's really going on, I'll look for Angela for a few more days, but that's it. I'm keeping the money you gave me and you can have the rest. What does Raskin do for Sergei?"

"Well, I'll make an educated guess for you, Rick, since you seem unable to make one for yourself." A smile that showed irritation instead of the usual smugness. "You say that Theodore Raskin has started a cryptocurrency exchange. Well, I'm not really up on the technology, but I do know that the true identity of people buying cryptocurrencies is hard to detect. Everyone uses a pseudonym. And, although the Feds are starting to catch up, an exchange would seem like an easy place to launder ill-gotten gains for those who choose such a life."

A life hardly foreign to Stone.

"And when is Sergei supposed to get out of prison?"

"Friday."

"Well, Friday came early." I watched his eyes. A flash of surprise, then quickly back to flat. Lifeless. If I hadn't been watching him intently, I might have missed it.

"How do you know?" Not the hint of a tremor or concern in his voice.

"Because he sat in the recliner in my house at two this morning while one of his killers held a gun to my head."

"What did he want?"

I appreciated Stone's concern for my welfare.

"You."

"You're still alive." His eyes narrowed down to stiletto points. "You must have given me up to him. Do you need to make a phone call, Rick?"

He slowly moved his right hand into his jacket pocket. No doubt now around the grip of a gun.

"How could I give you up to him?" My own gun was in a shoulder holster inside my coat. Stone, already holding his, had the edge in a quick draw. I had the edge in age and athleticism. But a gun in the hand is worth two aging jocks in the bush. I kept my hand in my lap. "I have no way of contacting you and no way of knowing when you're going to show up."

"Like I said, you're still alive. How did Sergei leave it?"

Stone, Sergei, my family. The man I owed my life to, the man trying to kill him, and the people I'd put in danger by being in the middle of the two of them. My debt to Stone had already been prepaid when he tried to kill me before he saved my life. Could I really give him up to

Sergei? In the world of karma, Stone was well past his due date to die for his sins. But in the real world, that was God's decision, not mine.

"He told me to set up a meet with you at my house the next time you contacted me."

"And you think you'd walk out of your house alive after Sergei's minions were through?"

I'd considered that Sergei wouldn't let me live. No witnesses. But I don't think he'd go after my family if I gave him Stone. If he knew I killed his daughter, he'd kill my family in front of me, but everything else was business.

"It doesn't matter what I think. You're still alive, but he threatened my family. How long do you think you're going to live with Sergei looking for you? You shouldn't have come out of hiding."

Stone looked out the windshield down on Balboa. He didn't say anything for a while. He took his hand out of his pocket. Empty.

Finally, he spoke.

"Sergei's *why* I came out of hiding."

CHAPTER 19

"WHAT DO YOU mean?" Why would Stone leave witness protection, where he was seemingly safe, knowing Sergei would soon be out of prison and looking for him?

"Every time I have to put the pieces together for you, I have less and less confidence that you can do the job I'm paying you to do." He frowned at me. "Think about it. Who orchestrated Sergei's early release?"

"The DOJ."

"Correct." He nodded. "And what is the law enforcement arm of the DOJ?"

Civics 101 with State's Witness Peter Stone.

"The FBI." I let that roll around in my head for a few seconds. "So, you're saying that Sergei gave the FBI something that is going to take down someone big, and as compensation they not only let him out of prison but gave him the address of the witness who put him behind bars? I agree that the FBI has been flexing its muscles in places where they don't belong lately, but this is too much even for me. Accomplice to murder?"

Stone didn't say anything, so I continued my takedown of his paranoia.

"Besides, you said yourself that the U.S. Marshals run the WITSEC program."

Stone stared down at Balboa again. His face gave away nothing. But I had the feeling that he was deciding what truth he could tell me again as opposed to constructing another lie.

Finally, "Special Agents Dennis Sorensen and Charlene Bowden paid me a visit a week ago."

"The two Feds you claimed not to know when I asked you about them a few minutes ago?" Did Stone lie to me then, or was he lying to me now?

"The same. You're on a need-to-know basis, and five minutes ago you didn't need to know. Now you do."

"What did they want?"

"Theodore Raskin."

Raskin again. My instincts had been right. He was the key to the whole affair. Stone, the FBI, Sergei Volkov.

"Why is everyone so interested in Raskin? Is he the real reason you came back to San Diego?"

"I came to San Diego to try to find Angela so I can get the kidney transplant and live long enough to see Sergei die. The Feds didn't tell me why they were looking for Raskin, but Sorensen made subtle threats about my safety."

Sorensen had made a not-so-subtle threat to me about jail time. The same threat multiple law enforcement agencies had made to me over the years. But none of the ones that weren't bent had ever threatened my safety. I guess intimidating Stone required a sharper angle.

"Subtle threats as in, 'By the way, Sergei Volkov is getting out of prison Friday, and it would be a shame if he found out where you live'?"

"I said subtle threats." Stone's face squished up in derision. "I already knew Sergei was getting out before the Feds arrived at my front door.

I have a connection at the Federal Bureau of Prisons. I've known for weeks."

He had more moles in hidden places than a vacant dirt lot in Southern California.

"Whatever Sorensen and Bowden are up to, their behavior doesn't comport with normal FBI standards. Threatening you, shacking up in a dive hotel in Pacific Beach. There's something off about them."

"How would you know where they're staying?"

Stone would never buy that I answered the Feds' questions in my home and snuck out and followed them in the car I'd been driving when they tailed me an hour before.

"Someone followed them after they left my house."

"And who was that and how much does she know about who you're working for?" The edge in Stone's voice sharpened.

He said "she." He knew that Moira and I worked together. He knew too much about everything.

"They don't know anything. Just that I was being followed and I wanted to find out where the people following me went in an effort to find out who they were."

"I think it's best if you stay away from the FBI and all law enforcement going forward."

"So do I. I hope they stay away from me, too. Back to my original question. Why is everyone so interested in Theodore Raskin?"

"I don't know." He lied. "I've been patient and answered your questions because you claimed to need to know everything in order to find Angela. I doubt any of the information I gave you will help in that endeavor, but I answered the questions, nonetheless. Now it's time for you to tell me where you are in finding Angela. I paid you a lot of money for you to ask me irrelevant questions."

I told him about Angela's vacant condo, her neighbor and the man in the Maserati, my talks with Steven Albright and Lyndsey Breck. I didn't tell him about following Cassie Albright. I'd follow her to find her mother if I had to, but I wouldn't let Peter Stone get any closer to her than I'd let Sergei Volkov get to my family. She was out of bounds for Stone. Barely in bounds for me.

"That's not very much information for the money I'm paying you."

"That's one day's work, and it's a start."

He frowned, shook his head, then reached into his other coat pocket, not the one that I was sure held a gun, and handed me an old-fashioned flip phone. A burner. Non-traceable. I didn't even recognize the brand. "There's one number in the memory. Call it nightly with a report. And answer it when it rings."

"You going to fix your Sergei problem?" The words came out of my mouth hard like billiard balls dropped on a pool table. If I didn't give up Stone, Sergei was my problem, too. Unless Stone still had the muscle to erase that problem.

"Yes." Matter-of-fact. "But I may need your help setting it up."

"Done." Accessory to murder. I'd pull the trigger if I had to in order to save my family.

I'd done it before.

CHAPTER 20

AFTER STONE DROPPED me back home, I went inside and pulled some duct tape out of the toolbox I kept in the hall closet, then opened the door and peeked outside. Stone was gone. I walked to the driveway and opened my car's passenger-side front door, then taped the phone underneath the passenger seat. If Sergei showed up at my house again and one of his crew searched me, a burner phone that connected me to Peter Stone would be a death warrant.

After I made sure the phone was secure, I restarted my walk to Enterprise and rented a white Ford Focus sedan. Stone told me to stay away from the FBI, but if they were connected with Sergei Volkov, I needed to know. If they weren't and were just doing their job while shacking up in a cheap motel on the side, it would make things a lot easier.

I hoped for easier.

I made the twelve-minute drive to the Mission Bay Motel. The motel was on the west end of Pacific Beach, a bit north of Mission Beach and only a couple blocks from the ocean. And a couple generations from modernity. The whole block was a mishmash of buildings from different time periods, from weathered turn of the century, the one two turns ago, to brightly colored signs on mini-mall boxes.

The motel complex consisted of two two-story sun-bleached white rectangular buildings slammed together at an angle. There was another wing next to a squat office and a pool. The motel was older than me and aging about as well.

I circled the block and didn't see the black Chevy Tahoe or Moira's white Honda Accord. Not in the parking lot or on the street. My phone buzzed as I approached the motel for the second time. Moira. I put in earbuds and took the call.

"Tahoe is on the move. Heading north on Mission Blvd. Just passed Diamond Street."

"Do you think they made you?" I drove north on Mission but hit a red light at Garnet.

"No. I parked half a block south and watched the motel through my binoculars." A slight edge to the machine gun response.

"Were they carrying any luggage when they got into the Tahoe?"

"Just a briefcase. Looks like they're coming back. The guy is dressed in khaki slacks and a sweater and the woman is in jeans and a leather jacket."

"Roger. Maybe they're going to get breakfast. If they're still heading north, I doubt they're going back to sit on my house. They would have turned on Grand or Garnet. Maybe breakfast and then my house."

"Still heading north. Passed a bunch of breakfast joints. They're going somewhere else. And they're not dressed in Fed attire, so I doubt it's FBI headquarters in Sorrento Valley. They would have taken Garnet to get to the 5 freeway."

"Yup."

"They're stopped at the light on Turquoise. In the left-hand turn lane. I'm four cars back."

"Wherever they're going, we're gonna find out."

"'We're?'"

"I'm about five blocks behind you in a white Ford Focus."

"Roger."

Moira called off the blocks as the Feds made their way into La Jolla via La Jolla Boulevard. I was within two and a half blocks of Moira by the time she called. "Turning right on Pearl."

"They could be taking the long way up to FBI headquarters," I said as I closed in on Pearl.

"Wrong clothes for that." Moira, annoyed staccato. "And why bother with the long way? The Feds seem to like to go from point A to B without throwing in an A plus or minus."

Another possibility that put a wiggle in my stomach popped into my head. What if they were heading to La Jolla Shores? And Steven Albright's house. Cassie Albright's house. I checked the clock on my dash. Eight-twenty-two in the morning. La Jolla High would have already started classes. But maybe they were headed to Steven's office on Prospect Street. If Moira called out a left on Girard, Albright's office and home were possible targets.

"Crossed Girard and going up the hill into the residential area." Moira's words cut off my thoughts and settled my stomach. They weren't looking for Angela Albright. At least it seemed that way. Good. I didn't want a kid, possibly just missing her mom, getting pulled into a federal investigation. Or whatever the two people in the Chevy Tahoe were up to.

"Roger. I'm a block behind you. I'll try to catch up so we can switch positions."

"Shit."

"What?"

"They just turned right onto Cabrillo Avenue. I'm pretty sure there's no outlet."

"There isn't." I had a buddy on my high school football team twenty-five years ago who lived on the street.

"Maybe they did spot me and turned onto Cabrillo to wait for me to turn down it and confirm that they have a tail. I'm slowing down and am going to pass by and look to see where they are."

"Roger."

"They went down a driveway at the end of the block. It looked to have hedges on both sides. Couldn't see the house from here. I'm pulling over on Pearl. I don't think they went down the street to trap me. I switched cars with Luke last night. I'm still pretty sure they don't know I'm on their tail."

Luke was her twenty-six-year-old son who drove a 2019 black Mazda 3. Like the Honda Accord, a ubiquitous car and shape in Southern California that would be less likely than most cars to stick out.

I cleared Girard and headed up the steady hill. Moira was parked a quarter block north of Cabrillo Avenue.

"I got you. I'll turn onto Cabrillo and see what I can see." I did as stated. I drove all the way to the end where Rhoda Drive shot up a hill and ultimately dead-ended at La Jolla Country Club.

No black Chevy Tahoe in view. A hill covered in dense foliage rose up from the end of the street to give a sense of privacy. A few of the houses had been remodeled since my high school pal lived on the street, but nothing else had changed. Still a feeling of seclusion at the end of the street.

The driveway to the last home on the right was anchored by tall, thick hedges and was long and turned slightly to block the view of the house.

What were the shady Feds up to?

I thought about parking on the street and sneaking down the driveway to get a look at the hidden house. Then I noticed a small security camera atop one of the brick pillars that stood sentry in front of the driveway. I kept the car moving, circled around, and drove down the other end of the street. I turned left on Pearl and parked about a half a block down from Cabrillo.

"Well?" Moira in my ear.

"Still hidden from the street by the hedges. A pillar at the front of the driveway has a security camera. New one. Looked like Arlo Pro 3 or 4."

"Then whoever is inside, including the Feds, could have seen you."

"Maybe, but I kept moving. My visor was down. Different car than the one they saw me in yesterday. Different look from yesterday. Just someone who made a wrong turn down the street."

"Roger."

I hung up and pulled up PropertyShark, a pay website on my phone that has residential real estate property ownership records.

I searched the site and got a little surprise when I found the owner of the Cabrillo Avenue house. It was owned by a commercial business. A company called Sterlingshire Inc. I looked them up and found that they were an investment management company that had been in business for little over a year. I dug deeper. Apparently, the firm specialized in real estate. Mostly residential. They'd owned the house for eight months but hadn't had a tenant, as best as I could tell.

I called Moira and told her what I'd found out.

"I've heard that huge investors are buying up residential real estate to flip or turn into multi-family units." She rattled off the words. "That's one of the reasons housing prices have skyrocketed. But what are those two doing there? Looking for a love shack in La Jolla?"

"I don't know. Something else a little strange about Sterlingshire Inc. There're only three or four mentions of them online, and their managed assets aren't listed anywhere. Not even on their website."

"That is odd." Moira digging in. "Every investment management company I've ever investigated has shouted their assets from the rooftops. Even when they weren't that impressive."

"Yeah. Me too."

"Where is their headquarters?"

"Wilmington, Delaware." I glanced at Cabrillo Avenue. "Tax, regulations, and anonymity advantages. Only one name associated with the company. Keith Barent Johnson."

"Anything on him?"

"Not much. Forty-seven years old, divorced, no children. Just a couple old postings on social media from 2021 about his real estate investment company flipping a few homes in Dallas."

"And now he's owner of Sterlingshire Inc.?" Moira said. "Whatever that is."

"He's listed as director. You only need to list one name as the registered agent when you incorporate in Delaware."

"Seems strange that Sterlingshire Inc. doesn't have more of an online presence."

"I agree. Or that Keith Barent Johnson doesn't either." My brain clicked over. "Wonder if it's all a cover for the Feds."

"I was wondering the same thing. Angus once told me that he knew of a federal prosecutor who used kind of a stash house to interview witnesses on RICO cases to keep them under wraps."

Attorney Angus Buttis who Moira sometimes investigated for and who let Moira use his offices to meet with clients.

"That's a possibility. Those two are hard to figure."

Dive motels, possible witness stash houses in upper-class neighborhoods owned by a Delaware incorporated investment company. Special Agents Sorensen and Bowden were a team with many disparate pieces.

CHAPTER 21

AN HOUR LATER, I was back circling La Jolla High School. I spotted Cassie Albright's car parked a block down from the high school parking lot in front of a house that looked to be as old as the school. I was sure I'd parked my car in the same spot twenty-five years ago when the parking lot was overflowing. As had a lot of kids before me.

The cars changed over the years, but the house didn't. Only it's appraisal value. It could now be a two-million-dollar teardown. The ground in La Jolla would eventually always be worth more than anything built on top of it.

I found a spot five or six houses down and watched Cassie's green Kia Soul. The car stayed where it was. No Cassie by 12:30 p.m. I called Moira for an update on Cabrillo Ave. The Feds were still at the house. I hung up and waited some more.

Nothing.

I pulled away from the curb at 1:13 p.m. Cassie had either stayed on campus during lunch or left with friends. Either way, I doubt she met her mother, unless Angela picked her up at the school. Not likely if she was serious about staying hidden.

*   *   *

Moira called as I hiked up Balboa Ave. on the way back to my house after dropping off the rental at Enterprise. She had the Feds alone now. I'd spend the rest of the afternoon waiting for Cassie Albright to get out of school, then go to her tennis practice, and finally follow her home. She didn't know my car, and the rental cut into Krista's future fund.

"The Tahoe's on the move." Machine gun Moira.

"Where to?"

"On Torrey Pines Road right now."

"Maybe they're finally heading up to FBI Headquarters in Sorrento Valley."

"Let's find out."

Moira gave me the play-by-play. 52 East, 805 South, 163 South. My stomach started to tighten, and I picked up the pace. Sweat dotted my forehead on the cool November afternoon. Not from the exertion.

"They just got off on Tenth Ave." Slightly above a whisper. I sped up into a trot and hit Moraga Avenue. Thirty seconds later. "They're on Broadway."

I broke into a sprint to get to my house. And my car. I knew where the Tahoe stopped well before Moira said it through a strangled voice.

"They went into the garage at 1480 Broadway."

An underground parking structure for a downtown condo complex.

The underground garage where Tatiana Volkov died. Where I laid in wait and shot and killed Tatiana and her bodyguard five years ago.

CHAPTER 22

"I'M NOT GOING down there." Moira was the only person on earth who knew what I'd done that night. And knew why I did it. Or so I thought, until Peter Stone knocked on my door yesterday morning.

Moira and I had only talked about it once. But once was enough. A justification that only I, alone, could see. It almost ruined our friendship. Ripped a crevasse between us. A wound that took months to heal and left a scar. Still visible, but never discussed. With the best friend I'd ever had.

And now the scar was raw again as Peter Stone and some twisted FBI agents were sniffing around my dark past. A past I'd commit again under the same circumstances. Righteous. Justified. Survival.

"You're damn right you're not. There's a camera in there." One I disabled five years ago. "Wait them out until I get there."

"Why are you out of breath?"

"I ran up a hill to get to my car." I jumped in my Accord and punched the ignition.

"You think this is just a coincidence?"

"I don't know what it is." I got onto Moraga and headed for Balboa and Interstate 5 South.

Fifteen minutes later I pulled up across the street from 1480 Broadway. The building was beige and tan and had a welcoming lightness to it. I'd never seen it during the daytime before. Only at night. Or the early morning hours. When it was darkness and shadows. When evil lurks and upright citizens are home asleep in bed.

I hadn't been home that early autumn morning five years ago. Or the two that preceded it. Those mornings, I'd done reconnaissance work. When the third morning arrived and the black Hummer entered the garage, I was ready. To sell off a piece of my soul and keep Moira, and myself, alive.

Moira was parked half a block to the east. She called me a couple minutes after I arrived.

"Unit number 2627 is owned by Sergei Volkov." Tatiana's old condo. Moira must have looked up the address on PropertyShark while I drove downtown. "He's owned it for nine years. I guess Tatiana lived there on Daddy's dime while she was there."

"Mmm, but we don't know if they went in there to meet someone in unit 2627."

"Yeah." She stretched out the word. Like I was being naive.

But I wasn't. I wasn't even lying to myself. I just didn't want to say the scary part out loud. Why were Sorensen and Bowden meeting someone in the building where Tatiana Volkov was murdered? Possibly in the condo she'd lived in.

"Any names of occupants over the last five years? Renters?"

"No. Sergei's is the only name listed."

Sergei certainly hadn't been there in at least four years. He probably let one of his crew live in the condo like Tatiana had. Tatiana hadn't only been Sergei's daughter. She'd also been one of his capos. The family business.

Was this where Sergei deposited himself when he got out of prison? Were Special Agents Sorensen and Bowden inside questioning Sergei on official business? Or were they there on unofficial business? Their business. Dirty business.

If they weren't talking to Sergei, who were they talking to? Was it a coincidence that they were inside a condo complex where a unit was owned by Sergei Volkov, the Mob boss who the Justice Department just let out of prison? I didn't believe in coincidences. I believed in the truth. And the truth was that both the FBI and Sergei Volkov visited my house on the same day. Were they working together? Or were the Feds on official government business?

Maybe to the former. *Probably not* to the latter.

Moira and I stayed radio silent for the next hour.

I checked the time on my phone. 2:24 p.m. Cassie Albright was probably about to start tennis practice. I had to get up to La Jolla High School before she went home. Or had a rendezvous with her mother.

I called Moira.

"What?"

"I have to head up to La Jolla High to follow a sixteen-year-old girl in hopes that she'll lead me to her mother so I can tell a former casino boss turned mob informant who tried to kill me where his daughter, who doesn't know he's her father, is."

"All in a day's work. I got it from here."

"Maybe you should head north behind me, and we can two-car Cassandra."

"Afraid you'll get made by a sixteen-year-old girl as she shoots videos of herself driving for TikTok?"

That wasn't what I was afraid of. Not as I sat outside the building housing a condo owned by a Russian Mob boss who had enough blood on his hands to keep his bathroom sink permanently stained pink. I knew what Sergei and his men were capable of. I'd killed his daughter because of what she'd been capable of. And because of what she'd done. But Moira, as smart and tough as she was, hadn't been up against that kind of evil before. Few people had.

"These kids are pretty sharp. Follow me up to La Jolla. Stone's paying me to find Angela Albright. Sorensen and Bowden are sidetracks." But I knew they were somehow involved in the bigger picture that Stone wouldn't tell me about. I just didn't want Moira being too close to that picture.

"You know they're somehow connected, Rick. What's up?" Concern instead of the normal dismissiveness.

"If the two Feds are connected to Sergei Volkov, it changes things. A lot. I don't want you sitting in your car without backup if something goes wrong."

"I'll be fine." A hint of sweetness. "I don't take chances like you do. Go find Angela Albright. I'll check in every half hour."

"Give them another hour and call it a day."

"I'll take that under advisement." She hung up.

I started my car and drove down Broadway with my eyes in the rear-view mirror for as long I as could see Moira's car.

CHAPTER 23

CASSIE ALBRIGHT'S METALLIC green Kia Soul was still parked on the street below the high school parking lot when I got there at 3:02 p.m. I decided to sit on the car instead of watching practice. She had to come to her car eventually. I parked a block down on Westbourne Street and waited.

Moira checked in. No movement. I told her to go home. She hung up.

A half hour later, after girls I recognized from tennis practice yesterday drove away from the high school, I questioned the decision. Maybe Cassie didn't have to come back to her car. Because she still hadn't a half hour after all her teammates had already left. Had I missed the chance to find Angela by sitting on the car instead of the kid?

Maybe. Didn't have a choice now. I had to wait and see if Cassie ever picked up her car. And see if someone dropped her off.

Moira checked in two more times while I waited. She had news on the second call.

"I was afraid they left through another exit, so I went down into the garage. I—"

"There is no other exit." I discovered that when I reconned the building five years ago.

"You didn't let me finish." Rapid fire. "I found that out when I went inside. But I also saw the Tahoe parked in the space for unit number 2627."

"Shit." Tatiana Volkov's old parking space. The one where she and her bodyguard died. The one that belonged to the condo owned by Sergei Volkov. "Go home. Get the fuck out of there. Now."

"Settle down. I'm back on the street in a different spot. Nobody saw me."

"You've done all you can. We'll deal with it as a team tomorrow." A different tack. "I'm sitting on Cassandra Albright's car. It's five-twenty and all her tennis teammates have already gone home. I think she might have met her mother and they went somewhere in Angela's car. I need you back here in case Angela drops her off. We need to follow Angela, but she's been in hiding. She'll be wary. We need two cars."

"What makes you think that Cassandra didn't just go off with a boyfriend?"

"Maybe she did. I'll know when someone drops her back at her car. I can't afford to miss it if it's Angela. And I need your help to follow her if it is. Finding Angela is what we're getting paid to do."

An exhale. "All right. I'm heading up. I have to stop at a Starbucks first to pee and get some tea. You want anything?"

I hadn't eaten since breakfast and hadn't even thought about it. That happened to me often on surveillances and stakeouts. My appetite went into hibernation for eight, ten hours. The same with my bodily functions. I could hold my urine like a dog stuck in the house all day waiting for his 8–6 master to get home from work.

Now with the mention of both, I was suddenly starving and had a bursting bladder. Moira could get me something to eat, but she couldn't pee for me.

"I'll take an everything bagel. Thanks."

"Roger." She hung up.

Moira was out of danger. For now. But what about tomorrow? What were Dennis Sorensen and Charlene Bowden up to? Were they playing chicken with the Russian Mob? Or were Moira and I the ones playing chicken? With the Russian Mob *and* the FBI.

I leaned over and reached under the front passenger seat. My hand found the burner phone Stone gave me. I carefully peeled back the duct tape so that I'd be able to put it back without having to retape it. I tapped the only number stored on the phone.

Stone answered on the second ring.

"I hope you have news for me." The smooth condescension.

"The two Feds that followed me have been up at Tatiana Volkov's former condo for the last couple hours. The condo still owned by Sergei." I laid on my own condescension. "You want to stop playing games and tell me how they and Sergei are connected?"

"I don't play games." The scythe edge I'd only heard in Stone's voice a handful of times. When the mask of smug civility slipped and I got a glimpse of his soul. The thrumming darkness. "I hired you to find Angela, not spy on irrelevant fantasies. Have you found her yet?"

"I'm not fantasizing about the Feds' rental parked in Tatiana's old parking space. Tell me about them now or I'm dropping the case."

"You took twenty-five-thousand dollars of my money. You're not dropping anything."

"I'll give you back your money, minus two days of work. Where do you want me to send it?"

A long empty of silence. I thought about the thick envelope in my gun safe at home and did the math in my head while Stone was silent. I'd be in the hole if I returned Stone's money after that two thousand dollars I gave Moira. She'd give it back if she knew. I'd have to tell her.

"Progress report on Angela." Now he sounded more tired than angry. I didn't know how to process that. I don't know which made him more dangerous.

Peter Stone was still a client. Different from any other I'd ever had, but the same in that I'd taken his money in good faith to do a job. I updated all my clients with reports. All my clients.

"I've been tailing Angela's daughter."

"Cassandra."

I didn't like hearing the sixteen-year-old child's name coming out of Stone's mouth. An innocent stuck in the middle between her mother and me. And Peter Stone. But I didn't have a choice. And she *was* his granddaughter. Even if she didn't know it. Or if anyone else did.

"Yes. I find it hard to believe that a mother would drop off the grid for a month and not contact her daughter."

"And has she contacted Cassandra?"

"Not as far as I know."

"What about tapping Cassandra's phone?"

"That's against the law, and I'd have to have physical access to her phone to install monitoring software or know her iTunes ID to do it remotely." My other phone pinged the arrival of a text. I looked at the screen. Moira.

"I have it on great authority, my own."—a snicker—"that you've been known to break a law or two. In fact, God's most important Thou Shall Not."

"But I've never broken any of my own. And Cassandra's a sixteen-year-old girl, and I wouldn't even consider invading her privacy that way."

"I'm running out of time, Rick. I need to find Angela." Desperation mixed with anger.

"I'm working on it, Stone, but I need to know what the Feds in the SUV have to do with Sergei Volkov."

More silence. Shorter this time.

"They're out of the Seattle FBI Field Office." Calmer. "Of course, they lied to me about why they came to my home. But I played along to see if I could figure out what they really wanted. And I did."

"What did they really want?"

"A piece of the action."

CHAPTER 24

"What action?"

"My guess is that they think Theodore is committing fraud on his crypto exchange."

"Why do you think that?"

"They seemed to be pretty interested in it, and I could smell the greed seeping through their pores." A chuckle. "I know greed, and I know corrupt cops. Sorensen and Bowden are dirty."

"What did they want from you?"

"Theodore's whereabouts."

"Did you give it to them?"

"I couldn't. I haven't seen him in years. I don't know where he is."

"Well, they must think you do because they flew down here from Seattle looking for you. But they're holed up in a run-down motel sharing a room. Not the usual nice accommodations we taxpayers foot the bill for." That and the way they treated me seemed to corroborate Stone's take on the two Feds. Still, I felt Stone was hiding something from me.

"I agree with your assessment." No snark. "They must think that I left Spokane to try to find Theodore."

So Stone had been holed up in Spokane, Washington, for the last five years. Too nice a town for him to get his hooks into.

"Why would they think you'd want to find him unless they think that you're in on the fraud?"

"I'm sure they do think I'm in on the fraud."

"What do you think they're doing at Tatiana Volkov's old condo? Meeting with Sergei?"

"No. Sergei wouldn't go back to the condo downtown. All of his enemies know he still owns it." No condescension in Stone's voice. Rare. I think he was telling me the truth. But I'd been wrong about him before. Too many times. "Sorensen and Bowden might have a mole inside Sergei's organization who has access to the condo. Someone high up. The mole and the crooked Feds are probably in this together."

"In what?" I thought I knew but wanted to see if Stone would spell it out.

"The BitChange chase. Everybody wants Theodore Raskin and a piece of the fraud action. Plus, I wouldn't be surprised if he was siphoning off the money he laundered for Sergei's syndicate. Sergei was in federal lockup. None of the people who worked for Sergei when I knew him were terribly bright. Theodore probably put away a nice retirement fund when nobody was looking. Our friends Sorensen and Bowden are trying to find dear Theodore to shake him down for a piece of the action. Both actions."

"Why come to me and not the FBI?"

"What do you mean?" It came out as a question, but he knew what I meant.

"The FBI has unlimited resources. They could find Angela in a day or two. Credit card usage, digital footprint, backtracking calls to Cassandra Albright or Angela's best friend, Lindsey Breck." I paused to give him a chance to play along. Instead, he silently played stupid. "Why not trade them what you know about Sorensen and Bowden and what you think they're up to in exchange for the FBI tracking down Angela?"

"My case manager never told me that Sergei was getting out." The knife edge came out again. "I found that out on my own. I don't trust the FBI. I trust Sergei more than I do the Bureau. I'm Sergei's number one priority. Whoever killed his daughter is one-A."

He stuck the dagger in just deep enough.

"I'll call tonight to let you know if sitting on Cassandra Albright's car pans out."

CHAPTER 25

I CHECKED MY watch. 5:47 p.m. It was getting late. Rush hour out of downtown would be sticky. Still, Moira should have gotten to the high school by now. Past now. My stomach rumbled for food. My bladder pressed south, begging for relief. Another five minutes and it would be dark enough for me to answer nature's call behind a bush.

I pushed Moira's number.

"I picked the busiest Starbucks in San Diego. I'll be there in fifteen, twenty minutes. I think your bagel is stale, but I bought it anyway."

"Right decision. Park on the corner of Westbourne and Draper when you get here."

"Roger." She hung up.

The answer to my hunger was on the way, but my bladder still needed relief. I waited another few minutes until the evening sky turned to night. I looked up and down the street and saw no one or any cars approaching. Convinced I had a few precious seconds of solitude, I slipped out of my car and snuck over to a hedge of spiraling Japanese yews in front of a home that had shown no signs of life the whole time I'd sat in the car waiting for Cassandra Albright to return. One quick thought to the possibility of paying a five-hundred-dollar fine and/or being charged with a misdemeanor, then a quick unzip.

Headlights lit Draper Street five seconds into my relief. I had cover from the hedge unless the car turned onto Westbourne Street. The car did turn onto Westbourne, but left toward the high school, instead of right toward me.

I finished my business and peeked through the hedge as the car, a late model Nissan Sentra, pulled to a stop next to Cassie Albright's Kia Soul. The car didn't belong to Angela Albright. She owned a Tesla Model S. I looked at the license plate and memorized it. Whispering it to myself over and over.

The Sentra sat there for fifteen to twenty seconds until the passenger door opened and Cassie got out. She was still in her tennis black skirt and red top. She slung her racket case over her shoulder, shut the door, and waved as the car turned into a driveway and did a three-point turn.

Cassie got into her car and the Sentra turned right on Draper heading back the way it came. I got a brief glance of the driver as the car drove away. Woman. Blond hair. That's all I could make out, but it was enough.

Angela Albright.

Had to be. Electricity vibrated along my spine. I could feel the blood pumping through my veins. The charge of the hunt.

Cassie drove her Soul onto Draper following the Sentra's path. I ran to my car, punched the ignition, and turned onto Draper. Cassie was a hundred yards ahead. The taillights of what I hoped was Angela's Sentra were another couple hundred yards beyond. I closed the gap on Cassie's Soul but didn't want to get too close and draw attention to myself.

The Sentra turned right on Genter Street, and I lost sight of it. My guess was that Angela, or who I hoped was Angela, was making her way to Torrey Pines Road and then onto the 5 or the 52 and then the 805. If it was Angela, I doubted she was staying in La Jolla or Carmel Valley. The towns of her two last residences. Where whoever else was looking for her would look first. She had to be headed to a freeway, and I needed to get close enough to her to keep track of her before she did.

The Sentra drove a few blocks through town and turned right on Torrey Pines as I anticipated. I now had two lanes in which to maneuver to close some ground on the Sentra. I passed Cassie with my head turned away from her and picked off another car before the red light at Torrey Pines and Ivanhoe stopped me. I was pretty sure it stopped Angela too. Just barely. I figured she was the first or second car from the light in the right lane. I was at least five cars back.

The light changed and the Nissan Sentra went a block then passed under the green light at Prospect. I punched the gas and swerved to my right for an open shot to make the light. Yellow. Five car lengths out. Red as I broke the plane. No horns. No sirens. The Sentra was in sight a few cars ahead. Cassandra Albright was lost somewhere in the background.

The Sentra finally got onto Interstate 5 North. I'd been right, but wished I'd been wrong and that Angela *was* staying in a hotel somewhere in La Jolla. I realized I was still whispering the license plate number that I'd seen on the Sentra over and over.

Trailing Angela on the freeway as the night darkened and all taillights looked the same was going to be challenging. And annoying on an empty stomach. But there was one benefit. If I was able to keep track of her on the freeway, my headlights would blend in with hundreds of others. The outline of my car would be indistinguishable from all the other sedans on the road, and I could slip right behind her.

My phone rang right after I hit Solana Beach. Moira. I'd forgotten all about her. I took the call through the car's entertainment system.

"You must be doing a really good job of hiding. I don't see you anywhere." Annoyance in her fast twitch voice. "Did Cassandra go home, or did you give up?"

"I'm pretty sure I found Angela Albright."

"What!" Her voice bounced around the inside of my car.

"A blond woman in a late model Nissan Sentra dropped Cassandra at her car about twenty-five minutes ago. I'm tailing her on I-5. We're passing through Solana Beach."

"You want me to get onto 5 North and try to catch up?" The excitement of the chase in her voice. The brief few minutes of a private investigator's day that made the ten hours of boredom worth it. Something I felt at that exact moment.

"No. I have no idea where I'll end up. She could be driving to LA. But see if your connection at LJPD can look up the plate number on the Sentra. If Angela owns it, maybe her new address is attached." I recited the license plate number. It would be stuck in my head for a while.

"Okay. But he's off for the rest of the night until tomorrow."

"An address will be good to have if I lose her. But if she stops at a hotel somewhere tonight, I'll knock on her door. I want to get Stone what he needs and move on from this case."

"What about the shady Feds?"

"I'll leave that to the sunlit FBI."

"Really?" The tone of her voice conveyed more than just a question or surprise. Disappointment? In me?

"Yeah. Stone is paying me, us, to find Angela. The rest isn't our concern."

"You mean, you don't want to know what they are up to?" Same tone. "You're going to quit before we learn the truth about two shady government agents? That doesn't sound like you."

"It's the new me." I tried to make the words sound like I was capable of change. I had to be. I was quitting my job as a private investigator and moving to Santa Barbara. I didn't have a choice. I couldn't allow myself to have a choice.

"Yeah. Right. Call me when Angela lands somewhere."

"Roger." I tried to concentrate on the car five car lengths ahead of me instead of the life-changing event looming in front of me. "And could you please keep Midnight for one more night? I have no idea when I'll be home."

"Of course." She hung up.

The back end of the rush-hour traffic kept the flow between bumper to bumper and twenty-five miles per hour all the way up through Oceanside. Angela was well beyond her Carmel Valley condominium and still heading north. I checked my gas tank. Over three quarters full. I figured I had around three hundred miles left. Possibly more once the traffic cleared and if Angela stayed on the freeway.

We passed San Clemente, San Juan Capistrano, Mission Viejo, and kept heading north. I'd been correct about Angela getting on a freeway, but I had no idea where she'd get off. Somewhere in Los Angeles made sense. Big city. Easy to get lost or stay lost, and still within a couple hours of her daughter.

The traffic turned to sludge around the City of Commerce and stayed that way all the way through Glendale and lightened up around San Fernando. Los Angeles was quickly receding into the darkened background of my rearview mirror.

The traffic thinned considerably when we passed Santa Clarita and started climbing up I-5 toward the Tejon Pass and the Grapevine. Angela Albright could be headed anywhere now. Bakersfield. Fresno. Sacramento. San Francisco. If so, she had to stop for gas sometime soon.

The tiny town of Gorman passed by in the dark. Over the 4,000 foot elevation of the Tejon Pass. At the top of the pass, the Sentra got off on Frazier Mountain Park Road heading west. There was a truck stop, a thin strip of retail, quick dining, a couple of hotels, and three gas stations, which was where I thought Angela was heading.

That could be a problem. If Angela was getting gas, I needed to get some too. I couldn't afford to track her up I-5 another two hundred miles and run out. But I didn't want her to spot me. Not yet. If I surprised her in the middle of nowhere late at night and started talking about Peter Stone, she might freak out and rabbit. Peter Stone could have that effect on people. Sometimes, so could I.

But she passed by the gas station and continued west on Frazier Mountain Park Road. Where was she going? I'd never been on the road, though I'd passed by the freeway exit dozens of times going to and from Northern California.

There were only a couple other cars on the road as I followed the Sentra farther away from the freeway. Structures peeled back into the rearview mirror as we dug west through a valley between squatty mountains with scattered pine trees.

I lagged back about a quarter mile so that my headlights weren't so bright behind the Sentra. The two-lane road was a steady climb as it pulled away from Interstate 5. Occasionally, homes a couple steps up from ramshackle would pop up in my headlights. The farther I pushed away from the eight-lane concrete metropolitan lifeline of I-5, the more I wondered what people out here did for a living and how far they had to drive to do it.

The Sentra braked and made a right turn after about ten or twelve miles. A small wooden road sign read MIL POTRERO HIGHWAY when I caught up to the turn. After the mostly straight, steady climb up from the freeway on Frazier Park Mountain Road, the two lane "highway" was twisty and mostly downhill with occasional short bumps up and then back to the downhill curvy toboggan ride. I'd lose the red taillights around a turn and catch them again as I weaved down into the valley. Each time I caught site of them, they were a little bit farther away than before.

The pine trees that had been in the distance on Frazier Park were now tight to the road and claustrophobic. The pilot of the Sentra must have had local knowledge or was a daring, reckless driver. A recklessness that was also a part of my DNA, which I had to constantly combat to make sure I could be a steadier influence in Krista's life.

And, maybe again, in Leah's.

CHAPTER 26

A FLASH OF a round sign next to the road on my left read PINE MOUN-TAIN CLUB. I think. It wasn't lit, but a swath of moonlight hit it after filtering through the pine trees. The sign was possibly a horizontal slice of a tree trunk. I didn't know what kind of club might be out in this wilderness, but I hoped it meant there was civilization nearby and that the Nissan Sentra was going to light soon.

Sure enough, I came to a short strip of a town. A quarter mile down the road, a large wooden sign in front of a parking lot for a small row of buildings read: WELCOME TO PINE MOUNTAIN, VIL-LAGE CENTER. Apparently, I was in Pine Mountain and it had some sort of club.

I had a sense of a golf course on my right but couldn't be certain. The downtown passed by in less than ten seconds and a residential area west of it in another minute, and then we were back to just asphalt and pine trees.

The Sentra turned down a road to the right. I sped up to get to the turnoff. Pineview Court. The name told me that there were homes down the street and probably no outlet. "Court." Good. We may have finally reached our destination.

I slowed into the turn and saw a couple darkened homes to the left side of the road. No cars in the driveways. No homes on the other side of the street. I edged slowly farther down and saw a Nissan Sentra parked in the driveway of a modern ranch house. A person went up the stairs onto the porch. A woman. There wasn't enough light to get a good look at her, but she was average height and could have had blond hair. Long dark coat and probably blue jeans. She disappeared into the house as I drove past. She could have been Angela Albright. And she might not have been.

I checked the license plate of the Sentra as I passed by. Same as the one I'd been following all night. There were three more homes, all darkened, all on more than an acre of land. The road dead-ended into a forest. I made a three-point turn and went back the way I came. I slowed as I passed the home that the woman went into.

Decision time. I checked the clock on the dashboard. 10:13 p.m. Should I disturb whoever went into the house, hoping it was Angela Albright and that she'd be willing to talk to me this late at night two hundred miles away from her home? Or wait for the light of day when people are more receptive to talk to strangers or someone they haven't seen in a decade?

I couldn't risk losing her. Not when I was so close to completing my mission. My last mission.

I took off my Padre hat, finger combed my hair in the rearview mirror, and tried to look nonthreatening in my jeans and bomber jacket. A hard sell, but at least I looked presentable. A smile would help. I got out of the car and the air hit me with a crisp pine-scented slap. I could see my breath. Thankfully, I thought the November morning in San Diego was "cold" enough for me to put on the jacket when I left my house. Although, it was kind of my uniform. Along with jeans and a T-shirt. Some wore a suit and a tie to work. I wore jeans, T-shirt, bomber jacket, and a ball cap.

I embraced the temperature change and walked toward the house with the Sentra parked in the driveway.

Lights were on inside the house, but I couldn't see past the white curtains covering the windows. I went up the wooden stairs onto the covered porch and noticed the Ring doorbell camera. Someone inside could get a look at me and decide whether or not to answer the door. Good.

I knocked on the front door, pulled out my wallet, and removed my laminated private investigator's license, issued to me by the Bureau of Security and Investigative Services of California. I held the license in front of me so that it was clearly visible to the Ring camera.

The door had a picture window in it that was covered by a white lacy sash. I couldn't make out anything beyond the sash. I knocked on the door and waited. Nothing. No sound from inside. I rang the Ring doorbell and heard it echo inside the house.

Nothing. No reason to knock or ring again. I was certain whoever was in the house was now checking me out on their Ring feed. I waited some more.

Fifteen seconds later, a woman pulled the sash back from the window in the door. Blond. Blue eyes. About forty years old. Pristine model beauty. And not Angela Albright, but close enough in general appearance that she could have been the woman I saw in the Sentra driving away from Cassandra Albright's car earlier tonight and later entering the house she now stood in. She wore jeans and a yellow blouse. She could have taken off the coat when she went inside.

I lifted my P.I. license up to the window, even though I was pretty sure she'd already looked at it on her Ring feed.

The woman opened the door about six inches. The length of the security chain attached inside. Those chains were easily breached, but I was glad she had a sense of security so that she might talk. Whoever she was.

"May I help you?" A wary, confused expression on her face.

"May I speak with Angela Albright?" I put my license back in my wallet and handed her my business card.

"Who?" The woman's eyebrows knitted close together in confusion. Or feigned confusion. She looked at my card.

"Angela Albright. She lives down in San Diego. Is she a friend of yours?"

"I'm sorry, I don't know anyone by that name." She stepped back and started to close the door.

"I apologize. Could I ask you one more question?" I smiled.

The door stopped a couple inches from closing.

"I suppose." A frown. "What is it?"

"Have you ever been to La Jolla?" I kept smiling. "It's in San Diego."

"No, I haven't." A quick shake of her head. "Now I have a question for you. What makes you think that this Angela Albright person is in my house?"

"Because I followed the Nissan Sentra in your driveway two hundred miles from La Jolla tonight after the driver dropped off Angela's daughter at her high school at six o'clock."

"The car in the driveway is mine, and it didn't go anywhere near La Jolla or San Diego tonight." Her porcelain beauty turned hard. "And if you don't get off my porch and leave me alone, I'm going to call the police."

I'd never heard of Pine Mountain until I saw the sign at the general store. But one thing I was 100 percent certain of—the tiny town was too small to have its own police department and had to rely on a sheriff's department for law enforcement. My guess was that we were in Kern County and that Pine Mountain wasn't afforded its own deputy to patrol the ten-second drive through the town every day. If she called "the police," we'd both have a long wait.

But being the smartest person standing on the porch wouldn't get me any farther than I'd already come.

"If and when you see Angela, tell her Rick Cahill needs to talk to her. Thanks." I turned and exited the porch. I didn't hear the click of the door closing until I was on the walkway that led to the street.

CHAPTER 27

THWARTED, BUT NOT beaten. The woman lied to me. Angela might not be in the house, and the woman herself may not have dropped off Cassandra Albright at La Jolla High School tonight, but her car had made the trip. I rationalized that the lie, and Angela possibly being within my reach, was reason enough to commit a little misdemeanor. Even as my new life stretched out in front of me, my rationalizations became easier and easier to make.

I opened the trunk when I got back to my car and grabbed a small gray duffle bag from the spare tire wheel well. What I called my "black bag." For black ops. A bag no one else had ever seen and only Moira knew about. And even she didn't know all of its contents.

One of the items in the bag was a geo tracker. I grabbed it, put the bag back, and closed the trunk then walked toward the house and driveway where the Sentra was parked, checking windows of homes as I went. All dark. My guess was that many of the homes up in Pine Mountain were second vacation homes for people who needed to flee LA or other metropolises a few months a year.

I ducked behind a pine tree on the front lawn of the woman's neighbor, hunched down, and scrambled through the grass onto the driveway where the Sentra was parked. I used my phone's flashlight app to look inside the car. Nothing on the front or back seats. No lingering sign of

Angela Albright. I pulled the magnetized GPS tracker, a little smaller than a cigarette pack, and placed it inside the wheel well of the rear driver-side tire.

I snuck back to my car and exited Pineview Court and went westward on Mil Potrero Highway. A quarter mile down, I did a three-point turn and parked on the opposite side of the road with a view of the entrance to Pineview Court. I figured if Angela Albright was inside the Sentra house and decided to bolt, she'd head east toward Interstate 5.

I opened the app connected to the tracker on my phone. A red light blinked on a map showing Pineview Court. I watched it blink for about ten seconds, then went online and pulled up PropertyShark and used the address to look up the owner of the home where the Sentra was parked. Allen Barnes Pettis. I googled the name and found someone who was an entertainment attorney in Los Angeles. Sixty-three, divorced three times.

Angela's new boyfriend? Her neighbor, Alaina McCreery, said that the man who drove the Maserati was a "looker." The photos I found of Allen Pettis showed a gray-haired roundish man. To each his or her own, but I wouldn't call Pettis a "looker." Still, I felt I was getting close to finding Angela. Too late to contact Alaina McCreery tonight and send her a photo of Pettis. I'd try in the morning.

I shut down my phone and watched the entrance to Pineview Court in darkness for a solid half hour. No cars entered or exited the street. I was tired, but wired and hungry, and I'd put a tracker on the Nissan Sentra. If someone took off in it, I'd be able to tail it remotely. Time to find out if the ten second strip of a town had a hotel.

I drove back to town and parked in front of the general store in the Village Center parking lot and looked up hotels in the area on my phone. Found one for Pine Mountain Inn that was about a hundred or so yards from where I was parked. A two-story all wood structure that fit right in amongst the pine trees. I walked up to the office and found a locked door, but a sign on it that had a phone number to call for after hours. 11:00 p.m. was clearly after hours in Pine Mountain.

I called the number and a man with a British accent said he'd be down in five minutes. I checked the GPS tracker using the app on my phone. No movement from the Nissan Sentra. Still parked at the house on Pineview Court owned by Allen Barnes Pettis.

Five minutes almost on the nose, a burly Brit dressed in a Pendleton and dark corduroy pants appeared, red-faced and smiling. He must have walked down the hill above the little spread of town in the chilled night.

"Thomas Foster." He stuck a hand that I shook. "Nice to meet you."

"Rick Cahill. Sorry to bring you out this late at night."

"Nothing like a brisk walk in the cool mountain air."

We went inside the office, which was cozy and mountainy with wood paneling. I gave him a credit card, which he slid into a reader then handed back to me along with a key and told me we'd settle up whenever I checked out. Old-fashioned hospitality. I hoped I wouldn't have to chase Angela Albright more than another day or two but couldn't be sure of anything.

My room upstairs was nice with a rock fireplace and a small balcony for stargazing. But I wasn't on vacation. If I were, I would have had luggage. And a toothbrush.

I sat on the bed and checked the geo tracker app. The car was still in the driveway of the home owned by Allen Barnes Pettis. The hunger I'd put on hold four hours ago kicked in with grinding tenacity as soon as I hit my room. Nothing looked open when I pulled into "town," but I had to eat. Something. Anything. Soon.

I went downstairs, got into my car, and took a chance that the Jack in the Box I'd seen on the overpass when I turned off the I-5 was still open. Twenty-five minutes later, I found out. Jackpot. Open. As well as a gas station where I filled up my car.

I ordered a Jumbo Jack, large fries, and a large chocolate shake. I figured the carbo load would fill the hunger pangs and put me to sleep on a night when I was still riding the high of the chase. Something I thrived on. Something that gave my life meaning when the truest meaning of life, that of a father, was absent me with Krista in Santa Barbara. But all I felt when she was gone was ache. Not the rewards of being a father. Only the responsibility and a painful void.

On a case, doing work that was important to those who paid me, making a difference in their lives, was the best I could do to fill the emptiness of missing Krista. A feeling I'd soon lose if my move to Santa Barbara and a change of careers came to fruition. I'd be closer to Krista. And Leah. But my family still wouldn't be whole. In Santa Barbara or not, I'd still need something to fill that void.

I took down a quarter of the Jumbo Jack in one bite and was almost halfway done with it before I left the parking lot. All that was left when I got back to the inn was a couple ounces of the chocolate shake. Which I finished up in my room.

The geo tracker app still had the Nissan Sentra at the house outside of town. I was about to put my phone on the nightstand and turn on the TV and hopefully drift off into a carb coma of sleep but pulled up Leah's number instead.

I hovered my finger over it. She'd no doubt still be furious with me for putting her and Krista in danger. Even if it wasn't my fault. But I guess it was. I took the case. I didn't have to. Peter Stone. Enough red flags for a Chinese Communist Party parade. But the money would be a step toward helping provide for Krista's future. After I was gone.

And, maybe, I wanted to be back on the chase.

Leah and I didn't make a practice of talking on the phone anymore. Texts every couple days to check up on Krista. Skype calls with Krista once a week with whoever had her holding the phone. I'd broken the rules by going to Leah's parents' house last night. And then blown everything up with the phone call to her father early this morning. I'd said what I needed to last night. And so had Leah. I was quitting my life's ambition and moving to Santa Barbara. She was consulting with a divorce attorney. What was there left to say?

Maybe what I should have said to her last night. Face-to-face. That I still loved her and wanted to start fresh. Again. But what good would it have done? She was, if not on a different path now, at least exploring one. Words wouldn't sway her now. Only actions. If at all.

I put my phone on the nightstand and turned on the TV.

CHAPTER 28

I WOKE UP on top of the hotel comforter, still in my clothes from yesterday. The first thing I did was check the geo tracking app on my phone. The Sentra was still at the house. Which wasn't too surprising because it was only 6:57 a.m.

I'd slept in. I usually couldn't sleep past 6:00 a.m. even if I tried. This morning, I could have rolled over and gotten another hour, but I didn't want to give the Sentra driver too much of a runway.

I got out of bed and took a much-needed shower after spending all day yesterday in a car. Unfortunately, when I left the bathroom, shiny and clean, I had to get back into the same clothes I wore yesterday. One exception. I went commando and hoped I'd find somewhere nearby to buy some new underwear.

And, I didn't have any deodorant.

The General Store didn't open until 8:00. I needed something to eat and went looking on foot. I found a bakery a couple buildings down from the hotel called Bear Claw Bakery and had a ham and cheese croissant for breakfast. My first. I'd been missing out, or maybe I just had to drive two hundred miles to find the right bakery. I bought a half a dozen chocolate donuts and an orange juice then topped off my gas tank at the town's lone gas station. No indoor plumbing, so I used the porta potty at the end of the parking lot to drain what little liquid was left in my internal tank

If Angela Albright or her look-alike took me for another long tail, this time I'd have a full tank of gas, an empty bladder, and a box of donuts. I was ready for anything.

I just wouldn't be fully clothed.

I entered the General Store at 8:00 a.m. on the button. The store was smallish and fairly general, but, as expected, it didn't sell underwear. Or much of any wear. However, it did sell toothbrushes and toothpaste, so I bought one of each. The only clothes it sold were Pine Mountain Club T-shirts and sweatshirts, as well as hats. Whatever this club was in Pine Mountain, the locals seemed pretty proud of it.

I grabbed a maroon T-shirt with a picture of a black bear on it and a blue hoodie that, in addition to the Pine Mountain Club Script, had "Est. 1971" on it. I grabbed a light gray hat that read the same. Whatever this club was, it had been around longer than I'd been alive. Luckily, the store also sold some stick deodorant, which I happily grabbed. I put everything in my basket along with two liters of water and went to the cash register. The guy manning it was in his early twenties. Curly brown hair with the hint of muttonchops and an obligatory stud earring in his left earlobe.

I set the basket's contents down on the counter.

"Find everything you were looking for?" He had a friendly smile, and the question came off as sincere, not rote.

Underwear? Better to keep it to myself.

"Yeah, thanks."

He rang up my items and asked me if I wanted a bag. California. I said "yes," and he rang up the extra ten cents then started putting my booty into a black plastic bag.

I watched the three Pine Mountain Club items go into the bag, and my curiosity got the best of me.

"What is the Pine Mountain Club? I saw a sign for it last night, too. Is it like the Kiwanis or something?"

"Kiwanis? Is that in Hawaii?"

"No, it's a charitable organization." I guess I showed my age. "What is the Pine Mountain Club?"

"Oh!" The kid threw back his head and laughed. "No. That's the name of the town. You're in Pine Mountain Club, California. Welcome." Another laugh ending in a smile.

"Thanks. I apologize. I'd just never heard the name before."

"No one has. That's how most people up here like it. But we here in the General Store are always happy to see new faces."

I went back to my car, rolled on some deodorant, and put on my brand-new Pine Mountain Club T-shirt. Still could use some new underwear. Or at least clean ones.

I got back onto the road at 8:10 a.m. and drove west of town along Mil Potrero Highway. I drove past Pineview Court and took up my spot from last night, about a quarter mile down the road.

I did a deeper search on Allen Barnes Pettis and found out he'd represented Harvey Weinstein on the business side. Not the creepy side. Although, the two sides did end up meshing together. Nothing else too interesting about Pettis except that he also repped James Cameron for a few years.

Pettis didn't have a social media presence. Old school. Grudging respect. After I finished the search, I found the piece of paper with Alaina McCreery's phone number in my wallet and called her. No answer. I left a message on her voicemail for her to call me, then texted a photo of Pettis and asked if he was the man in the Maserati who was dating Angela. Hopefully, she would get back to me soon.

I sat in the spot for over an hour without seeing a car. A white Ford F-150 drove by headed toward town about 9:45 a.m. That was it for the morning's action. Nobody entered or exited Pineview Court.

My phone rang at 11:03 a.m. Moira.

"There was a fire at the Cabrillo house last night." Her snare drum greeting. "One body found. Burnt almost to ashes."

"What? Do you know who it is? Was it one of the two FBI agents?"

"I don't know. My contact at LJPD won't give me anything, but he did give me the name and driver's license for the owner of your Nissan Sentra. Clairice Bethany Timmins. CDL picture on the way."

The name of Allen Barnes Pettis's most recent ex-wife according to what I found online last night. She lived in the home he still owned. Some divorces end up that way.

My phone pinged a text a couple seconds later and I opened an image of Clairice Bethany Timmins's California driver's license. The photo matched the woman in the Sentra house.

"I talked to Clairice Timmins last night," I said. "And she lied to me about where her car was last night. At the least. At most, she lied about knowing Angela and dropping off Cassandra at her car."

I told Moira about my conversation with the woman I now knew as Clairice Timmins.

"So, either she lent her car to Angela or drove down to La Jolla and spent time with Cassandra Albright on her own?" Moira.

"Right." Now the hard part. "You can call it a day on your end. You're officially off the case. It's a police matter now."

"I'm not officially off anything." She was revved up. Just what I feared. "I'm heading back to the Mission Bay Motel to see if the Chevy Tahoe is parked in the lot. If it is, I'm sitting on the Special Agents until I find out if there's still two of them left. I am officially still on the case."

"It's over, Moira." Stern. Real irritation bubbling up. Along with anxiety. "Let the cops handle it. In fact, once you find out who was murdered at Cabrillo you should go to the police and tell them what you know."

"Stop." A snap. "I'm following through on this. If the two Feds in the Chevy Tahoe really are crooked, then I want to bring them down. There's too much corruption in these governmental agencies now. And no one is ever punished. It's offensive."

Moira's late husband, Clint, who'd been considerably older than she, served in military intelligence before he retired and went on to become a private investigator. I'd never met him, but I knew that even a decade after his death, his service to our country still motivated Moira. She was on a mission now. One I wouldn't be able to talk her out of.

"I got you into this and now you're on a crusade." I didn't try to hide my anxiety. I *had* gotten Moira into this, even though the invitation was only for that first day and she jumped on for the rest of the ride on her own. She was involved because of me.

It wasn't the first time I'd pulled her into potentially dangerous situations. The outcomes of a few of the others had left emotional scars. Deep ones. But Moira stuck with me. Had my back. Always. And she was one of the few people left on earth who loved me and whom I loved. She was family after I'd lost mine and before I found my new one. I couldn't let her get hurt. And I knew I couldn't stop her when she set her mind to something.

"Don't worry about me. I'm not reckless like you are." She snorted a laugh. "Do you think your friend at Channel 6 News can help us out? She's got great sources."

Cathy Cade, investigative reporter. Hardly a friend, but we'd traded information a couple times.

"Worth a try but may not be worth the trouble. When I show interest in the murder, she'll know I'm somehow connected and start sniffing around in our business."

"And that could be dangerous if word got out to the wrong people."

"Yup." As always, she was right with me or a step ahead. "I doubt it's a coincidence that someone suddenly died in a fire at the house where you tracked the two FBI agents who Stone claims asked him about Theodore Raskin, the cryptocurrency guy. The DB has got to be either Raskin or one of the Feds. Stone's got a connection to all of them."

"The Medical Examiner should be able to get DNA off the body and make an identification, no matter how bad it's burned. Even if there's no soft tissue left, there's still the bones."

"Yeah, but the ME can only make an identification if the body's DNA is in CODIS or some other database."

"You're right." A splinter of irritation in her voice. "You really think Stone could have something to do with the dead body?"

"I don't know what to believe. But what I do know is that Stone never tells the whole truth or gives the whole story." Kind of like when I talked to the police. "I want to believe that he's trying to track down Angela for a kidney transplant. He doesn't look well. He may actually need the surgery. But what if he doesn't? What if there's another reason he wants to find Angela? Odds are the reason would be in his best interests, not hers. What if I lead Stone right to her and she gets hurt?"

"So, what are you going to do if you do find her?"

"Warn her."

CHAPTER 29

I PULLED UP the driver's license photo Moira sent me. Clairice Bethany Timmins. DOB November 29, 1979. She'd be forty-four in a few weeks. Older than she looked.

I googled her name and a few pages came up. She was now a real estate agent who had once been a model. Just like her looks suggested. Some small clothes catalogs that I hadn't heard of, but a model nonetheless. She certainly had the figure and the beauty for it. My guess was that she wasn't tall enough to make it to supermodel status. I put her at 5'4", maximum.

She didn't have a Wikipedia page, which I thought was a bit strange because everyone who'd ever been in any portion of the public eye seemed to have one these days. Well, almost everyone.

Her name was a bit unique, so I was able to attach her to a high school in Kingsburg, California. In Fresno County, about a hundred and fifty miles north of Pine Mountain Club. She and Allen Pettis were married for eleven years. Divorced for three. No children that I could find.

I didn't find a college for her either, so she might not have gone to one. She had a brother and a sister, both younger, who lived out of state.

I looked her up on social media and found her to be quite active on Instagram and Facebook. After having my head in my phone for the last half hour and not watching the entrance from Pineview Court onto the highway, I checked the GPS tracker again. The Sentra was still in the driveway.

Clairice Bethany Timmins had over five hundred followers on Instagram and thirteen hundred–plus friends on Facebook. I ate my second chocolate donut of the morning and took a deeper dive into the owner of the Nissan Sentra that I'd trailed for two hundred miles last night. I didn't have anything better to do, but I had to save the rest of the donuts for later in case this turned into an all-day surveillance.

The first thing I learned about Clairice Bethany Timmins was that her friends called her Claire. She posted a lot of photos of hiking in the mountains on Instagram. They could have been from around Pine Mountain Club or somewhere else in California. Plenty of pine trees with the California hardscrabble underbrush. I didn't know enough about the area and hadn't had a chance to explore yet to know how close to home the photos were. All the shots were of her hiking alone and had the arm-stretched, downward angle of selfies.

I went over to her Facebook page. Again, a lot of shots of her in the mountains. Some of her with gal pals whooping it up in a bar and in bikinis around a swimming pool. The pool shots were from two and three years go. None after that. The pool was large and in a rolling backyard that had views of mountains. The house on Pineview Court didn't have the same angled view of the mountains. The one on Facebook was much higher up. My guess was the home the pool belonged to was somewhere in or around Pine Mountain Club.

I didn't recognize anyone else in any of the photos, going back a couple years. Something odd struck me when I scrolled back through her page that I hadn't noticed on first glance. There were no new posts on Timmins's Facebook page in the last three weeks. I started scrolling again, checking the dates of posts. Before the last three blank weeks, in the last two years, the longest she went between posts was six days.

I jumped over to Instagram. Same thing. Three weeks since her last post. I went back to Facebook and went onto Timmins's friend list and started scrolling, looking for Angela Albright. I typed in Angela's name into the friend search box and nothing came up. Then the name on her birth certificate. Nothing.

I tried a few combinations of the two names and nothing came up. Not everyone uses their real name on social media, so I decided to do it the hard way and started scrolling through Claire Timmins's friends by looking at their pictures. Going through thirteen hundred pictures looking for the one needle in the photo stack was daunting, but I had nothing but time on my hands.

I took a break after three or four hundred photos and checked the GPS tracker for the hundredth time. Still blinking in place. I looked at the time on my phone: 1:47 p.m. I compromised with myself and ate half a donut and drank the rest of the orange juice.

I went back to scrolling. Twenty minutes in, I stopped on a photo of a blond woman in her late thirties. At scrolling speed she could have passed for Angela Albright, but when I stopped I saw that she wasn't. But that wasn't what held my eye now. The name of the next friend down the list did. At least the last name. Lisa Raskin.

Raskin. The same last, somewhat uncommon, name of the man that the Feds and Sergei were looking for. Theodore Raskin.

I studied the woman connected to the name. In her late thirties, early forties. Attractive. And there was something familiar about her or my imagination was at work again. I went back to Claire Timmins's Facebook posts. Sure enough, a woman who could have been Lisa Raskin was in one of the swimming pool photos. In the background on a chaise lounge. Just far enough back for me to not be sure. Timmins hadn't tagged or named anyone in the post. There was only a caption that read: "Pool Party!"

I pulled up Lisa Raskin's Facebook page and started scrolling through posts. I didn't have to check her friends' list because I already knew she and Claire Timmins were friends. Unlike Timmins, her most recent posts were from the last few days. I went back in time and found the same pool shot that Timmins had posted with the woman I knew was Lisa Raskin in the chaise lounge. Again, no shout-outs or tags.

I checked her profile for a family listing, but she didn't have one. Most people don't bother to fill in the "about" page. But I knew in my gut that Theodore Raskin was the reason Angela Albright was in hiding and the key to her whereabouts.

I googled Theodore William Raskin and took a deeper dive online than I did yesterday. There still wasn't a whole bunch about his background that I could find. I got onto a paid people finder website that I regularly used and found out he was forty-five years old, was born in Las Vegas, and had lived in many places since. The most recent being Rancho Santa Fe in San Diego County. A wealthy, ruralish enclave known for its horse country.

His Vegas roots made his supposed connection to Peter Stone believable, as Stone spent over half his adult life in Vegas before being pushed out of town when he was forced to sell his interest in the Starlighter casino to a mega corporation that famously razed the structure by imploding it, then building a huge, shiny, new family-friendly gambling edifice in its place.

Raskin's age meant he could have been a young man as described by Stone when he worked for him. Stone sold his shares in the Starlighter around twenty years ago. Unfortunately, Theodore Raskin of Las Vegas didn't have any sisters.

But he did have an older brother, Allen Joseph Raskin.

I searched Allen Joseph Raskin and found biographical information on Theodore's brother. Married to Emily Judith Raskin, nee Emily Murphy. Tall, dark hair, brown eyes, and looked nothing like Facebook's Lisa Raskin. However, I dug deeper. Emily Murphy was Allen Raskin's second marriage. His first was to Elizabeth Drucilla Shon. I found twenty-three-year-old wedding photos of the bride. Dark hair and eyes, wearing a lacy head covering. I zoomed in on the images on my phone, which slightly distorted them. The woman could have been a very young Lisa Raskin. And might not have been. I looked up Elizabeth Drucilla Shon online and couldn't find any more images. Only that she was forty-three and born in Las Vegas.

That made sense for her to meet and marry Allen Raskin, but it didn't shed any more light on whether Elizabeth Raskin could be Lisa Raskin. For one thing their first names didn't match. The diminutive of Elizabeth was Beth or Liz or Eliza. But maybe I was wrong and there were more. Liz was close to Lisa. I googled nicknames for Elizabeth and there it was. Lisa.

Still not 100 percent there but getting closer. Much closer. What if Lisa Raskin was Theodore Raskin's ex-sister-in-law? What would it prove? Nothing really. But it was still too much of a coincidence for me. There had to be a connection, some membrane that held all the events of the last few days together. I knew I was right.

I searched for Theodore Raskin on social media. There were a few hits, but none that matched cryptocurrency mastermind Theodore Raskin. I went back to the people finder website I'd been on earlier and took a screenshot of Raskin's photo. I called Alaina McCreery again. This time she answered.

"Hello?"

"Miss McCreery, this is Rick Cahill. I asked you some questions about Angela Albright a couple days ago."

"You don't have to treat me like I'm senile, Rick." The sweet tea-tinged accent. "I'm not that old. I just got back from babysitting my grandkids and saw your message. The picture you texted me is not the man I saw with Angela."

"I have another photo to send you. Can you tell me if the new one is the guy in the Maserati?"

"Sure, hon." Extra sugar on *hon*. "Text it on over."

I sent her the photo of Raskin and waited. It wasn't an ideal way to identify someone. There was a reason police used lineups and photo six-packs to identify suspects. It forced the witness to be certain. There were options to choose from. With one photo you could be less discerning. Although if the person didn't look anything like the suspect, one photo was as good as six.

"That's him," Alaina McCreery responded within five seconds of me sending the text. "He's a little older now. Some gray around the temples, but that's him. I'm sure of it."

Bingo. My Raskin theory was proven correct. And a whole new world of possibilities and questions about where Angela Albright was and why opened up.

"You didn't happen to get a license plate number on the Maserati, did you?"

"What kind of a neighbor do you think I am?" A little laugh. "I didn't bother to check the license plate, but it was a four-door sedan, metallic black, and had a grille like a shark's mouth. A lot of teeth. Kind of sleek. And sexy."

"Thanks, Alaina. You've been very helpful."

"Do you think Angela's with Mr. Maserati?" Her voice dropped. "Do you think he'd hurt her?"

"I don't know where she is, but I don't think she's been hurt." But she was probably in danger. The forces that swirled from and around Peter Stone were never benign.

CHAPTER 30

I WAS ABOUT to call Moira and fill her in on the Theodore Raskin connection when I glanced up and saw the Nissan Sentra emerging from Pineview Court onto the highway. Shit. If it turned right, it would come toward me. If Timmins saw me, word would get back to Angela or Raskin or whoever was pulling the strings that I hadn't just asked some questions then gone back to San Diego. They'd know I was staking out the connection to Angela's daughter and was determined to find Angela.

The Sentra turned left and headed in the direction of the tiny town of Pine Mountain Club. Too far away to be certain that no one was in the passenger seat, but I sensed it was empty. For whatever that was worth. My senses were hit and miss lately. Out of practice.

I checked the tracking app on my phone. It showed the red dot for the Sentra moving east on Mil Potrero Highway. Good. It worked. Follow the Sentra and whoever was driving it from afar or break into Claire Timmins's house and look for signs of Angela? Or anything else that could help me figure out what was going on?

I started the car and pulled onto the highway. Twenty seconds later, I turned left onto Pineview Court and parked under a pine tree two houses up from Claire Timmins's home. Out of range from her Ring doorbell camera.

I put on the PMC ball cap. I wanted to change my appearance enough from last night. The Pine Mountain Club sweatshirt would help, too.

I got out of the car, opened the trunk, and pulled up the covering exposing the spare tire well. I unzipped the duffle bag and rummaged through what police would rightfully call a burglar kit. The duct tape and plastic cuffs would signal something more sinister than burglary to the police. I had a different intent for the items, but there wouldn't be a good explanation for anything in the bag if I was ever caught with it.

I pulled out a couple black nitrile gloves from a box and put them on. Next, I found the small plastic case containing my lock pick set. I slipped the set in my back pocket. Lastly, I pulled out the latest addition to my black bag. A home security alarm jammer. It was black, about three by five inches with three straight black antennae sticking out of the top. Not infallible, but it had worked the one time I'd used it.

I stuck the jammer in the Pine Mountain Club hoodie front pocket and went behind the first house and walked under pine trees outside the backyard fence. The lot was huge, as was the next, and it took me almost a full minute to get behind Claire Timmins's house. I hoped she didn't have a Ring alarm or any security camera in her backyard. Or a dog.

The yard was anchored by a pine fence about six feet high and well over a hundred feet long. I put my gloved hands on top of the fence and went up on my tiptoes and peeked over into the backyard. It was made up mostly of a large, lush lawn. There was a wired-off herb garden and a large redwood deck with a built-in grill, outdoor kitchen area, and high-end patio furniture.

No dog or any signs of one. No sign of security cameras, either. There were two doors leading out to the backyard from the house. One, sliding glass, would be easy to breach unless it had a secondary deadbolt that was set into the frame of the house. Without that, you could simply jiggle open most sliding glass doors by pressing your hands against the glass and pushing the door up and down. No chance with a deadbolt.

The other door was wooden and had a picture frame window in it like the front door, complete with white sash.

I wasn't 100 percent certain that there was no one in the house. If I had, indeed, seen Angela Albright driving the Nissan Sentra last night from La Jolla, she might still be inside. But after Clairice Timmins's lies last night, I doubted that Angela would answer the door. And I couldn't get caught on the Ring doorbell camera if she wasn't home once I decided to break in.

I needed to make a ruckus in the backyard to draw someone to the window or outside. Luckily for me, there were plenty of projectiles within reach. I picked up three of the freshest looking pinecones off the ground. Ones that looked least likely to break apart when they were thrown against something hard. Less mess to clean up when I'd be in a hurry.

Another look around my surroundings. Not even a squirrel. I glanced back over the fence, then lowered my soles to the ground and threw a pinecone the hundred or so feet onto the roof of Claire Timmins's house. A loud bang and trundle as the cone bounced up the roof after impact then rolled down onto the deck with a thump. I peeked over the fence and studied the windows that opened onto the deck. No movement of sashes. This time I launched a pinecone onto the corner of the deck away from the windows. It banged off the deck and bounced against the adjoining wall then clattered along the redwood flooring. No sash movement, no doors opening. No sounds of a barking dog.

No one was home. I dropped the last pinecone.

Good news and bad. No Angela, and it also meant that, more than likely, Angela had never been in the house and the woman I'd followed up from La Jolla was Claire Timmins. That is, unless Angela was in the

Sentra with Timmins right now. That was the bad. The good was that I could breach the house certain no one was inside it.

I looked three hundred sixty degrees around me one last time to make sure no one was watching. I didn't see a soul. The neighborhood was empty except for a guy about to jump over a homeowner's fence and commit a crime. I hoisted myself up and over the fence and landed on the grass, stumbled, fell, and went into a controlled body roll and back up to my feet. Not quite as agile as I was ten years ago, but still capable enough for the job. Any job I took on.

I scrambled up onto the deck, grabbed the two pinecones, and threw them back over the fence. Then I turned on the alarm jammer and pressed my nitrile-covered hands against the sliding glass door as a first option. As expected, it barely moved when I pushed up and down. Bolted secondary lock.

Next, I moved over to the picture frame wooden door that probably led into the kitchen. Before I went to work, I checked the GPS tracker on my phone again. The Sentra was still moving east on Mil Potrero Highway. Now three miles away from me, just outside of town. The blinking red dot looked like it would hit Pine Mountain Club within a minute.

If Claire Timmins was just going to town to get groceries from the General Store, then I might only have another fifteen or so minutes to breach and search the house. If she was headed to the freeway, I didn't want to let her get too far out in front of me. I might be able to track her in my car using the GPS tracker, but if she was a half hour to an hour ahead of me, she'd be able to meet someone, do whatever business the two may have, and then get back on the road without me knowing who she met.

I needed to be quick inside the house under either scenario.

I hadn't used the lock pick set in a couple of years. I slipped the tension wrench in the bottom of the keyway, then the rake above it. I used the back-and-forth method with the rake, but I was definitely out of practice. Nonetheless, one pin at a time, I finally got the door unlocked in a couple minutes. In my prime, I could have done it in under a minute.

I held my breath when I turned the knob and pushed the door. It didn't open.

Deadbolt. Damn.

I worked the wrench and the rake and unlocked the deadbolt in a little less time than I did the door lock. Again, a deep breath. I pushed the door open. No beeping alarm. Either Claire Timmins didn't have an alarm, it was turned off, or the jammer worked. If there was an alarm in the house. I didn't have time to go searching for a wall panel. Most people had it mounted on the wall near the front door, but some hid it away in hall closets or other secreted areas.

Alarm hidden or not, I was safe. At least for now. The house was open to me.

But I hesitated before I entered it. An image of Krista and Leah flashed across my consciousness, blinding me to all else. Breaking into someone's house. Breaking the law. Pursuing the truth no matter the cost. To the innocent. To me. To my family. The damage it had already caused all of the above. Especially my family. But this was it. The final quest. After I found Angela Albright and warned her about Stone's pursuit, I'd be done. No more private investigator work. No more risking everything for something I couldn't touch. Something that wasn't more important than my family. Until my pursuit made it so. No more. This was the last.

I went inside the house.

CHAPTER 31

THE KITCHEN WAS a large chef's kitchen with a massive granite island and stainless-steel Wolf and Sub-Zero appliances. There was a large brick Tuscan arched opening into the living room. From the outside, I'd expected rustic American styling, not Tuscan. I scanned the kitchen for a desk space, but there wasn't one. Just a small alcove that had a wine rack and shelving for cookbooks. There was a walk-in pantry with a sliding barn door in the back. Nothing to search anywhere in the kitchen that would give hint to the whereabouts of Angela Albright.

I went into the plush carpeted living room and flash checked the tracker. Timmins's car was now parked in the General Store parking lot. I set an alarm on my phone for fifteen minutes.

The living room was large and open to the foyer. Again, the styling and furniture were Italian-ish, and the accent wall behind the brick fireplace was a massive mural of a vineyard that climbed all the way up to the A-framed ceiling. Nothing in it hinted at Angela Albright's presence.

I went down a hall and found a large room that looked like it had once been an office but was now in transition. A very masculine office. Dark wood paneling and wainscotting. The floor had been ripped up to the concrete and some of the paneling taken down from the walls.

An erasure of the ex, which would be complete when the remodeling of the room was done.

There was what I'd describe as a sunroom on the other side of the hall that had probably once been a game room. There were indentations in the carpet that looked like they'd come from the feet of a pool table. Further eradication of the ex. Two bathrooms filled out the rest of the downstairs. No sign of Angela or anything interesting on the first floor.

I went up the staircase off the foyer onto the second floor. Three bedrooms, a guest bathroom, and a laundry room. No clothes in the washer or dryer. The first guest bedroom had a queen size bed that was neatly made. Throw pillows at proper attention. No clothes in the bureau or closet. Nothing in the nightstand. The carpet still had a plush feel underfoot. The room felt like it had never been slept in.

The second guest room was larger and felt more lived in. The carpet not as spongy. The queen bed was made but not as crisply as the bed in the other room. The throw pillows looked to have been placed haphazardly or in a hurry. I lifted up the comforter. The sheet wasn't tucked in all the way up the side. The pillow and sheets hinted at women's perfume. I didn't recognize the scent, and there was no way I could pin it to Angela Albright who I hadn't seen in ten years. Even if I could, women change their scents.

There was a single book on the nightstand. A novel by Megan Abbott. Also a box of Kleenex, but nothing else. Only some loose change and a pen in the nightstand's two drawers. There were a couple mismatched colorful knee socks, a knit cap, and a pair of women's sized mittens in the top drawer of the bureau. Nothing else in the other drawers. The closet was empty except for an extra set of sheets and blanket. But it had forty or fifty plastic hangers hanging on the closet pole.

I checked the en suite bathroom. A fleck of toothpaste in the sink, and the mirror had fingerprint smudges on it. The medicine cabinet had a toothbrush, new tube of travel size Crest, and a square of dental floss. Nothing else. I pressed the bristles of the toothbrush on my left wrist above the bottom of the nitrile glove. Slightly damp.

There were two towels on the rack next to the shower. One was also damp.

Someone had used the toothbrush and the towel this morning. I was certain someone had stayed over in Claire Timmins's guest room last night and had left just the slightest trace of themself behind.

A woman? Most likely. But if true, where was she now? Had she been in the passenger seat of the Sentra when Timmins drove to town? I thought the passenger side was empty when I saw the Sentra make the turn onto the highway, but I couldn't be certain. Did someone pick up the woman last night or this morning? Uber? A taxi? Did they even have either up here? Did someone else pick her up? Theodore Raskin?

Too many questions. No answers. Maybe I'd find some in the rest of the search of the house.

I checked the GPS tracker before I went into the master bedroom. The Sentra was still parked at the General Store. I didn't know if that was just the first of many stops for Timmins or the only one.

I hurried down the hall to check out the master bedroom.

It took up about half of the upstairs floor and had a walk-in closet that was almost as large as the first guest room. The California King bed was made and had about double the throw pillows of either of the beds in the two guestrooms. I took a picture of the arrangement of the pillows atop the bed, then removed four of them and pulled back the covers. The sheets were tucked in all the way up to the bed pillows, unlike the bed in the second guest room. I sniffed the sheets and the pillows. A scent, more soap than perfume, and not the same as on the sheets in the guest room.

Claire Timmins had most likely slept in her own bed last night, not the one in the guest room. Someone else did, and that person also took a shower in the guest bathroom this morning.

I snugly remade the bed and rearranged the throw pillows to match the photo I'd taken.

An old-fashioned rolltop desk and wingback chair sat in front of a window that looked out over the backyard. There was a closed laptop computer on the desk. I opened the laptop and a password box came up on the screen. No use even trying. I didn't know enough about Claire Timmins to even venture a guess at a password. I'd never even heard of her until last night. I closed the laptop and moved onto the other objects on the desk.

There was a leather organizer next to the computer. It had a thin stack of real estate flyers inside it with Timmins's name and photo on the upper left corner. I hadn't seen many homes in the area, but there might be more higher up in the mountains.

I opened the drawers of the desk. Nothing of interest. The bottom right drawer served as a filing cabinet. I fingered through the files. Most were buyer and seller contracts, offers and completed sales. Nothing hinted at Angela Albright.

I looked through the organizer, going back a month. No appointments listing Angela's name or any secret code that I noticed. Just client appointments and open houses for a busy realtor. I checked the real estate flyers. They were copies of a single one-sheet with a dozen boxed photos of homes for sale.

Pine Mountain Club looked like a hot market. Six of the boxes had bold sold signs across the photos. In the bottom right corner of each of the sold photos someone, presumably Timmins, had written in initials in blue ink. Not hers. There were different initials in each box. Maybe the initials of the clients who bought the homes. Maybe something completely different.

Most of homes on the flyer were in the $500K to $700K range. In San Diego or LA, they'd go for double that price. One of the sold homes stuck out, though. Forty-five hundred square feet and it sold for $2,200,000. Much larger than all the others and a lot more expensive. There was only the one photo of the home, probably from a drone. It was from above and at an angle that made the house look secluded and high up in the mountains. The initials in the bottom corner were BR.

An elite weekend getaway for an LA bigwig or home for a Pine Mountain Club local? An alarm suddenly beeped, and I swung my body around in the desk chair. Then I laughed. The fifteen-minute alarm I'd set on my phone. I pulled out the still beeping phone and turned off the alarm.

I checked the GPS tracker to see how far away from me the blinking red dot was. Not far at all. It was coming back in my direction on Mil Potrero Highway and was only about two miles from the house.

CHAPTER 32

I PUT THE file back in the organizer. My brain flipped in reverse, and I scanned the bedroom looking for anything I might have disturbed and not put back in place. Clear. Next, I sped through the second floor doing the same. All clear. I thundered down the stairs and sped through the kitchen to the door into the backyard. I opened it and twisted the flange on the knob lock, exited, then closed the door behind me. The door locked. I spun to run for the back fence then stopped.

The deadbolt. Shit!

I turned back to the door and whipped out the lock pick set from my jeans. Locks can be relocked by reverse picking them. As long as the pins weren't damaged in the original pick. I slipped the tension wrench in the keyway and pushed in the opposite direction as before and went to work with the rake back and forth.

I counted out loud, a number a second, giving myself a minute to relock the bolt. I figured I had a max of four to five minutes before Claire Timmins rolled back up into her driveway. And I'd already lost about a minute. I felt one pin trip at twenty-three seconds. The next at forty-four. Sixty-seven. Three more pins to go. I didn't have another minute to spare.

I'd have to leave the deadbolt unlocked.

I jammed the pick set back into my pocket and sprinted for the fence. Maybe two minutes before Timmins turned down Pineview Drive. Even less until she saw the entrance to the highway. I could scale the fence and disappear into the pine trees, but my car was parked up the street from her house. None of her sometime neighbors were in the neighborhood right now. Looked like they hadn't been for a while. She'd notice a stray car parked on the block. The *only* car parked on the block. One she'd never seen her neighbors drive. She'd wonder who it belonged to and where the person driving it was.

I had to get to my car before Timmins got within sight of Pineview Court. I leapt at the fence in a full sprint and hit it near the top, then vaulted myself over. The momentum tossed me into the underbrush beneath the pine trees. I hit the ground at an angle and twisted my left ankle. I went down in a heap. No controlled roll and back up to my feet this time. Pain throbbed all the way around my ankle as I laid on my back. I grabbed it and could almost feel it swell beneath my fingers.

No choice. I had to get back to my car. Now. I struggled up to my feet, grunting to give release to the pain. I shuffle-ran along the fence and then along those of the next two homes. A clenched-mouth grunt with each stride. Finally, I broke left around the last home and saw my car parked across the street under the tree forty yards away. My college football forty time decades behind me and a sprained ankle in front of me.

I pushed toward my car, then noticed the nose of another car turn onto Pineview Court. I dove behind a lilac bush on the edge of the lawn of the first house on the block. Not close enough to be completely obscured by it if someone was looking in my direction. My right cheek flat against the ground, I saw the bottom half of the gray Nissan Sentra slow to a stop for an instant, then proceed down the street.

Busted? No. Timmins was probably looking at my car, which was parked across from me. I kept my head down as the Sentra passed out of sight, then scrambled up to my feet and limped over to the porch of the empty house.

A couple seconds later, I heard the metallic clunk of a car door close. Just one. Timmins, or whoever had driven the Sentra back from town, was alone. I listened for the sound of feet shuffling upstairs onto the porch. And waited. No clunk of a car trunk signifying the collection of grocery bags. No, my bet was that Timmins, or whoever, was looking at my car.

I waited, seemed like more than a minute, but was probably twenty seconds or less. Once she went up the stairs onto the porch, she'd lose her sightline to my car. Finally, the sound of footsteps, a pause, then the thump of Timmins's front door being closed.

I broke into a full gallop-limp-sprint and hopped across the street to my car. I pushed the ignition on and did a three-point turn and exited Pineview Court, my eyes in the rearview mirror the whole way.

If Claire Timmins heard my car, she didn't bother to run out of her house to get a look at it. If she noticed the deadbolt to the back door unlocked, she might not have to see me to know someone had been in her home. And now she'd recognize my car if she saw it again on the road. I'd have to follow her from afar using the GPS tracker and the map on my phone or at night.

I turned left onto Mil Potrero Highway and headed back to town to reassess my plan on how to find Angela Albright.

CHAPTER 33

I PULLED INTO a parking space in front of the inn, still riding the adrenal blast of almost getting caught burglarizing Claire Timmins's home. My ankle throbbed, and my conscience was slightly bruised. I'd broken the law, felt slightly guilty about it, but still savored the buzz. And justified it by convincing myself I'd broken the law in order to find Angela Albright and keep her safe. The kind of feelings and justifications I wasn't supposed to have anymore. The kind I couldn't allow myself to have anymore.

I had to get used to the fact that there was a slower, safer, law-abiding life ahead of me.

I opened the car door and pine-scented mountain air hit me in the face. I took a deep breath for the first time since I'd gotten to town last night. I'd been so on the go for the last twenty-four hours that I didn't appreciate where I'd ended up at the end of surveilling the Nissan Sentra.

The angst drained from my body with each pine-scented inhale. My shoulders dropped and the tension oozed out of my neck down my spine and into the ground. I looked around, the pine trees on the mountains, the rustic little town. I noticed, really noticed, the beauty of this mountain oasis for the first time. For an instant, I felt the way a mountain retreat was supposed to make you feel.

Relaxed.

In happier times, Pine Mountain Club would be an ideal spot for Leah, Krista, Midnight, and me to get away for a weekend. Krista's first foray in the mountains. Wide open nature for Midnight to explore. A romantic hideaway for Leah and me to rekindle the love that had once burned so deeply. A love that I still felt every day and that I hoped, against logic and reason, could help mend our broken marriage.

I grabbed my luggage, which consisted of a Pine Mountain Club T-shirt, my bomber jacket, and a bag full of four and a half donuts, a liter and a third of water, and Stone's burner phone from under the passenger seat. And the Ruger SP101 .357 Magnum in my shoulder holster. I shut the car door and took a step toward the inn. And almost went down over my twisted ankle. The pain vibrated up my leg.

A jolting reminder that these weren't happier times. And that reality was painful.

I limped up to the inn, passed the manager's office, and made a slow turn to the staircase.

"Mr. Cahill?" A woman's voice. I stopped and looked into the office. An attractive woman in her fifties with an engaging smile walked out from behind the polished wooden counter. Her light brown hair framed an intelligent face with the crinkle of an honest life well-lived around her eyes. Her attractiveness was matched by her warmth. "I'm Colleen Foster. I own the inn with Thomas. Did something happen to your leg?"

Colleen. The name of my first wife who was murdered. Another reminder of how dark life can get.

"Yes." I forced the grimace into a smile as I took a step toward the outside staircase. "I just twisted my ankle. Nothing major. Thanks."

"Ooh." She made her own grimace. "Sprained ankles are painful. I wish I could move you to a downstairs room, but they're all full. We require people with dogs to be downstairs for obvious reasons."

We shared a laugh.

"Upstairs is fine. Thank you." I smiled. "I can manage with the hand-rail, and the room is just across from the stairs. Thanks for your concern."

The stairs were tough, but the railing helped take the weight off my ankle and kept me steady.

When I finally made it up to my room, I sat down on the bed to get the weight off my ankle. I checked Stone's burner phone. One missed call. Shit. Stone. No message. The voicemail wasn't activated on the phone. One less possible breadcrumb for someone to connect Stone and me.

Someone knocked on my door, delaying me the anxiety of calling Stone for at least a few seconds. I got off the bed and gingerly shambled to the door. No peephole. I decided to live dangerously and open the door. Why change now after all the success I'd had living recklessly?

Colleen from the manager's office stood holding a plastic grocery bag and a small, folded towel with a little plastic wrapped two-pack of Motrin.

"For your ankle. There's an ice machine downstairs, but I wanted to make sure you got a head start." The warm smile.

"Thank you so much." I took the Motrin, bag of ice, and towel from her. "That was very thoughtful."

"You're welcome. Let me know if you need anything else."

"I will. Thanks." I smiled and shut the door and was now worried that I'd be murdered in my sleep. These people in Pine Mountain Club were just too damn nice.

I tossed the ice and towel onto the bed, ripped open the Motrin pack, and downed the orange caplets with a swig from one of my water bottles.

My ankle needed a break. I collapsed onto the bed, took off my shoes and socks. My left ankle had a golf ball growing out of its side and was already hueing black and blue. I put the ice bag onto it, laid on my right side, and pulled out the burner phone. Stone picked up on the third ring.

"Rick." The baritone ooze. "You've been a bad boy. You didn't call me last night, and you didn't pick up when I called earlier. You're supposed to check in every night and not ignore my calls. I'm very disappointed."

"I went on a wild goose chase last night, Stone. Followed someone who I thought was Angela up to Santa Barbara. It took me all day to finally get a close enough look at the woman to confirm that it wasn't her. I left the phone in the trunk of my car." Lying came easily to me when talking to Stone, as it probably did for him when talking to me. Or anyone.

"I'm beginning to think I made a mistake hiring you, Rick. You've been on the case for three days and haven't come up with anything but went on a wild goose chase wasting my money. And I paid you a lot of it. I expect results."

"I understand. But our arrangement also calls for you to tell me anything that could possibly help me find Angela." Not specifically, but it was implied.

"I don't know what you're talking about." He sounded sincere.

"Somebody ended up dead in the house on Cabrillo Avenue in La Jolla that your Fed friends spent some time in yesterday." Lie detector time. "I'm sure you heard about it on the local news. Body was burnt to ashes."

"Why would you have followed the special agents to a house in La Jolla?" An underline of anger. "I told you to stay away from them and concentrate on finding Angela. That's what you're getting paid for."

"It wasn't me. It was the person who followed them from my house."

"Moira MacFarlane."

"No. Somebody else."

"You're a bad liar when you're lying about someone important to you." A mocking jab.

"Did you hear about the dead body or not?"

"You're assuming I'm still in San Diego."

He wanted me to go down his semantic maze. Always a dead end.

"In or out of town, you still have connections. You must have heard about the dead body."

"Where's this all going, Rick?"

"Who died?"

"You tell me."

"Do you think these FBI agents are capable of murder?"

My personal cell phone vibrated an incoming call. Moira. As much as I wanted to talk to her, I couldn't until I got rid of Stone. And somehow extract more information from him than he wanted to give me.

"Stupid question." Syrupy dismissal.

"Why?"

"You've been in the game long enough to know that anyone is capable of murder under the right circumstances."

I had my own circumstances to deal with.

Stone was looking for Angela Albright. Two crooked Feds who Stone claimed asked him about Theodore Raskin, a former employee of his who ran a cryptocurrency exchange, showed up at my house the same day Stone did. The occupant of a car belonging to a woman in Pine Mountain Club met with Angela Albright's daughter in La Jolla. The same woman had a friend who might have been related to Raskin by marriage. Angela's neighbor claiming to be 100 percent certain that she'd seen Raskin pick up Angela many times. Some maybes, some yesses, and too many coincidences.

Stone's desire to find Angela now seemed to be about more than his supposed need for a kidney transplant. Theodore Raskin was that *more*. That put Angela in danger. And me alongside her.

She needed to be warned. I already had been. From my years of dealing with Peter Stone.

"I'm just trying to collect as much information as I can. I told you how I worked. I need to know everything. Is it possible that Angela knows Theodore Raskin? From what I've learned so far, Angela disappeared around the same time Sorensen and Bowden questioned you about Raskin. I'm at a dead end, Stone. I'm looking for any connections I can find."

"I can't imagine how Theodore and Angela could have ever met." Disdainful. His default attitude toward me or trying to cover up the truth? "I'm running out of time, Rick. And so are you. I need to see some progress soon."

He hung up.

Progress. I was making progress. Progress that, if relayed to Stone, could put Angela Albright's life, and my own, in worse danger than they already were.

CHAPTER 34

I COULDN'T CON myself. Stone had me rattled. I'd just lied to a man who'd once tried to kill me and who I'd seen kill men in front of me. In self-defense, but without remorse or conscience.

I couldn't leave Angela Albright's fate in the hands of Peter Stone.

I did have another option. Give Stone to Sergei Volkov. But like Stone told me earlier, Sergei wouldn't leave a witness behind. I'd be more than a witness, though. I'd be an accessory if I set Stone up for his death. That might be enough for Sergei to let me live. A business deal.

Had the evil I'd been battling for decades soaked so deeply through my pores that I could send someone to their death for just the chance of saving my own life? It wouldn't be an innocent life I'd trade for my own. Would that make a difference come judgment day? Or had I already been judged for my past sins?

Either way, if it was my family or Stone, or even an innocent man, there wouldn't be a decision to make. Just action to take. Thankfully, it hadn't come to that.

Yet.

I checked the GPS tracker. The Nissan Sentra was still sitting in the driveway of the house on Pineview Court.

My stomach suddenly reminded me that I was hungry. Returning Moira's call would have to wait. I eyed the bag of donuts I'd left on the little desk next to the door. Then I thought better of it. The donuts would keep. I needed some food that was a bit more nutritionally balanced, but I had to be able to get to my car to go find some. Pine Mountain Club was a small town. Tiny. I doubted their restaurants delivered. How much work could a delivery driver generate in a town of a hundred people?

I took the bag of ice off my ankle and rolled it up in the towel innkeeper Colleen gave me. The ice had been on my ankle for about a half hour. The golf ball was still there, but it hadn't gotten any bigger. I delicately rolled my foot around. My ankle radiated pain and had diminished rotation. Minimal mobility, but the pain was tolerable. The Motrin and the ice had done some good. Progress. I needed to be ambulatory. I slid over to the edge of the bed and hung my legs down onto the floor.

One step onto the hardwood floor and my ankle gave out and I almost went down. The pain woke up. I'd sprained my ankles plenty of times playing high school sports and college football. There was always a trainer handy to wrap the ankle up and send me back into the game. Going right back into action kept the ankle loose until it blew up later after the game in the locker room.

Rest *was* necessary to treat a sprained ankle. But it was also debilitating on a fresh sprain when you needed to move around for a short time. I forced myself to gimp around the room. The pain pushed grunts out of my mouth.

I didn't know what tomorrow would bring, or even tonight, but I knew with Peter Stone, Sergei Volkov, and crooked Feds in my life right now, I needed to be able to move around and stay upright on two legs. And if that wasn't possible, I'd have to do it on three.

I checked the time on my phone. Almost 5:00 p.m. The sun had already sunk below the horizon. Fall nights got dark early in the mountains.

I put my shoes and socks back on and tested my ankle again. My gait was a short step with my right foot and a slide with my left. Not the mobility I was hoping for and needed. I put the bag of ice in the tiny "freezer" compartment of the mini fridge, grabbed my keys, and shuffled out of the room.

The staircase was only six feet from my door. I navigated the distance in four dragged steps. Going downstairs was easier than the reverse. I held onto the railing and hopped down on my right foot, keeping my left in the air. The seventy-five feet to my car was much more difficult, painful, and time consuming.

The drive to the golf course a quarter mile down the street took less time than the "walk" to my car. I gritted my teeth and limped from my car to the golf pro shop. When I was ten feet from the pro shop, a man in his late twenties wearing a Titleist hat and a Pine Mountain Club golf shirt exited it and stuck a key into the glass door's lock. He sensed me behind him and turned around.

"Sorry, we're closed for the day. We open at eight a.m. tomorrow morning." He gave me a Pine Mountain Club warm smile.

"I just want to buy a putter. It will take me ten seconds. Cash or credit, whichever is easiest for you." I gave him a wounded private investigator smile.

"It will still be there tomorrow morning. I promise."

"Does the General Store sell walking canes?" I asked.

"Huh?" He tilted his head like a confused Labrador retriever.

"I need a cane. I figured a putter was the closest thing I could find in town." More injured smile. "I doubt the General Store has any. Am I wrong?"

He looked me in the face then shifted his eyes down to my legs. All my weight was on my right leg and my left heel was off the ground.

"I can't say I know every item in the General Store, but almost. I think you're right about canes." He turned back to the door and slipped the key back in. "Cash would probably be best, so I don't have to open up the register again. I can add it to tomorrow's sales in the morning."

He swung the door open, flipped on the lights, then held the door for me to enter. I wobbled in, and he walked over to a putter rack. I followed him over as best I could.

"Wow." He watched me limp over. "That looks pretty bad."

"It's manageable. A putter will help. Thanks."

There were about seven or eight putters on the rack. A couple Odyssey, some Ping and Tour Edge putters. My new friend grabbed a Tour Edge Anser–style putter.

"This is the cheapest one I got." He checked the price tag glued around the putter shaft. "It's sixty-five bucks, but I can give it to you for the member price of fifty-five. Plus tax, of course."

A Ping or Odyssey would have been at least a hundred-fifty dollars more.

"Thanks."

He took the club over to the counter and picked up a handheld calculator and tapped away on it. "That will be $59.68."

I pulled out my wallet and gave him three twenties and two fives.

"Keep the change. I appreciate you opening up for me." I handed the money to him.

He counted out the three twenties, put them in an envelope, and held his hand holding the two fives out to me.

"No worries, man." The smile. "Not a big deal."

I was now more certain than ever that I was going to be murdered in my sleep. Pine Mountain Club folk were just too nice.

"Keep it. You did me a solid. That's the least I can do."

He looked at me, then at his hand holding the money. He left his arm sticking straight out for another second or two, then finally shoved the money in his golf slacks.

"Thanks, man. As soon as your leg's better, come out and play a round. I'll give you the member rate."

"Deal."

CHAPTER 35

I WALKED UP the long ramp that led up to the General Store entrance, leaning on the putter head with my right hand. The butt end of the rubber grip made for solid traction with the ground. I doubted the Ping or Odyssey would have felt any sturdier. My ankle still hurt, and I was hardly Fred Astaire, but I could function on three legs and go where I needed to without losing too much time.

My guess that the General Store wouldn't have canes was correct, but it did have Ace bandages. I bought one, a bottle of Motrin, a couple more liters of water, and another Pine Mountain Club T-shirt, then tap-danced out of the store.

I stopped at the Mexican restaurant on the way back to the inn and had a couple of chicken enchiladas that were the most nutritious things I'd eaten in over twenty-four hours. My waitress, of course, could not have been nicer or more complimentary about my idea for an impromptu cane. I over-tipped her and even got a thanks for coming in from the chef who came out of the kitchen as I left.

I made it up the stairs at the Pine Mountain Inn and into my room with my putter-cane, Ace bandages, and water and called Moira. Voicemail. I left her a message to call me back ASAP. I unstrapped my shoulder holster holding the Ruger .357 and plopped down onto the bed.

The water in the shower got hot in a hurry and felt good after a day of some action and a lot of sitting, all while going commando in my jeans.

I limped into the bedroom with my cutting-edge putter-cane. The hot shower water wasn't the best choice for a recent ankle sprain. Still cold treatments for the next three days, then warmth to help with blood flow and mobility. Right now, more blood meant more swelling.

I was clean and naked and limping. The only clean piece of clothing I had was the Pine Mountain Club shirt I just bought at the General Store. Saving that for tomorrow. I didn't know if Pine Mountain Club had a laundromat, but even if they did, I doubted anyone wanted to see me waiting for my clothes in the dryer dressed in a T-shirt, a hat, and nothing else. Naked in my room, it would have to be. I caned over to the mini fridge and fished out the bag of ice from the upper "freezer" area. The ice was now mostly ice water.

Shit.

I dumped the water in the sink, put on my pants and new favorite sweatshirt, grabbed the ice bucket and my putter-cane, and hobbled downstairs to the ice machine. The wooden steps were cold on my bare feet. The temperature had dropped at least fifteen degrees since I came back from dinner.

Going back up the stairs was tougher with the ice bucket and cane. I didn't have a free hand to steady myself on the railing. Slow, wobbly, and in pain. My reality for the next couple days. Where those days would be spent, I'd yet to determine.

My cell phone had a red dot on the phone icon when I got back to the room. I grabbed it off the desk and found that I had a voice message from Moira.

"What's so urgent?" Moira could be Hemingwayesque in her use of language.

I sat on the bed and called her back.

"I see you're still up in Pine Mountain Club or Pine Mountain Association or whatever they call it up in the middle of nowhere."

"It's Pine Mountain Club." I realized I felt protective of this little mountain hideaway. "And how did you know I'm still up here?"

"We have Find My Friends on our iPhones, remember?" Her big-sister-talking-to-slow-younger-brother voice. "I showed you how to use it last year."

I'd forgotten. I wasn't very tech savvy, but I wasn't a Luddite, either.

"Oh, yeah." I found the app under "utilities" and opened it, then tapped "people" and then Moira's name. She and Leah were the only people I'd ever connected. Made sense. They were the only two adults I contacted somewhat regularly. "Did you find out who the dead body was at the Cabrillo house?"

"Only that it's a male. All of my PD contacts are playing dumb."

"You think it's Special Agent Sorensen, and the FBI has pulled a press blackout because he's dirty?"

"That's exactly what I would have thought if I hadn't seen him and Bowden get into their rental Chevy Tahoe at the Mission Bay Motel this afternoon and then drive up to the FBI Headquarters in Sorrento Valley."

"What?" Ironically, that was the last place I expected the two Feds to go. "Stone made it sound as if those two are rogue agents, and they certainly have been behaving that way. Why the hell would they go to headquarters? Did you sit on them?"

"For an hour. Then I had to leave. Luke was having a meltdown over his girlfriend. He needed his mom."

Luke was basically a good kid, but on the emotionally immature side. He and Moira had a complicated, seesaw relationship since his father died of a heart attack ten years ago. Moira seemed to be constantly trying to regain the closeness they had before her husband's death.

"Is he okay?"

"He's calmed down some. He's over here talking to her on the phone in his old bedroom. Crisis averted." She let out a grunt. "For now. Anyway, back to the case. Why are you still up in the boonies? Are you getting closer to finding Angela?"

"I think I am." I told her that the photo I'd seen of Lisa Raskin on Clairice Bethany Timmins's Facebook page was close enough to match a younger version of her in the wedding photos of her to Alan Raskin, Theodore's brother, and that I'd discovered a damp towel in Timmins's guest bathroom along with fresh toothpaste in the sink.

I left the kicker until the end.

"I texted a photo of Theodore Raskin to Angela's neighbor." I paused to let the tension build. Just to be a jerk. A kid brother. "And she's 100 percent certain that Raskin is the guy who picked up Angela multiple times in a Maserati."

"Holy crap! That could put a whole different spin on why Peter Stone wants to find Angela, couldn't it?"

"Bingo."

"And don't think you can slip past the fact that you were in Timmins's guest bathroom in order to feel the damp towel." Big sister. This time busting the little brother for sneaking out at night. But in this case, I snuck in. "How did you get inside her house? Knock on her door again hopping in place and ask if you could use her bathroom?"

"Not exactly."

"Dammit Rick, if you get arrested in a place like that you could spend a month in jail before they give you an arraignment." An extra sizzle to her machine gun voice. "And the local defense lawyer is probably the brother-in-law of the prosecutor."

"Funny."

"I'm not joking. Be careful up there." Her voice softened. "When are you coming home?"

Home. My onetime sanctuary that was now just a place for Midnight and me in our final years to be left with memories of hugs and giggles and ball tosses with Krista. And unrestricted love from Leah. That home, of the lived memories, of a loving, functioning family, had only been for two years. But they'd been the best two years of my life. And I'd give anything to live them all over again.

"I don't know. I still think Angela is up here somewhere. I've got a tracker on Claire Timmins's car, but so far, she's stayed pretty close to home.

"Have you talked to Stone?"

"Yes. Lied to him about where I am." I told her about my lie to Stone about following someone to Santa Barbara.

"Do you think he believed you?"

"Yes, but he's not happy with my progress."

"Can you quit? Give him back his money?" Concern in Moira's voice. Moira concerned made me concerned, but I'd already beaten her there. "I'll give you back the money you gave me. I didn't even want to take it in the first place."

"I thought about it, but I'm not sure it would do any good. At some point, I'm going to have to deal with Stone, but you don't have to." I tried to keep a lightness to my voice I didn't feel. "Keep the money and walk away. Whatever Sorensen and Bowden were up to, they've checked in with San Diego FBI Headquarters. The Special Agent in Charge in Sorrento Valley can take over from here. All you have to worry about now is your son. Thanks for having my back."

"Unfortunately, for some reason that I've never been able to understand, I feel responsible for you." More agitation than tenderness in her voice. "I felt that way from the first day we met when I went over to your house and reamed you out for stealing one of my clients. I—"

"I didn't even know they'd talked to you. I—"

"Jesus, Rick, of course I know you didn't do it on purpose. We've been over this already. Why do you have to make everything so hard?" Now more tenderness than agitation. "The point is, somehow you became family to me. Maybe because it had only been a year since Clint died when we met, and I was still trying to figure out how to navigate my new life. Not only did I no longer have my life partner, I no longer had my business and investigative partner. I lost some old clients and could barely put food on the table for a son who now hated me for reasons I still don't completely understand. Then I met you—someone even more messed up than me who needed someone to look out for him. I guess, over time, you became my new project." She chuckled. "A project I've clearly failed at, but I'm still trying to make you into a fully formed human."

"You can't win them all." I laughed myself because I didn't want to address the emotion in Moira's voice.

"Yeah." No laughter now. "Anyway, I'm in this as long as you are. We need to find Angela Albright and warn her that Stone is looking for her. And if Stone is into something illegal, something that puts people's lives in danger, then we go to the police. And we need to figure out what to do about Sergei Volkov."

"I'll figure out what to do with Volkov when the time comes. Keep your head down in the meantime." I hung up and opened the Find My Friends app and checked the whereabouts of Leah's phone. In the mountains above Santa Barbara. She and Krista were still safe. For now.

CHAPTER 36

"BILLY." I DIDN'T know if I said the name subconsciously or out loud. Whichever the case, it woke me up. I squinted my eyes down to slits and looked at the glowing fuzzy red numerals of the clock on the night-stand from a foot away. 2:08 a.m. Then I heard them. Footsteps on the wooden walkway outside my room. They stopped. Next to my door. I thought I heard the twist of the locked doorknob. I jackknifed off the bed and grabbed my .357 Ruger from the nightstand.

Two quick limp steps to the door and I leaned my ear against it. I either heard whispers through the door or a wisp of wind. A creak on the walk-way outside. I unlocked the door and whipped it open, the Ruger at my side. A shadow on the staircase across the way. My glasses, still on the far nightstand. My once blind vision, now uncorrected at 20/200, forced me to squint down for more clarity. The figure backlit by the dim lighting on the stairs. A masculine sense. The upper half of a man?

"Hey!" I kept half of my naked body behind the cracked door. My right half showing, with the Ruger in my right hand down against my leg.

The figure turned. A halo of light around it. A blurred angel.

"Wrong room. Sorry." Man's voice just above a whisper. The hint of a foreign accent? Israeli? Or an American one obscured by the whisper?

The figure turned again and clambered down the staircase.

I shut the door, spun, and dove onto the bed and snatched my glasses off the nightstand. I put them on and speed-limped over to the wood-framed sliding glass door that opened onto the deck. Blackout curtains blocked the view. I threw them back, unlocked the door, and hobbled out onto the deck.

White Christmas lights lined the pine trees in front of the inn, throwing faint illumination onto the small parking lot. No movement. No sound, but for an icy breeze ruffling the needles on the pine trees.

I stood, watched, and listened for thirty seconds, a minute. The cold wood of the deck ran a chill from my feet up my whole body. The pain in my ankle now awake after the adrenal blast of a possible intruder had worn off.

I gimped back into my room, shut the sliding glass door, locked it, and pulled on the handle to check the lock. Next, over to the front door, locked the knob and the bolt, then checked them both.

The bed was warm back under the sheets, comfortably inviting much-needed sleep. But my pulse still revved under my skin and my eyes searched the darkness above me. People accidentally trying to get into the wrong hotel room happened all the time. I once walked into a neighboring apartment room in college, went into the kitchen, opened the refrigerator, and passed out. Woke up with talking heads staring down at me. Alcohol had been involved. Gallons of it.

I didn't know what the bar scene was like in Pine Mountain Club, or if there even was one, but the time was right for a drunken mistake. 2:08 in the morning. Bars in California close at 2:00 a.m. Last call and then a stagger over to the inn where you were staying. The whole town was one street. No need to drive. Get drunk and approach the inn from the wrong side, try to get into a locked room, and encounter a naked man with a .357 Magnum dangling at his side. Happened all the time. But still, I couldn't sleep.

Peter Stone and Sergei Volkov were back in my life. Ordinary mistakes didn't seem so ordinary anymore. When I checked into the inn, Thomas Foster said I could have my pick of upstairs rooms, implying no one else was staying up there. Maybe someone checked in after me. Certainly possible. Common. Except the man had gone downstairs after his "mistake," not over to the other end of the hall to find his upstairs room. But, there was another staircase. Maybe in his potential drunken state, the man had to use the other staircase to reorient himself.

Completely understandable.

Except Peter Stone and Sergei Volkov were back in my life.

CHAPTER 37

BIRDS WERE TWEETING when I woke up the second time that morning. Bucolic. And safe. The clock read 7:44 a.m. My body let me sleep in to try to make up for the sleep I missed due to my mind's preoccupations for an hour and a half after my early morning visitor.

I checked the GPS tracking app on my phone. The Nissan Sentra was parked in the driveway of Claire Timmins's house on Pineview Court. I wondered if she noticed that the deadbolt on the door going into her backyard was unlocked. And if she did, if she attributed it to whoever had been in the lone car parked on her street when she got home yesterday. And if she made the connection to me.

My heart raced back to 2:08 a.m. this morning at the possibility of someone breaking into my room just ten hours after I broke into someone else's home. No ambiguity about that break-in. My excuse was that I was doing it for the greater good. To try to find Angela Albright so I could help keep her safe.

A rationalization. I'd broken the law. Even worse, I'd breached someone's home. Her private sanctuary. Gone through her things. In a world where privacy was now the rarest of possessions, had I committed an even greater sin? She hadn't left her back door open like we all do on our computers and smart devices so spies, legal and illegal, can slither in and commoditize every facet of our life while we scour the metaverse jonesing for our next dopamine hit.

I grabbed the ACE bandage out of the grocery bag and sat on the bed, trying to remember how all the athletic trainers I'd had over the years wrapped my ankles. When my memory failed, I looked up how to do it on my phone. I learned very quickly it was difficult to do on your own ankle when you were in pain. But I managed to use the figure eight method and feel that my ankle was more secure than without the wrap.

I had to loosen the laces of my left shoe to fit the extra wrapping in but managed to get dressed. My attire, old pants, socks, and shoes, and my new PMC T-shirt. Next, the article of clothing that I was just starting to get used to again. I slung on my shoulder holster and secured the Ruger in it. Two small leather pouches hung down from the holster under my right arm. I unsnapped each and made sure they held the two five-cartridge speed loaders for the revolver. Loaded. My bomber jacket provided perfect concealment and much-needed warmth in the mountain air.

I dragged over to the mini fridge, grabbed two litters of water and the bag of remaining donuts from the top of the dresser and put everything into the plastic bag. The bedside clock read 8:12. Time for breakfast and a question.

I took my bag and improvised cane and went downstairs. The top half of the Dutch door to the manager's office was open. Colleen Foster stood next to the counter talking to a man and a woman. I only got a look at the woman's profile and the back of the man's head. She was in her twenties. Attractive with amber hair cut in an old-fashioned bob. The man had dark brown hair and was average height and wiry. The conversation ended, and the couple walked out onto the deck off the side of the office. A gray haze that reminded me of San Diego hung over the morning. Except this one had an icy nip in it.

I entered the cozy office.

"Mr. Cahill." Colleen greeted me with her warm smile. "How's your ankle?"

"Better. Thanks." Moderately at best. "And you can call me Rick."

She looked at the upside-down putter I leaned on.

"I see you've made some accommodations, Rick." She gestured to my "cane."

"Make do when you can."

"Yes, we all must." She opened her hands toward a table lined with baked goods and a coffee maker plus a small rack of coffee and tea pods. "Please help yourself to a sweet start to the day. Everything is from the Bear Claw Bakery."

"I plan to." I stood where I was. "But can I ask you a question first?"

"Of course."

"I got the impression that I was the only guest upstairs." I tried to keep it light. "Did someone else get a room up there after I checked in?"

"As a matter of fact, yes. The young couple out on the deck right now." She nodded outside. Concern in her eyes now. "Did something happen?"

I looked through the glass door at the male half of the couple. I could only see a partial profile and the right back half of his head. He could or could not have been the man in the staircase at two this morning.

"Just a misunderstanding. Someone tried to get into my room last night while I was in it." I smiled like it was no big deal. And now it looked like it wasn't any kind of a deal. "I opened the door and the man said, 'sorry, wrong room.' I wasn't wearing my glasses, so I can't tell you if it was the man out on the deck or not, but it makes sense now that it was."

"Oh. He seems like a very nice young man." A smile. This one more perfunctory. Like I'd just become a potential problem guest. A whiner. "But, I'm so sorry. I hope the situation didn't disturb your sleep."

"Not at all." I couldn't get back to sleep for an hour and a half. "The only reason I asked was because after he realized he had the wrong room, he went downstairs instead of walking to the other room at the end of the hallway."

"Oh, I see." A little warmth returned to her face. "They're staying in the Jordan room, which is across from you on the other side of the building and has a separate staircase."

"Ah, that makes sense." Now I felt like an idiot. "I didn't mean to make a big deal out of it. Thanks for straightening me out."

"Oh, not a worry." She started to walk out from behind the counter. "Have you decided if you're going to be staying with us again tonight?"

"Unfortunately, I don't know yet." I smiled. "My work here is a bit open-ended."

"What is your work here, if you don't mind me asking?" She asked in a friendly way. Not like a sheriff who was about to ask you to leave town.

An opening.

"I've been hired by someone to try to find a family member." I had to be careful. For a lot of reasons. Things had changed with Stone. This had been a discreet investigation from the start. I couldn't put up posters of Angela on telephone poles with my phone number to call, *If you see this woman.* If Stone was telling the truth about Theodore Raskin, I probably wasn't the only one looking for Angela. Sergei Volkov's men and two potentially crooked FBI agents would looking for her to find Raskin or looking for them both. I had to find her first. As quietly as I could. I took out my phone, pulled up the most recent photo I had of Angela, and showed it to Colleen. "Have you seen this woman around town? Or anywhere?"

I was pretty good at reading people, but I'd been wrong enough to get burned. And to get other people burned. But I had a sense about

Colleen. The moment I met her. She had a kind soul and genuinely cared about people. She'd want to do the right thing.

She studied the photo for a good five seconds, then shook her head. "I don't think so. As you know this town is tiny, and my husband and I live right up the hill. We know pretty much everyone here by name. She doesn't look familiar. What's her name?"

Another decision. Each piece of information I gave her, the less discreet my investigation became. That could put Angela in danger. And me, too. But I went with my gut on Colleen Foster. I pulled my private investigator's license out of my pocket and handed it to her.

"I just want to show you that I'm legit." She studied the laminated card then handed it back to me. "This is a delicate investigation. I'd appreciate it if you don't tell anyone else about this. I know you'll tell your husband. That's a given. But, please, no one else. The person I'm looking for could be in danger, and I don't want to draw any attention to her."

Colleen's eyes got big, and she nodded. "Okay. I promise."

"The woman's name is Angela Albright. She's from San Diego and has been missing for about a month." I spoke in a low voice. "Does the name ring any bells?"

"No."

One last bit of information that could endanger Angela and me. I pulled up a photo of Theodore Raskin and showed it to Colleen. "How about this man? Ever seen him?"

She looked at the photo for a few seconds then handed me back the phone. "I've never seen him either. Who is he?"

"He may be a friend of the woman I'm looking for."

"Well, I'll be on the lookout for both of them." Colleen smiled. "And if you text me both photos, I can show them to a few people I know who can keep a secret and find out if they've seen either of them."

"No. I can't do that." I looked her straight in the eye and didn't say anything for a couple seconds. "You have to keep all of this to yourself. I probably told you more than I should have. I'm not the only person looking for Angela. The other people who are don't have good intentions. So, please, forget what I told you."

"Okay." Eyes wide again.

I gimped out to my car, silently cursing myself for giving up too much information. I got back much less than I gave. I didn't know any more than before I told Colleen Foster why I was up in Pine Mountain Club. She hadn't seen either Angela or Raskin up on the mountain. But I'd gotten her involved by telling her things I shouldn't have. Not only had I upped the danger profile for Angela and myself, I might have put Colleen in danger.

Of course, if I'd gotten valuable information from my actions, I might feel differently.

The side of myself that edged up along the line of darkness. The truth no matter what. The side I needed to lock up. For good if I was going to have any chance to make my family whole again.

The side that slipped into the background when I became a father. But it never went away. Like it should have. Fatherhood changes you. But it didn't change me enough. The darkness was still inside me. Could I keep it at bay?

CHAPTER 38

I GOT INTO my car and checked the GPS tracker one more time. The Sentra was still in place at Claire Timmins's house. I drove the two hundred feet to the one gas station and topped off my gas tank.

I got back into my car and was just about to punch the ignition when the name Billy bubbled up into my consciousness again. First it came last night when the poor guy who thought he was unlocking the door to his room was met by a naked man with a .357 Magnum at his side, and now again in my car.

Who was Billy, and why was his name bumping around inside my head? Oddly, I didn't know anyone who went by Billy. If I'd been born twenty years earlier, I'd probably know a bunch of people named Billy. It was quite popular before I was born.

I couldn't think of a single William I knew, so no Billys. Then it hit me.

Alaina McCreery, Angela's neighbor, thought Angela's boyfriend who drove the Maserati, who I confirmed was Theodore Raskin, was named Bobby or Billy. That's what my subconscious was telling me in my sleep. Theodore William Raskin. Billy Raskin.

BR.

The initials on one of the photos in the flyer of the homes Claire Timmins had sold. Could the BR on the photo stand for Billy Raskin?

Had Timmins sold him a home up in the mountains above Pine Mountain Club? Maybe, but how was I going to find out? The address of the house was on the flyer that was in the organizer on her desk in her bedroom. Should I break into her house again? What if I was wrong and I gave myself another opportunity to get arrested? The Kern County sheriff's deputies would have a long way to drive once someone called the police. But it wouldn't matter when they got there if I was identified. They'd put a BOLO out for me, and I could run or possibly do jail time and never put my family back together.

Duh. It wasn't going to be that hard.

I grabbed my phone and googled Claire Timmins, Pine Mountain Club realtor. The information on the flyer was probably on her website. Every realtor I'd ever known, including a woman I'd once been in love with, kept score on their websites. Show potential customers how many homes you've sold and for how much and what you were representing.

I found Timmins's website and scrolled down the first page. Twelve years in the business. Then a tab for home sales. There it was. The information formatted exactly as it had been on her flyer. The home "Sold" in the lower right of the flyer that I remembered having BR inked across it. The memorable home because it was three times as much as any other home listed.

I logged onto PropertyShark and found the home. And the new owner.

Sterlingshire Inc. The same company that owned the house on Cabrillo in La Jolla where the burnt corpse was found.

I didn't believe in coincidences. Even less so when it came to cases I was investigating. And, even if I did, I'd never believe that Sterlingshire Inc. just happened to own a house in La Jolla that crooked FBI agents spent an afternoon in where someone died and also owned one in Pine Mountain Club that might have a connection to Theodore "Billy"

Raskin. The house sold by Claire Timmins, whose car dropped Cassandra Albright at her own car behind La Jolla High School two days ago, and the realtor who wrote the initials BR across the photo of the house after she sold it.

No, these weren't coincidences, but the listed director of Sterlingshire Inc., incorporated in Delaware, America's version of the Cayman Islands, was Keith Johnson. KJ, not BR. But Claire Timmins wrote BR. There had to be a connection.

Everything I'd learned in the last two days in the mountains were guideposts along the trail to Angela Albright. And I had to find her before anyone else did.

I tapped the address into my iPhone map app and connected it to my car's entertainment center, then punched the ignition. Then I called Moira and left a message on her voicemail to call me ASAP.

Apple Car Play connected to my phone and the address came up on the dashboard's navigation screen. The home was about seven miles out of town, and the GPS said it was a twenty-one-minute drive. It looked like the last stretch of the drive climbed up a sharply winding mountain road.

I grabbed a chocolate donut from yesterday's bunch out of the plastic grocery bag and started driving. The texture of the donut had tightened a bit, but it was still tasty. I drove west on Mil Potrero Highway, the ambitiously named two-lane road. A quick check of the GPS tracker on my phone to make sure that I didn't have to make an executive decision if the Sentra was on the move. It wasn't.

I passed by Pineview Court a few minutes later and wondered when Claire Timmins was going to get back into her car and whether she'd be alone.

A couple miles later, I turned left onto Cerro Noroeste Road. The road wound up a pine tree-studded mountain and narrowed as I drove higher and higher. Barely enough room for two cars to pass going in opposite directions. The pine trees grew thicker and closer together as the road climbed steeper. The only semblance of modern civilization, the old asphalt road I traveled upon. My car's entertainment system buzzed an incoming call as the valley below dropped farther and farther away from my car.

"You called?"

The trace of tenderness in Moira's voice from our last conversation gone. Like it had been a mirage or never been there at all. Normal for our relationship. As if every outward show of affection was a sign of weakness. But I never took them that way. Moira was mentally and emotionally the strongest person I knew, even when she showed vulnerability. There was no one I'd rather walk down a dark alley with or have talk to the police on my behalf after I'd straddled the thin blue line.

"Yeah. Found out something interesting. Remember when I told you about finding the damp towel in Claire Timmins's house yesterday?"

"Oh god." Dramatic. "Not sure I want to hear anymore."

But I knew she did. As much as I wanted to tell her.

"I found something else." I told her about the realtor flyer in Claire Timmins's desk and the sold property marked with the initials "BR" and that Angela's neighbor had referred to Raskin as Billy or Bobby.

"Is the wind blowing all the way out there on that limb?" A lilt in her voice. "This is a sad grasp at a rainbow even for you."

"Yeah, you may be right." Hint of the forlorn in my voice to set the hook deeper. "But the new owner listed for the house on 1 Cerro Noroeste Road is Sterlingshire Inc., the same entity that owns the house on Cabrillo Avenue in La Jolla.

"Holy crap!" The response that I'd been hoping for. The one that was worth the wait. "Are you sure?"

"I'm only as sure as PropertyShark is."

"This is pretty spooky, but what if the initials written across the sold homes by this Timmins woman aren't initials for the name of the homeowner? If they were, wouldn't the picture of the Sterlingshire Inc. home have an SI written across it instead of BR? Or even a KJ for Keith Johnson?"

I hadn't thought to check the names of the owners of the other homes that showed as sold on Claire Timmins's flyer because I didn't remember them. Just the initials of the two-million-dollar home that was three times as expensive as any other home on the flyer.

"Shit. I didn't think of Sherlingshire." I told her why I remembered the initials BR. "But you have to admit, this is all too coincidental for there not to be a connection to Raskin. Maybe this Keith Johnson guy is the Delaware face of Sterlingshire and Raskin is the money."

"I guess it's possible."

The road ahead almost U-turned 180 degrees. I slammed on the brakes and laid down rubber to keep from flying off the side of the road and landing at the bottom of the mountain much sooner than I wanted to. I settled my breath and waited for my heart to catch up. No wonder it took twenty minutes to travel seven miles from the Pine Mountain Inn. Every turn was potentially your last. I eased the gas back up to fifteen miles an hour and crept along the twisted spiraling road.

"What was that?" Moira asked.

"Nothing. Just checking my brakes."

"Jesus, Rick. Where are you?"

"On my way to the Sterlingshire Inc. house. Wrong initials or not. I'm about six minutes out."

"Good lord." Deeper than her normal tenor. "What are you going to do when you get there?"

"Probably knock on the door and see who answers. Or if no one does, check the garage for a Maserati."

"BR again. You know this Sterlingshire Inc. may just own a lot of homes in Southern California and have nothing to do with Raskin."

"Yeah. Right." Another tight turn ahead that looked out over the next vista. I braked hard again and saw the first sign of human life I'd seen in ten minutes. A redwood roof and deck of a house slightly below the level of my car. Had to be the Sterlingshire Inc. home. The only house I'd seen since I passed by Pineview Court. Out in the middle of nowhere. A perfect place to hide out if you didn't want to be found.

"Found it."

"Wha…" Her voice sounded blocky and echoey, then the call ended.

I hit a button to call her back. Nothing. Not even a ring tone. I pushed the button anew after every new turn when I had a few feet of straightaway on the road. Nothing. Must have found a dead cell area. Off the grid. A brief repast of no outside world interference that should be savored. Like when I was a kid and time was infinite and I had zero responsibilities. I didn't have much need for a phone back then, but if I did need to use one, it was connected to a wall in the kitchen or on the nightstand next to my parents' bed. Before they started sleeping in separate ones. In separate rooms.

My return call to Moira would have to wait. Besides, I was a couple minutes away from possibly proving my thesis. But, even if I did, and the house around the next few turns *was* Theodore "Billy" Raskin's, it didn't guarantee that Angela Albright would be inside it.

The pine trees closed in on the road as I wound farther up the mountain. I spotted the roof of the house again around another bend. The isolation grew more intense. The road now twisted downhill as I drove closer to where the house must be. Somewhere amongst all the trees. Just twenty minutes from the town of Pine Mountain Club, but I had the sense of being on an endless road to nowhere. A beautiful, pristine nowhere.

But *nowhere* was a destination, and I found it. A clearing, off to the right. Finally, after one more turn of the asphalt road. In fact, the asphalt ended and turned to dirt for about thirty yards until it ran into a long, paved stone driveway that led up to the house I'd seen on Claire Timmins's flyer. And it was more impressive in person. It looked to be built almost entirely from redwood with a grand deck that wrapped around the side of the house to the back. A two-story river rock and redwood façade surrounded a ten-foot-tall, polished redwood front door with three thin, rectangular windows in the upper third. Two large windows bracketed the door. Closed blinds shut off visibility into the house.

The garage had four doors, but I guessed they could park cars two deep behind each door. Was there a Maserati sitting behind one of those doors?

The house was a deal for 2.2 million. In LA, San Francisco, or San Diego, it would be three to four times that much. And a lot easier to find.

I sat in my car and let it idle at the end of the dirt road in front of the driveway. I grabbed my small pop-up opera glasses from the glove compartment and scanned the front of the house. No security cameras visible or a Ring doorbell, which was odd. Even lost out on the edge of a mountain, a home like this needed security. Particularly lost out on the edge of a mountain. If I could find it, so could anyone who really wanted to. Especially with it listed on a realtor's website and flyer. But I guess they'd have to know who the realtor was first.

I used the opera glasses to look inside the house through the three windows in the front door. The windows were so high that I could only see the upper part of the living room, and a huge window in the back wall that had a view of pine trees.

I checked the outside of the house and found what I'd missed on first glance. Security cameras. Hidden up under the eaves on the right corner of the house and the left corner of the garage. The housings of the cameras were painted a cinnamon brown to match the color of the redwood.

Aesthetically pleasing but an odd choice for security cameras. Homeowners generally wanted them to stick out to act as deterrents. Even out here on the nowhere mountain, where it would take a sheriff's deputy at least a half hour to an hour to arrive on the scene, video could still be used after the fact as evidence. Any crook with a break-in under his belt would know that. So, why hide what could be a deterrent?

Whatever the reasoning, if I could see the camera, it could see me. Or at least my shape in my car, which had a license plate in the front. I was probably a solid hundred feet from the house, so it was possible the camera couldn't get a clear picture of my license plate.

But the chances were that I'd already been made by the security cameras. If someone was home watching me from the redwood eye in the sky right then or checked it the next time they were home, they'd soon learn who I was.

So why not cut to the chase. I pulled my car up the luxurious polished paved stone driveway and parked in front of the house. I got out with my putter-cane and hobbled onto the deck, knocked on the front door, and waited. Nothing. I rang the doorbell, which bonged inside. Nothing.

I got on my tiptoes and looked through the bottom of the windows. A grand foyer opened into a large living area. A dark wood staircase wound up to a second level on the right. The back wall was all glass except for a floor-to-ceiling fireplace that matched the stone and redwood façade bordering the front door. Dark wood flooring against off-white walls on the sides of the living area.

Nothing was on the walls, and the only furniture in the room was a sofa facing the fireplace. There was a TV arm mount attached to the fireplace, but no TV. No plants in the house that I could see either.

It looked like someone was living in the house but hadn't moved in their possessions or done any decorating yet. Raskin? Angela? I'd like to get a look upstairs. See what kind of clothes were in the closets. Or if there were any clothes at all in them. Maybe no one was living in the house yet and the sofa was a leftover remnant of the last owner. There were answers upstairs, and I had the lock pick set and an alarm jammer in the secret duffle bag in my trunk. But unlike at Claire Timmins's house, this front door had a hotel-like card reader for entry. No keyhole. A high-tech house up in the mountains on the outskirts of nowhere.

One grunt at a time, I walked around to the garage and peeked in between the door and the jam on all four entrances. I didn't see any slivers of cars. Just polished cement flooring, but nothing else all the way to the back wall, which had some steel shelving but nothing on it.

I'd just turned my innocent stop and knock on the door into casing the house caught on video. And all for naught.

CHAPTER 39

ON MY WAY back to Pine Mountain Club on the winding road down the mountain, I stopped my car around the first turn that had a view of the Sterlingshire Inc. house. Hadn't seen another car since I left town, so I figured I was safe to park in the middle of the road.

I got out of the car, opened my trunk, and grabbed my Nikon binoculars, which were about four times more powerful than my opera glasses. The right side of the house was at least five hundred yards away as the crow flies. I zoomed the binoculars in on the highest capacity but could only see the first ten feet or so into a room off the deck. I couldn't see enough to tell what kind of room it was, but I figured it was a second-story bedroom.

I moved the binos to the left and caught pine trees protecting the house. But something caught my eye before the trees. I slowly moved the binoculars back to the left and stopped. There it was inside the room, a few inches from being blocked by the pine trees. The sole of a shoe lying on its side.

Judging by its size, it was a woman's.

Left behind by the last occupant? Possibly a man with small feet or a child with big ones? A kid leaving a shoe behind in the old home made a lot of sense. Kids left all sorts of things everywhere. Something missed on one last check before the movers came? Maybe. But the shoe was about two feet in from the window. If there were curtains and they were closed, it was unlikely that the shoe could have been behind them.

No, my bet was that there was someone staying in the house. And that someone was a woman. Angela Albright? Possibly. Was she in there right now? Maybe, but from the outside, the house had the feeling of emptiness. Maybe she'd been in a room watching me on her computer via the security cameras. It was just a gut feeling that the house was empty, and my gut had been wrong enough for me to question its pangs.

Besides, how would Angela have gotten there? I was pretty sure she was with Claire Timmins yesterday morning on Timmins's drive to Pine Mountain Club. The damp towel in the bathroom indicated that she'd been at Timmins's house in the morning. Timmins's car had been in her driveway the whole night after I followed her up from La Jolla and didn't move until she drove west to Pine Mountain Club yesterday. Maybe Angela drove her own car and it had been in Timmins's garage that night.

I tried my phone again. Still no service.

I slowly drove down the winding mountain road, even slower than my ascent. I knew I had one more vista point around a curve to get another look at the right side of the Sterlingshire Inc. house. I glanced at my rearview mirror after each turn. Two more hairpin turns and there it was. I stopped my car and got out with the binoculars.

The house was now another five hundred yards away in direct distance, but the angle was more straight on to the right side of the house. I looked through the binos, still on full zoom at the bedroom window, which now looked to be a sliding glass door that led out onto the deck. The shoe was still there. And so was the end of a bed. Looked to be a twin size. And there was something hanging off the end of it.

The pink top of women's pajamas?

I lay down on the road in front of my car to try to get a more level view with the room, but the best I could do was see the top of the end of the bed. Couldn't see deep enough into the room to see anything else.

But I was now convinced that a woman was staying in the house or had been recently. I drove another hundred yards down the mountain, and the entertainment system of my car started telling me I had texts and missed calls. I listened to the texts via my car's mechanized woman's voice. All from Moira. All asking me what had happened and that she couldn't get through on the phone.

I started to tell my car to call her, but I slowed way down and checked the GPS tracker on my phone first. Working. And the Nissan Sentra was still parked in Claire Timmins's driveway. More office work, or was she just a homebody?

Next, I called Moira.

"Where the hell have you been?" The greeting I expected.

"I hit a patch without cell service."

"Whatever." Dismissive like it was my fault. "While you were off the grid and pretending that it was 1980, I learned some interesting information."

She wanted me to ask what it was. Of course, I bit. "What?"

"The reason the dead man in the Cabrillo Avenue home hasn't been identified yet is because he can't be identified."

"What the hell is that supposed to mean?" Although disturbing images started filtering through my brain.

"The body was burned to a crisp. And before that, just to make sure, someone removed the fingertips and most of the teeth, like they had taken a hammer and chisel to his mouth." Moira listed them off like reading a recipe for lasagna. She had a lot of levels. And sublevels.

The images in my head had been depressingly on the nose. If the body had had one.

"Anything left of the body for DNA?"

"My guy at La Jolla PD said they found a small amount and ran it through CODIS, and there were no matches."

The Combined DNA Index System is a DNA database run by the FBI. All DNA that police agencies collect from convicted felons or, in most states, upon the time of the suspect's felony arrest, are fed into CODIS.

"So whoever he is . . . or was, he didn't have a record. And removal of the fingertips and teeth indicated a mob hit. That would seem to rule out Sorensen and Bowden." I had to force myself to slow down and pay attention to the sliver of a road, but thoughts of Peter Stone and Sergei Volkov meshed with mob hits and pressed hard on my mind.

"Unless they or someone else wanted it to look like a mob hit," Moira said.

"Possibly, but grim business for the uninitiated. Did you learn anything else about the body?"

"They think the victim was between thirty and forty-five. Took care of himself. No clothes or personals left behind. Found him in the bathtub."

Between thirty and forty-five. That fit an almost unlimited number of men. But it also fit one single man. Theodore Raskin.

But Raskin had worked for Stone and Volkov for years. He probably would have crossed the line at least once and had his DNA on file. Then again, maybe not. Stone called him a computer whiz kid. Those types of assets are valuable, behind the scenes and protected. The crimes they usually commit are organizational, and they know how to not leave evidence behind.

"Hello?" Moira.

"What?"

"You were radio silent for thirty seconds. What's going on in that warped head of yours?"

"Was trying to figure out who the man without the teeth might be."

"And?" Big sister impatience.

"Was thinking it could be Raskin. The man everyone is looking for."

"That seems possible."

"Who's working the case for LJPD?" I asked.

"Detective Sheets is lead."

La Jolla PD Homicide Detective Jim Sheets and I went back a ways. It wasn't the worst relationship I had with a cop. In fact, it was better than most. He was an honest cop who always tried to do the right thing.

"He's a good cop."

"Agreed, but telling him the truth could be problematic and dangerous. Especially for you," Moira said.

Peter Stone and Sergei Volkov.

"You have to do what you think is right."

"Right for who?"

"For you. For justice, I guess."

"Don't get self-righteous, for God's sake. Let's be smart." A tinge of humor in her voice. "I'm just going to tell them that I followed the two in the Chevy Tahoe because my client asked me to after he discovered they were following him. Theoretically, you are my client because you're the one giving me money to investigate."

"They'll ask who you're working for, of course."

"Well, they'll have to beat it out of me." She sounded serious. "Anyway, I'm sitting on the two Feds right now. They went out for breakfast at the Broken Yoke in Pacific Beach, then headed back up to FBI Headquarters in Sorrento Valley."

"The more time Sorensen and Bowden spend at FBI headquarters, the less likely it is that they're running some rogue operation or are cold-blooded murderers. They might be corrupt with abuse of power like some of the leadership of the agency, but I now don't think they're killing people in the pursuit of robbing some crooked cryptocurrency mastermind. I think your time could be better spent watching Cassandra Albright. It's possible Angela isn't up here, but down in La Jolla."

"Best-use-of-time suggestions from the man chasing ghosts up in Pine Mountain Kitty Club on a mountain nobody's ever heard of."

"There might be some big cats up in the Kitty Club."

"What's that supposed to mean?"

I was going to keep the Shadow Man to myself because I wasn't really sure what his attempt to get into my room meant, and I didn't want to needlessly worry Moira. But I also wanted her opinion on it.

"Someone tried to get into my room around two this morning." I gave her the specifics all the way down to not wearing my glasses, holding the Ruger against my leg, and the slightly foreign whisper.

"Do you think he saw the Ruger?"

"I don't know. It was dark except for the lighting behind him in the stairwell. There was probably enough light to see it against my leg."

"Yes. Your very white leg." She snickered. My Irish fair skin was a constant source of amusement to someone who turned the color of a walnut in the summer. Or spring. "What did he say again?"

"'Wrong room. Sorry.'"

"Did he sound nervous or upset? Scared?"

"He whispered three words to me. Hard to get his disposition from three whispered words. Why?"

"Maybe not. Maybe the fact that he whispered tells us everything we need to know." A trace of worry in her voice.

"What do you mean?"

"Say you're a slightly drunk civilian trying to get into what you think is your room at a hotel and some guy whips open the door, showing a gun. Do you think you'd calmly whisper an apology or say something like, 'Whoa! Sorry. I got the wrong room. My fault! Sorry!' in a full voice?"

"I see your point." A little ping along my spine. "But it's possible that he didn't see the Ruger."

"Yes, it is and that's probably what happened." She tried to sound like she believed her words. "Nonetheless, be careful, Rick. In the meantime, I'm going to stay on Agents Sorensen and Bowden up here in Sorrento Valley. Don't answer your door naked without your glasses on anymore. Especially holding your gun. You may confuse visitors."

"Right. I'll check in later." My ankle hurt. My tolerance for sarcasm was low today.

"Don't get testy. I'll swing by the high school by 11:30 a.m. and let you know if Angela shows up or something exciting happens."

"Roger." I hung up and immediately called Special Agent John Mallon to find out if he'd seen Sorensen and Bowden at FBI Headquarters. No answer.

CHAPTER 40

I MADE IT back to the Pine Mountain Inn by 10:17 a.m. Time to recoup and plan the rest of the day. I lugged my bag of donuts and water up the stairs because I wasn't sure when my next stakeout would be, and I was hungry. And the donuts weren't getting any fresher sitting in the car.

My hands were full, and I had to get my room key out of my pocket. I shifted the putter over to my left hand but didn't get a good grip and dropped it. It clattered onto the wooden walkway and ended up on the welcome mat in front of the door.

Shit. Having to bend over on the sprained ankle was the rim shot to an already clanky day.

I roughed the key into the lock and opened the door, set down the bag just inside the room, then bent over to pick up the cane. I had to lift my left leg behind me to take the weight off my ankle and bend down on my right leg like a crane wading in a shallow pond.

That's when I saw it. A small, thin strip of black metal lying on the black doormat. It was about three inches long and had a ninety-degree bend and wavy twists on the end. I wouldn't have seen it if I didn't have to get so close to the ground to grab my cane.

I picked up the metal strip first. I didn't have to examine it closely to know what it was. Or examine it at all. I'd used something similar in the dark enough times to know what it was just by feel. And had used it during the daylight hours yesterday afternoon.

The strip of metal was a tool. A rake from a lock pick set.

I shoved it in my jeans pocket, picked up my cane, then looked around the second floor and stairwell to make sure no one was watching. Clear. I wobbled into my room and shut the door behind me.

Then locked it.

CHAPTER 41

My EARLY MORNING "Wrong room. Sorry," Shadow Man hadn't had the wrong room. He'd had the right one. He just didn't have a key to it, but he didn't need one. Just like me.

He must have dropped the rake when I whipped open the door at 2:00 a.m. this morning. Or, less probable, he left it there today when he knew I was gone and came back up to finish the job. I limped around the room sniffing the air for male scent. Cologne. Musk. Sweat. Nothing. I checked the doors of the dresser and the desk. There wasn't anything that looked searched through because I didn't leave anything in the room to be searched. Everything I had I was wearing or carrying.

Who was the Shadow Man, and what was his end game? Some random burglar in a tiny mountain town who didn't have to worry if the room he broke into was occupied because if the occupant called the police, he knew he'd have at least a half hour to flee before a sheriff's deputy arrived?

But was the potential bounty worth the possible consequences? A woodsy hotel in a tiny mountain unincorporated parcel of land that couldn't even be called a town, much less a resort area. Beautiful, but bare bones when it came to a small pool of victims. Was he hoping to find a couple hundred dollars in my wallet on the nightstand?

And with a lock pick set? The tool of a pro searching for bigger bounties or expensive secrets. Or, in my case, the truth.

The pick set said purpose, premeditation, not random opportunity. My room had been chosen. Either because I left something valuable in it for the Shadow Man—or I was the thing of value.

A shudder ran through my body that had nothing to do with the pain in my ankle. Someone had tried to get into my room while I slept last night. Did he know I was in there? If he did, he was coming to do me harm.

I'd fought for my life before. Many times.

The fear I felt was never in the moment. Fear was for the anticipation and the aftermath. Violence was my reflex. Always cocked and ready to fire back at a whiplash stimulus. The shaking hands and revving heart were after the fray. The attacks on my life had usually come violently and quickly out of the dark. No chance for the shake of anticipation. But now I had both. The before and the after. And I had time to think, not the instinct to react.

I had a responsibility to warn Angela Albright about what might be coming for her.

But first, I had to learn who the Shadow Man was and what he wanted. Did he want to find out if I knew where Angela Albright was? Was he connected with FBI Special Agents Sorensen and Bowden? Had they figured out the connection between Angela and Theodore Raskin?

Or maybe the Shadow Man was working for someone else. Someone more dangerous. Sergei Volkov. Had he come to the same conclusion as Peter Stone, that I had something to do with the death of his daughter? Was the Shadow Man an assassin? If so, why not try to kill me last night? Because I got the jump on him when I whipped open my door and he saw the gun I held to my side? He wouldn't know that I was legally blind without my glasses.

But if the Shadow Man was working for Sergei Volkov, how did he find me in the tiny town of Pine Mountain Club? Moira was supposed to be the only person who knew I was up here.

The only other people who knew I was in Pine Mountain Club were the few people I'd met there. None would have a reason to want to hurt me. Although Claire Timmins did seem to have a connection to Theodore Raskin. Did she tell him about me? Did he want me dead, or roughed up, or my room tossed to see if I was after him? Claire Timmins and Angela were connected. Either Angela or Timmins had met with Cassie Albright two days ago. That was a fact. The only thing in this case that I was certain of. Was Timmins behind the Shadow Man?

Without Timmins, no one who wanted to hurt me or find out what I knew could know I was in Pine Mountain Club. Or could they? Last night someone tried to break into my room using a lock pick set very much like my own. Maybe that wasn't the only similarity I was up against.

A GPS tracker.

CHAPTER 42

I GRABBED MY cane, unlocked the door, and hobbled downstairs to my car. Even though I doubted someone had gotten inside my trunk, I popped the hood to search it first. I once made the mistake of not looking for a second GPS tracker hidden on my car after I found the first one. Almost got me killed. I searched the trunk, pulled up the carpeting and checked underneath, even the spare tire well where I kept my black bag. Clean.

Next, I bent down using the side of the car to stabilize myself and slid my hands under the bumper. My ankle throbbed with the awkward angle, but I managed to check both bumpers and all four wheel wells. Clean. But I wasn't done.

I returned to the back of the car, took out my phone, opened the flashlight app, and eased my way down onto my back then slid under the car. I checked the muffler, edged forward on my back with tiny pushes from the heel of my one good foot and pushing off the ground with the palms of my hands, while the phone rested on my chest. Next were the rear axel, gas tank, undercarriage, front axel.

No GPS tracker. My car was clean. No one in San Diego could have tracked me up to Pine Mountain Club. But someone with ill intentions knew I was here.

I wiggled halfway out from under my car when I heard a woman's voice.

"Is everything okay with your car, Mr. Cahill?" I finished my exit lying on my back and saw Colleen Foster, holding a couple canvas grocery bags. "Our gas station is right around the corner and has an excellent mechanic. Danny."

I hoisted myself off the ground with the help of my cane and the back of my car.

"Everything is fine." I wiped loose dirt from the asphalt parking lot that had collected on the back of my pants and bomber jacket. Thankfully both pieces of clothing were dark and hearty. I was glad I never bought into wearing white jeans. Ever. "Was just checking something. All okay. Thanks."

"Oh good." The smile.

Colleen was always on the spot. A good hostess, who might be able to help me with learning the identity of the Shadow Man.

"Hey, I feel kind of badly about how things went down with the poor guy who mistakenly tried to get into my room last night. I bordered on being belligerent. Your inn has such a friendly vibe, and I want to positively contribute to it. I'd like to apologize to the gentleman if I get the chance. What's his name?"

"Oh, I'm sure he's fine." She twitched her shoulders. "No one likes to be awakened in the middle of the night thinking someone is breaking into their room."

"It's okay if you'd rather I didn't. I just want to let him know there's no harm done."

"That's very nice of you." She pursed her lips and her eyes looked upward to the left like she was thinking. Finally, "His name is Adam Samuels. He and his wife, Shelly, are from Glendale."

"LA or Arizona?"

"LA."

Glendale is a slightly upper income city in Los Angeles County south of Burbank. The type of place a couple would live who took a quick vacation an hour and a half away in Pine Mountain Club. It made perfect sense. Or was the perfect cover. I planned to have a little chat with Adam Samuels to find out which fit him.

"Thanks." We both started for the inn. "I may not be at 100 percent, but I could at least carry one of your bags for you."

"Oh, I'm fine. Thanks. Just take care of that ankle." She pushed ahead of me.

I plopped down onto the bed back in my room to take weight off my ankle and pulled out my phone. I googled "Adam Samuels, Glendale." I got an immediate hit. General manager of a sporting goods chain. In Glendale, Arizona. Oops. I narrowed the search to California and found a match. Adam Franklin Samuels. A twenty-nine-year-old software engineer. Married to Shelly Mundee, twenty-six. No photos.

I went onto Facebook and found Shelly Mundee quickly. She looked like the woman with the man who Colleen had talked to in the office at breakfast this morning. In fact, her most recent post was of her and Adam Samuels sitting on the deck off the Pine Mountain Inn office this morning.

I got onto a pay people search engine and found Samuels's address in Glendale, then onto PropertyShark and saw that he and Shelly Mundee owned the house. Bought it a year ago.

That seemed to clear everything up, but so did the one GPS tracker I found on my car a few years back without looking for a second. I didn't take anything for granted. Not anymore.

I checked my watch. 11:37 a.m. The weight off my ankle felt good, and I could have passed out on the bed for a couple hours to make up for the sleep the Shadow Man, possibly Adam Samuels, stole from me last night. But not when an unanswered question still hung in the air.

I got off the bed, grabbed my cane, and headed back downstairs. I went by the ice machine and took a left around the back of the inn and found the staircase Colleen Foster told me led up to the room opposite mine. I could see how someone could get confused late at night and go up the wrong staircase, especially if they'd had a couple drinks and never been to the inn before.

But if that was the case, and Adam Samuels was the Shadow Man, why was there a lock pick rake lying on my doormat this morning? Samuels was with his partner this morning. It would make sense that they came back to the inn together after being out on the town. Such as it was. I thought I'd heard more than one set of footsteps on the walkway this morning but couldn't be sure. Shelly Mundee? Possibly, but she was a petite woman. The set of footsteps I heard, the others I thought I heard, were heavy. They might have all been from one person, but the person definitely was someone who weighed at least a hundred and seventy pounds.

I managed my way up the stairs to the room on the opposite end of the inn, but across from mine. Noon on a vacation day, I doubted that Samuels or his partner would be in their room, but it was worth a try. I knocked on the door. Footsteps five seconds later, then the door opened.

Adam Samuels, the man I'd seen in the Pine Mountain Inn office this morning. Six feet, wiry. Short curly black hair. A hundred and seventy pounds would be his max. Could he have been the Shadow Man I saw this morning standing down a stair step across from my room? Possibly. I had a sense that the Shadow Man had more muscle than Samuels, but I saw him without my glasses. Everything mushes out. Blurs, shadows.

He gave me a smile on top of a confused look. No one staying in a hotel expects some rando leaning on an upside-down putter to knock on their door.

"Can I help you?" The smile stayed confused.

His voice was Southern California accent-less. No beachy stretched vowels or Valley Girl fry. I'd put it at a low tenor. The Shadow Man had spoken in a husky whisper. Hard to make a comparison between the two, but I remembered the feeling that Shadow Man wasn't a native speaker. None of that with Samuels.

Still, not conclusive.

"Yeah." I smiled with my mouth but studied Samuels with flat eyes. "Sorry to bother you, but I wanted to apologize for being a bit gruff last night."

"I'm sorry." His brow pinched down. "I don't understand."

"When you mistakenly tried to get into my room last night. I was a little gruff. It's a common mistake. I should have been more understanding."

He shook his head and looked truly baffled. "I don't . . . I didn't try to get into your room last night. We've been in this room since yesterday and didn't try to get into any other room last night."

"What's going on, honey?" Concerned voice, then Shelly Mundee's head popped up behind Samuels's shoulder.

"This guy thinks I tried to get into his room last night." Irritation now in his voice.

"What?" Mundee adopted his attitude.

I slipped my hand into my pocket and pulled out the lock pick rake. "So, this isn't yours?"

Trying to get a reaction to the rake was my equivalent to looking for the second GPS tracker. I was 99 percent certain that Samuels wasn't the Shadow Man, but I wanted that last one percent. No matter the social faux pas.

"No." Befuddlement creeping toward anger. "I don't even know what that is. Now, I've told you I didn't go to your room last night, so, please, leave us alone."

"Sorry for the misunderstanding." I smiled like it was all a mistake, which it was, and put the rake back into my pocket.

"Yeah. Sure." Adam Samuels closed the door.

I limped back down the stairs, then up the other stairs and into my room and sat on the edge of the bed.

Adam Samuels was innocent, and now he had a vacation adventure story to tell his family and friends about the weird guy who accused him of trying to break into his room. Not a complete bust for either of us.

But I still had an unanswered question that grew more ominous by the moment. Someone was out there, in the mountain shadows, waiting to do me harm. Who and why? And how the hell had he found me?

CHAPTER 43

I WAS TIRED and a little dusty after the search under my car. A long, hot shower suddenly seemed like a good idea. A much-needed restart to the day. I stood up from the bed, took off my jacket, and tossed it on the loveseat at the end of the bed, then my gun and shoulder holster, then my shirt. Someone knocked on the door before I could unbuckle the belt to my pants.

I limped three steps to the door without my cane. I didn't worry about grabbing the Ruger this time. I was pretty sure I knew who was on the other side.

I opened the door and saw Colleen Foster looking at me. No smile. Bingo.

She looked at my naked torso and her eyes went wide. Not because I wasn't wearing a shirt, but because she could see what my clothes always hid.

My scars. The jagged slash on my lower neck, the pink-red circular disruptions in my left shoulder and chest, the mash-stitched jigsaw on my left upper bicep. And finally, the ugly right-angle rip below my belly button. That's not counting the missing tip of my right middle finger.

The violent map of my life. The other scars from my journey of violence, my trail chasing evil, as I saw it, were etched along my psyche. And my soul.

I thought about limping over to the love seat and putting my shirt back on. For Colleen's benefit. But I figured our conversation wouldn't take very long. And, what she'd seen couldn't be unseen now.

She blinked and stopped staring. Then the reason she knocked.

"I just got a call from Ms. Mundee." No preamble. None needed. "And she's very upset. She said you accused Mr. Samuels of trying to break into your room. That's not the way you presented the situation to me. You can't go around disturbing other guests."

"That's not exactly what I said to Samuels, but I can understand the misinterpretation."

"The Pine Mountain Inn is a place of relaxation and neighborliness." She put her hands on her hips. "You misled me about why you wanted to talk to Mr. Samuels. I think it would be best if you end your stay here today. I can't have other guests harassed. I only charged you for two nights. You can take your time to get all your things together, but please leave by three this afternoon. I'm sorry about this, but it's our policy."

She took her right hand off her waist and handed me a curled paper receipt, then dropped both hands to her sides. Colleen Foster didn't look happy. She may not have ever had to throw a guest out before. A first for both of us.

I took the receipt.

She had every right to boot me. I'd disturbed another guest. Pushed a bit. But I liked Colleen, and with my new life just around the corner, it started to matter to me what people I liked thought of me. That bridges were best left unsinged. I transferred the receipt into my left hand and put my right in my jeans pocket and pulled out the rake.

"Have you ever seen one of these before?" I held the rake out for her to see. To take out of my hand if she wanted to.

Colleen let go a long exhale and looked at the rake in my hand. She seemed to be debating whether to engage me. Finally, "No. What is it?"

"It's called a rake. It's a tool used to pick locks. I found it on my doormat this morning when I came back to my room."

She looked at me, then back down at my hand, and picked up the
rake. She felt the wavy end between her fingers. "So, you think Mr.
Samuels tried to use this to break into your room last night?"

"No. I think someone else did. I just had to eliminate Samuels as a
suspect. I'm sorry it went sideways, but I had to make sure it wasn't him
before I could go forward. I can be out of here in a half hour. You still
might see me around town, though. My work's not done yet."

She looked down the walkway and the staircase, then back at me, my
exposed scars. "Do you mind if I come in?"

I glanced over at the loveseat. The compartments of the shoulder
holster that held the two speed loaders were exposed underneath the
Pine Mountain Club shirt.

"Sure, but give me a quick sec." I edged along the bed with my hand
to steady myself and shoved the shoulder holster under my bomber
jacket, put my shirt back on, then wobbled back to open the door wide
for Colleen to pass through. "Come on in."

Colleen stepped inside, and I closed the door behind her. She folded
her arms in front of her like she wasn't quite sure what to say. I waited.

"Do you think this person who tried to break into your room is
staying here at the inn?" A worried quiver in her voice.

"I don't know, but I doubt it. All the other guests were already here
when I arrived, right?" If someone tracked me from San Diego, they
couldn't have gotten a room at the inn before I did.

"Yes." Her lips pinched together. "Did you call the police about the
attempted break-in?"

"No. I doubt the Kern County sheriff would even send out a squad
car to investigate. No break-in. Some unknown person, unidentifiable
by me, claimed to accidentally try to open the wrong hotel room,
perhaps after a late night in a bar. The fact that I found a lock pick

rake on the doormat probably wouldn't carry much weight either. It could have been there for days, and the police might not even recognize it for what it is. Law enforcement agencies don't have the resources to investigate minor property crimes anymore. Much less, possible attempted ones. These are different times than when you and I grew up."

"Then what should we do?" Her eyebrows rose up. "Do you think whoever it was will come back?"

"Probably not. Especially if I'm not here."

"You don't have to leave today, Rick." Her voice softened as she looked at my shirt now covering the scars she'd seen. "You're welcome here at the Pine Mountain Inn. I can understand you needed to be careful and make sure Mr. Samuels wasn't the man who tried to get into your room. And you probably scared away whoever tried to get in here for good. This town, as idyllic as it is, isn't without crime. We have occasional shoplifting at the general store, and last summer some homes were burglarized. There's drugs, just like everywhere else. But I'm sorry someone tried to break in while you were here."

"Thanks, but don't worry about it." I was already worried enough for both of us.

Colleen Foster smiled a frown and left the room.

I was about to take a shower when I realized I still had the room receipt in my hand.

My credit card. That must have been it.

Colleen just ran my card, but I'd used it a few times since I'd been up on the mountain. Twice yesterday to get food and gas in town and twice the night I arrived over in Frazier Park. Someone must have tracked the transactions on my card and followed after me up the mountain. If they knew my car, they could have easily found it parked in front of the inn.

Who could get access to my records? Law enforcement. The FBI.

Sorensen and Bowden. They could get access to bank credit card accounts. They were the FBI. They had access to everything. And they had the legal means to get whatever they wanted. Or any means they needed. Either that or they pinged my phone off cell towers. Both would necessitate a warrant. But not from some FISA judge handing out warrants like your neighbor tossing candy into kids' bags on Halloween. They'd have to have a legit reason.

Unless . . . shit.

I called my next-door neighbor whose daughter sometimes watched Midnight when I was away on a case.

"Hi, Rick." Her usual friendly voice. She was a better neighbor than I deserved, considering she'd seen police cars and the coroner's van parked in front of my house more than once. And once was enough to give you a bad reputation in any neighborhood.

"Hi, Carol." I gave her my max friendliness. "I'm out of town. Did you happen to notice any black SUVs parked in front of my house yesterday or the night before?"

"No, but there was one parked across the street from the McCalls' the night before last, I think."

The McCalls lived two houses down from me. Our street was one of a few that stair-stepped down a hill and only had houses on one side of the street.

"Was it a Hummer or Chevy Tahoe?"

"Oh, I don't know the difference, but it was big and black." A quick breath. "Is this for a case?"

She thought being a private investigator was more exciting than it really was. Hours and hours of boredom interspersed with a few brief intervals of excitement. And occasional frightening moments of violence.

"It's minor thing. Thanks." I hung up knowing it wasn't minor at all.

CHAPTER 44

A BIG AND black SUV. No one on my street owned one, but there must be thousands of them in San Diego. And a couple among those thousands were occupied by FBI Special Agents Sorensen and Bowden, and Sergei Volkov and his men.

Either the Feds or Sergei's men could have broken into my house, gotten past the home security like I did at Claire Timmins's and accessed my computer. It was password protected, but there were ways a hacker could get into a locked computer without a password. No doubt Sergei had at least one hacker in his crew and the Feds would have access to computer security specialists. Once the hacker or specialist got in, he could find credit card statements on my email and look at my accounts. For convenience, I set my passwords to default on my computer when opening the accounts. I wished I'd made my life a little more inconvenient.

I skipped the shower and got fully dressed again. Deciphering how I'd been tracked to Pine Mountain Club revitalized me more than hot or cold water could. Now I had to figure out who tracked me. The Shadow Man was a blur last night. Sorensen's general physique could have fit him, and he could have altered his voice with the whisper. But he couldn't have known I was basically blind without my glasses and couldn't make out his face. He would have panicked and ran or come up with a story about why he was there.

One of Sergei's men? But the ones who'd spoken in my house all had Russian accents. I wasn't an expert on accents, but I was pretty good at them after spending years in the restaurant business and talking to people from all the over the world. The Shadow Man had sounded more Israeli than Russian.

Who was he, and who was he connected to? Whoever he was, he was still out there.

Tonight, I'd sleep on the loveseat pull-out bed. Angled at the door, wearing my glasses, with my gun at arm's reach.

*   *   *

The burner phone rang right as I was about to leave my room. Shit.

I answered.

"I'm beginning to think you don't like me, Rick." The usual undercurrent of rough nudging replaced with aggression in Stone's voice. Not a welcome change. "And I'm past beginning to think I've wasted my money."

"I'll give you back your money, Stone, and we can call it even." I took a beat, but not a long enough one to hold my tongue. "Even though I've been working your case twenty-four seven for four days. Having to try to figure out which side of your half-truths are true so I know what path to take."

I kept the attempted breach of my room to myself. And where I was staying, of course. My mission had changed since Stone hired me. I'd still find Angela and I'd tell her Stone's story about his supposed kidney need, but I'd warn her, too. Tell her that I thought Stone was probably lying or had an ulterior motive. She could make the decision how she wanted to go forward. But first, she had to know the truth. As I saw it.

"Your job is to find Angela with whatever information I give you and you've failed."

"Who's the dead charcoal skeleton on Cabrillo Avenue in La Jolla where your two FBI friends spent an afternoon a couple days ago? Why are you really looking for Angela? What does she have beyond a kidney that you really want? Theodore Raskin's whereabouts?"

"You're asking a lot of questions, Rick, but you've given me no new information. Where's my daily update?"

"I gave you your update. I'm withdrawing from the case." Even as I quit, I couldn't say the word out loud. Quitting was betrayal. To my client. And to myself. "Where do you want me to send your money?"

"1143 Portsuello Avenue, Santa Barbara, California."

My in-laws' house. Where Leah and Krista lived.

Nerve synapses crackled throughout my body. Heat flashed across my skin. Breath shotgunned out of my mouth. The room tinged pink. The beginnings of a red rage. The outward embodiment of my CTE.

"Is that a threat?" My voice a bestial growl. Saliva gathered in my mouth. I fought to rein in the building combustion surging in my body.

Peter Stone was a dangerous man. His wealth, his power, the darkness inside him deserved wary respect.

But I was dangerous, too. And like Stone, my clock was ticking faster than most. I had a lot left to live for, but a short time to do it. And the lives that went on after mine were more important than my own.

"Isn't that where you are now?" Scaled-down venom. He must have heard something in my voice he'd never heard before. So had I. "Spending my money on a road trip while you visit your family?"

"No, and I didn't visit my family while I was there." A truth inside a lie. The room stayed pink.

"Well, if you're not in Santa Barbara, where are you? What is my money buying? Perhaps a little miss on the side? Is that why the marriage went sour?"

"I've been trying to find Angela for you, but I just resigned." I tried to level my breathing and think rather than react. "I still don't know why you hired me. If you know where my family lives, you have access to information or people who know how to get it. I told you up front, there are plenty of private investigators in San Diego who are better at finding missing persons than I am. So, again, why me?"

"Because you care." A chuckle. "It's always been your biggest strength and your biggest weakness. But I'm learning it can't overcome your obtuseness and lack of elite intelligence. You're a blue-collar everyman with a chip on his shoulder."

Stone finally said something I couldn't, and didn't want to, argue with.

"You're right, I do care. I care about the truth, and you've either been holding it back from me or lying." I just threw away $50,000. I might as well get my lost money's worth. "Your rogue Feds, Sorensen and Bowden, are now reporting daily to headquarters in Sorrento Valley. Yet, it's kind of interesting that Sergei Volkov got out of prison the same time they started looking for Theodore Raskin."

"Sergei is not your concern."

"The hell he isn't." A gust of wind over the embers of rage inside me and my mouth tasted of blood. "He threatened my family. Like you just did."

"Settle down, Rick." A dismissive exhale. "I didn't threaten your family."

"Close enough." I tapped the burner phone to off and threw it down onto the hardwood floor with all I had. It smashed and tumbled along the floor, pieces of it turning into flying shrapnel, until it came to a stop against the wall, its innards hanging out.

I didn't have to worry about calls from Peter Stone anymore.

CHAPTER 45

I GRABBED MY personal phone out of my pocket and checked to see if the Nissan Sentra was still parked in front of Claire Timmins's house. It was. The best I could tell, Claire Timmins hadn't driven her car or left her home since she almost surprised me when I was inside her house yesterday. Every time I checked the GPS tracker, the red light blinked in place in Timmins's driveway.

Every time I checked.

But what about the times I didn't check? Data history. I hadn't used a GPS tracker in years and had forgotten that the trackers keep a history of all their movements.

The unrelenting surge of my CTE and the beginning of dementia, or just the normal memory loss that comes with human aging? I didn't know. In a way, I hoped I never would.

I opened the tracker app history and went backwards from present time. Sure enough, I'd been right about the Sentra for the last twenty-four-plus hours. It hadn't moved from Timmins's driveway.

But maybe Timmins had left her house. Maybe she had another car parked in her garage that she used for her realtor work? Or loaned to someone else. Like Angela.

I logged onto the same auto insurance company website I'd used to find out what cars Steven Albright owned and started the insurance quote process for a new car. I typed in Claire Timmins's address and the website asked if I wanted to start coverage on the one existing car or on a new one. The existing car was the 2020 Nissan Sentra.

Timmins didn't have another car. The parked Sentra was it. She hadn't driven her own car to go anywhere in twenty-four hours. What about before that?

I went back in GPS tracking history to the night I'd put the device on Timmins's car. Just to be thorough. I'd checked the app a couple times that night and early in the morning. The car hadn't moved.

Except it did. According to the GPS history.

The first morning at 6:03 a.m. while I was catching up on the sleep I'd lost, the Nissan Sentra took an early trip. South along Cerro Noroeste Road. The same direction I went when I found the Sterlingshire Inc. house on the end of the dirt road. There was nothing else on the road, except incredible views. I doubted Timmins was out sightseeing at the crack of dawn after spending the last month hiding from the world.

But according to the tracker, the Sentra never made it to the house. It looked like it turned around before it got there. My estimation was that it turned around about a mile away from the house.

Why? And finding a place to turn around on the narrow road before getting to the house would have been almost impossible. Maybe it didn't turn around.

Maybe it went all the way to the Sterlingshire house, and the GPS didn't pick it up because of the dead cell area. The tracking history stopped and started up again twenty minutes late right where I lost phone connection with Moira this morning. That short window of no connectivity.

The Sentra went to the two-million-dollar house that Claire Timmins recently sold. The one, according to the notes on the real estate flyer on her desk, she sold to BR.

Claire Timmins dropped off Angela Albright at Theodore Raskin's mountain hideaway the morning after I arrived in Pine Mountain Club. Or she drove there herself then quickly went back home.

Why? The first option made the most sense. She'd dropped Angela at the Sterlingshire house. I'd knocked on Timmins's door looking for Angela the night before, so the two of them must have decided Angela needed a new hiding place. And they had one. BR's brand-new house.

Was she still there? Had she spied on me from a second-story window when I knocked on the front door and peeked into the garage? Or had there been a car there waiting for her when Timmins dropped her off that first morning? If so, she could be back in San Diego by now.

Or she might still be up on the mountain. I knew one person who could tell me which. And she hadn't left her house in twenty-four hours.

I strapped on my shoulder holster and my bomber jacket and grabbed my putter, the newest addition to my uniform. Now almost as vital as my Ruger .357. I gimped downstairs to my car and drove west along Mil Potrereo Highway out of town toward Pineview Court and Claire Timmins's home.

My phone rang five minutes into the drive. FBI Special Agent John Mallon.

"Returning your call." Irritation in his voice. "What is it now?"

"I know Special Agents Sorensen and Bowden have been in your building a few times. What are they working on? Are they there on official business?"

"You know I can't answer a question like that." Irritation up a notch to anger. "You ask too much. I can't keep doing this."

"Don't you want to know if fellow agents are dirty, John?"

"They're not dirty!"

"So they're in San Diego on official business, investigating Theodore Raskin and BitChange?"

"They're in San Diego on official business. Don't call me again." Special Agent John Mallon, my only connection in law enforcement who sometimes helped me, hung up. Maybe for the last time.

But he gave me an important piece of information before he did. Sorensen and Bowden were clean. That meant the Shadow Man had been sent by Sergei Volkov.

Or Peter Stone.

A couple minutes later, I parked in front of Claire Timmins's house and got out of my car. No reason to hide today. The Nissan Sentra still sat in the driveway. I caned up to the door and knocked. Nothing. I double rang the Ring doorbell and noticed that the wispy linen sash in the door's window was torn at the top left corner. I angled my head to get a clearer look through the window.

And saw small, dotted stains on the carpet near the staircase. Reddish-brown. Shit.

I strained my head to the left, trying to see more, but I couldn't. The sash was in the way.

With no movement from Timmins in the last twenty-four hours and Peter Stone and Sergei Volkov in my orbit, reddish-brown stains on her carpet meant only one thing. Blood.

I prayed I was wrong.

Up in the mountains, at least twenty miles from the nearest sheriff station, I couldn't wait a half hour for a cruiser to arrive if Claire Timmins was inside bleeding out. I twisted the doorknob, careful to use just my fingertips on the rounded bulge so I wouldn't smudge any prints left behind by the person who caused the bloodstains on the carpet.

Locked.

I hustle-limped on my putter-cane to the trunk of my car. The lock pick set was still in my black bag in the spare tire well. A tool to use for meeting my ends. Always justified. Today I'd use it to try to save someone instead of rifling through her possessions. I put on a pair of nitrile gloves, grabbed the lock pick set, and went back to the house as fast as I could on three legs. Again, I was careful to touch the doorknob as little as possible. I went to work and got the door unlocked in about a minute.

I took a deep breath and stepped back when I felt the last pin drop into place. What would I find inside? Ebbing life or violent death? Were there killers inside?

I pulled my Ruger from its holster and used my fingertips to turn the knob and opened the door. I edged inside. One hand on my cane, the other holding the gun straight out in front of me. I stopped and listened. Silent as a closed casket. The house felt empty. I put the Ruger back in its holster.

I caned over to the dark spots in the carpet and pushed a nitrile-covered finger into one of them. A little of the semi-viscous material stuck to the glove. I knew what it was but smelled my fingertip anyway. A hint of iron. Blood. Maybe less than twenty-four hours old. Thus, no sickly sweet and rancid meat smell of a dead body.

But that didn't mean there wasn't someone dead inside the house. Only that they hadn't been dead long enough for decomp to set in. I took a deep breath and let it out slowly, then followed the stains. They stopped at the hardwood floor in the kitchen. Someone must have done the easy cleaning and run out of time when it came to the carpet.

I scanned the kitchen. No body on the floor, but I sensed death even if I couldn't smell it.

The pantry.

The distressed wooden barn door between the oven and the refrigerator in the corner of the kitchen. I limped over, said a silent prayer, and slid it open.

Claire Timmins lay on the floor, blood black and congealed beneath her head. Her blond hair turned rust-colored from the bloody wound on the right side of her head. Like a devil's halo. Eyes, dull and dead, stared at eternity. She was dressed professionally, in realtor's garb. Dark gray slacks and jacket. Light blue blouse. Pearl necklace. A bruise under her left eye that didn't have much time to blacken. She'd been beaten, then bludgeoned to death.

I didn't know Claire Timmins. I'd talked to her one time, and it hadn't been pleasant for either of us. But she'd passed through my universe when she helped Angela Albright, and she'd become a victim of the violence that swirled around me.

The Shadow Man? Maybe. The only thing I was certain of was that her killer hadn't been a rapist. She was fully clothed. Whoever had killed her wanted information, not violent sex. And if he got it, Angela Albright was in grave danger.

CHAPTER 46

I BACKED MY way out of the house, left the door open, and walked to Timmins's Nissan Sentra in the driveway. The air had an icy chill in it that I hadn't noticed when I arrived. Winter was coming. Raw and treacherous.

I had to head to the mansion in the mountains to try to find Angela. I wasn't the only one looking for her. Killers were, too. But first, one last bit of cleanup to perform. I eyeballed the neighboring homes even though I knew they were empty. Completely convinced, I dropped down next to the Sentra's driver's-side rear wheel well and removed the cigarette pack–sized GPS tracker. The tracker would be hard to explain to Sheriff's Deputies with Claire Timmins lying dead in her home.

I hustled over to my car and bolted out of Pineview Court, turned right onto Mil Potrero Highway, and sped toward Cerro Noroeste Road.

Claire Timmins was dead. There was nothing I could do for her now except treat her death with the dignity it deserved.

I called 911 dispatch and told the operator about the body and gave the address and my name. The rest I'd save for the detectives when I came back from the Sterlingshire house. Hopefully with Angela Albright safely by my side.

I called Moira.

"What now? I told you I'd call you if Angela showed up." Moira. "Obviously, she hasn't."

"Claire Timmins is dead."

"What?"

"Murdered. I'm driving up to the Sterlingshire house to see if Angela is there, then I'm going back to Timmins's house and tell the sheriff's homicide detectives everything I know about the case. All the way down to Peter Stone and Angela Albright, Sergei Volkov, and everything I've done."

Almost everything I'd done.

"What do you mean, *everything you've done*?"

Telling Moira about my break-in at Claire Timmins's house could make her an accessory after the fact. Even if she'd already figured out what I'd done on her own.

"I'm going to tell the police about my activities over the last couple days. I'll just leave it at that."

"Why? Why now? All of a sudden you want to become some kind of martyr?" Full auto anger. "What is the matter with you?"

"This is a homicide investigation now. Time for the police to take over. I'm going to tell them what I know and what I've done so they can eliminate me first and then go after Claire's real killers." I let out a long exhale. I didn't think Moira would like hearing what I said next. I didn't like saying it, but it had to be said and acted upon. "This is my last case. My odyssey's end. No more righteous quests. No more good versus evil. No more dead bodies on my watch. After I talk to the police today, I'm taking down my shingle. I need to find another way to make a living."

"Oh." Surprise and disappointment in one two-letter word.

"I'm going to sell my home and move up to Santa Barbara."

"That's great. You're moving back in with Leah and Krista?" She forced some joy into her voice.

"No. Maybe sometime in the future." But with each day that passed, the possibility of living together as a whole family again seemed more and more remote. Especially after forcing Leah and Krista into hiding because of this case. "I just need to be closer to Krista. And I don't want her to be stuck in a car for four hours each way to spend time with me. I want her to know that I'm there, within a few minutes if she ever needs me."

"What does Leah think about this?" The wariness in Moira's voice that I knew Leah felt in her heart.

"I told Leah about it Monday night when I drove up to Santa Barbara. She told me that she'd seen a divorce lawyer recently." My throat tightened. "She hasn't filed, but clearly she's considered it."

"Damn. I'm sorry."

"Thanks. No matter what happens with Leah, it's time for me to be a full-time father for Krista."

"You're doing the right thing, Rick." Her normal machine gun voice, now soft and measured. "If you're not going to be a P.I., what are you going to do for work?"

"I haven't thought that far ahead yet. I just know that I can't do this anymore and be the father Krista needs me to be." Or be the husband Leah wanted me to be.

"You'll find something." She sounded like she believed it.

"One last thing to put a lid on this case." I pushed my car up to seventy-five on the tiny two-lane highway. "You were right about my intruder last night."

"What do you mean?" She sounded like she didn't want to be right.

"I found a rake from a lock pick kit on my doormat this morning. The guy who wanted to get into my room tried to pick the lock."

"Talk to the Sheriff's detectives, then get the hell out of that town." Big sister urgency. "Come back home."

"I will, after I check to see if Angela's at the Sterlingshire house."

"Why not leave everything to the police now? You just told me that's the plan. Let them go to the house."

"I can't. Angela's my responsibility. She became that the second I said yes to Stone. I should have realized that from the start. I got caught up in how far $50,000 could go toward Krista's future instead of realizing that I'd be putting a target on Angela's back by taking the case."

"Turn around, Rick. I have a bad feeling about this." I could hear the worry in her voice.

I turned onto Cerro Noroeste Road.

"I'll be home tonight. I'll call or text when I leave. I'm gonna sign off now. Will be hitting the dead cell zone soon. Talk to you later."

"Dammit, Rick!"

"Goodbye." I hung up.

CHAPTER 47

THE SUN WAS dropping close to the tree line as it cast late afternoon shadows over the mountain. I drove right on the edge of reckless as I sped up the narrow, twisting road. Claire Timmins's killer or killers had found the connection between her and Angela Albright. I was sure of it. Wherever Angela was, she wasn't safe. If she was in the mountain mansion, I could pick her up and get her to the police, then explain to them how the pieces fit together. Try to convince them to put her in protective custody.

If they refused, she'd be my responsibility a little longer and that new life I wanted would start later. But it would start. My new life's mission.

Either way, Peter Stone would have to find another kidney donor. And another pawn in his game of life.

A view of the Sterlingshire house popped up around the next bend. I slowed to a stop, grabbed my binoculars, and got out of the car. This was the spot where I'd gotten a good look at the upstairs bedroom and saw the boot on the floor and the pink pajama top on the bed this morning. I wanted to see if the clothes were still there.

They weren't, but someone was. A woman sitting on the edge of the bed.

Angela Albright.

I hustled back into the car and tested that edge of recklessness even more on the drive to the mansion.

A few minutes later, I skidded to a stop in front of the house. No other cars. Everything looked exactly as it did this morning. But something inside had changed.

I hopped out of my car and hustle-caned my way onto the deck and to the massive redwood front door. I fought the urge to pound on the door and, instead, knocked firmly. One, two, three times. I waited. Ten, fifteen seconds. Nothing. No sense of movement inside. I knocked again and rang the bell. Still no answer.

I took a step back and looked up at the security camera under the eaves on the left side of the porch. I didn't know if the camera had a microphone, but I needed to take a chance.

"Angela. It's Rick Cahill. From Muldoon's." I spoke in a loud voice just under a shout, in case the camera didn't have a mic and she might hear me inside the house. I took off my hat and combed my hair with my fingers. We hadn't seen each other in ten years, but I recognized her immediately when I saw her through the binoculars. I hoped she'd do the same. "I need to talk to you. It's urgent. I just need two minutes."

No movement or sound from inside. I continued to stare up at the camera.

"Angela, I know you're in the house. I saw you in the upstairs bedroom a couple minutes ago." I opened my hands in front of me. "Please just give me two minutes to explain. You might be in danger. I can help you."

"Why should I trust you?" A woman's voice from a hidden speaker under the eaves. "You work for him."

"Who?"

"Peter Stone." An angry hiss in her voice.

She must have put two and two together unless Stone or someone else told her I was working for him.

"I did work for him, but I don't anymore. The only reason I'm here is to try to keep you safe. That's it."

"I don't believe you."

"Angela, you know me." I kept my head angled at the camera. "I helped you when you needed it most ten years ago. You used to bring Cassandra into my restaurant all the time. I have a daughter now. Krista." My voice caught in my throat without warning. I was only hours away from hopefully getting a step closer to becoming a bigger part of her life again. "I know what you're going through, not being able to see your daughter. I can help."

Silence.

"There are men looking for you. Dangerous men. Come with me and we'll go to the police." I turned and looked at my car and the road beyond the driveway. Clear. But for how long? I turned back to the camera. "Open the door and come outside. If you want, I'll wait by my car. You're in danger. We have to get out of here. Now."

More silence. I was about to speak again when I finally heard Angela's voice.

"I can't go to the police."

"Why not? They can keep you safe."

"I can't go to the police." Her voice pitched higher. "I can't leave."

"Then let me in and let's talk." Maybe I could change her mind face-to-face. If I had to, I'd tell her about Claire Timmins. Anything to get her to safety and get me closer to starting that new life.

"I always thought you were a good guy, Rick. But now you're working for Peter Stone. How can I trust you?"

"Because I quit working for Stone and I'm still the man who helped you ten years ago." But was I? Yes. Even with the things I'd done that could put me in prison for life, the goodness that compelled me to help Angela a decade ago was still inside me.

Silence. Then, twenty seconds later, the door swung open. Angela Albright stood in front of me. "Come in."

CHAPTER 48

I STEPPED INSIDE the large foyer, leaning on my putter. Angela closed the door behind me and put her hands on her hips, eyeing me. She looked much the same as the last time I'd seen her ten years ago. Beach blond hair, refined surfer-girl-next-door. Her skin a little paler than it was back when I knew her. Slightly deeper crow's feet around her eyes. In her early forties, just starting to look her age for the first time in her life. Comfortably attractive. She wore blue jeans, a gray cardigan, and black cowboy-style boots.

She led me over to the sofa I'd seen this morning when I peeked through the window in the front door. It was made of modest wool fabric. Not something that would survive the full move-in by Theodore Raskin.

There was a wooden coffee table in front of it that had an e-cigarette on it.

"Have a seat." She sat down on the sofa facing the majestic floor-to-ceiling windows with views of towering pine trees that scattered back to mountain ridges beyond.

I sat down and looked at the redwood deck that rose fifteen feet above the ground. No staircase. The only exit on level ground was out the front. We needed to get moving, but I wasn't going to kidnap Angela to do it. A different tact.

"Who have you been hiding from? Stone?"

"Yeah."

"Why?"

"He doesn't know that I know, but my mom told me before she died." She sprang up from the sofa, grabbed the e-cig off the coffee table, and started pacing in front of the massive window. "A deathbed confession that didn't make up for the awful person she was when she was alive."

"Know what?" I was 90 percent certain what she'd say, but I'd promised Stone I'd never tell her. Even as I quit on him and hoped never to see him again, I wouldn't break that one promise.

"He's my father." She spat the words out like she was trying to expel their truth from her body.

"He hired me to find you because he claims that he needs a kidney transplant. Did he talk to you about that?"

"No." She took a puff from her e-cig.

"Then why are you hiding from him?"

"I can't tell you." She blew out nicotine vapor.

"Did Stone introduce you to Raskin? How did this all start?"

"How do you know about Billy?"

"Everyone knows about you and Billy. That's why they're looking for you. To find out where Billy is."

Angela stopped pacing and looked at me for a solid ten seconds. She finally made a decision and sat back down on the sofa.

"Peter called me out of the blue about two years ago." She stared down at the coffee table. "I don't know how he got my cell number, but I guess you know enough about him to know that he can usually get whatever he wants. Anyway, he asked me to meet him in Washington. Bought me an airline ticket, so I went."

"Why did you go?"

"I owed him." Angela shook her head like she was trying to erase a memory. "He helped me through a rough part of my life before I met

Steven—a lifetime ago. I was a different person back then. Anyway, that's why I went to meet him. I flew into Seattle, then had to wear a blindfold for a four-hour drive in a limo to meet him."

"What did he want?"

"At first he seemed to only want to ask me about me and my family." Her eyebrows rose up. "He just seemed like a lonely old man who was ill and looking back at his life."

"Was this before or after your mother told you he was your father."

"Before. I wouldn't have gone if I'd known."

"Did Stone introduce you to Raskin?"

"Yes. He asked me to go to a charity event with Billy in La Jolla about four months ago." She frowned. "I went and enjoyed his company and we started seeing each other."

Stone as matchmaker? No, he didn't put people together so they'd find love; he matched people who, together, could benefit him in some way. Financially or to increase his power, control. One in the same to him.

"When was the last time you saw or spoke to Stone?"

"About five weeks ago."

Right before she disappeared.

"What happened then?"

"Why do you care about all of this?" Her eyebrows pushed downward. "None of this has anything to do with you. You can just walk away."

"Why can't *you* just walk away, Angela? Why can't you go to the police?"

"I can't talk about that."

"Does it have something to do with Raskin and BitChange?"

"I can't talk about it!" She got off the sofa and started pacing again.

Time was running out. I had to shock her no matter how much it hurt.

"I just came from Claire Timmins's house." I let the gravity for what I'd seen there fill my voice.

"What?" She must have read the pain on my face.

"Maybe you should sit back down." I motioned to the sofa.

"I'm not going to sit down!" A wounded shriek. "Did something happen to Claire?"

"She's dead. Someone killed her."

Angela wobbled, then collapsed onto the couch. She put her head in her hands and sobbed. I put my arm around her shoulder and pulled her close. I didn't say anything and let her cry. There were no right words to say. There never were.

Finally, after a couple minutes, she spoke in a wavering voice. "I've only known her for a few months, but I felt close to her. She's helped me a lot over the last month."

The men looking for Angela were still out there somewhere. I needed any leverage I could get if I had to go up against them.

"What does Billy have that everyone wants?"

She didn't say anything and puffed on her e-cig. Like a baby with a pacifier.

"Angela, whatever it is, there are men killing people trying to find it. Tell me. Tell the police. Tell someone so you can walk away from it."

She took the e-cig away from her mouth. "The keys."

"What keys?"

"The private keys authenticating transactions by users on BitChange."

"What does that mean? What could someone do with the keys?" I was in over my head, but I knew enough that having someone's keys meant access. To something.

"Billy accidentally found a way to uncover users' private keys when they're stored in their hot wallets."

"What's a hot wallet?"

"It's kind of like an online cryptocurrency bank account. But instead of storing money, it stores keys to unlocking the money."

I doubted the accidental part about Raskin "finding" a way to get into these wallets. Especially since he'd worked for both Stone and Sergei Volkov. The man who Stone called a "Whiz Kid." Whiz Kids don't find things by accident. They go looking for them.

"So, with these keys, someone could get access to the original transactions? The money?"

"From what I understand, it's a little more complicated than that." She brushed hair away from her face with her hand and hit her e-cig again. "But that's the general idea."

"How much money are we talking about?"

"Two hundred and thirty million dollars." She coughed out some fake smoke.

I almost coughed, too. Two hundred thirty million dollars wasn't just life changing. It was multi-generations changing. The kind of money that could lure Peter Stone out of his hidden lair and make a couple FBI agents with a taste of avarice go full-blown rogue. And somehow get a Russian Mob kingpin out of prison early?

Was it all connected?

"Did Stone ask you about the keys? Is that why you went into hiding?"

"He started asking too many questions about Billy's business." Her eyes squinted down in bitterness. "He pretended at first that it was out of genuine interest, but I knew what he really wanted. He wanted me to steal Billy's laptop and give it to him."

"What's in Billy's laptop?"

"Everything."

"What did you do?" I asked.

"I told Billy, and then I went underground."

"Up here?"

"Yes. Claire was a friend of Billy's and agreed to help us. Billy needed to take care of some things, and then we were going to move to an island in Fiji. Our own island. He wanted to fix the error in the blockchain that allowed private keys to become visible before we disappeared."

Close the back door after he already walked through it. And make off with everything in the house. That's how you can afford to buy your own island in Fiji. Now I knew why Angela didn't want to go to the police.

"How many people know about the keys? I haven't seen anything about it online or in the news when I searched for information about Raskin."

"That's because Billy never used the keys. He hasn't co-opted any of the transactions."

Doubtful.

"Well, somebody must have found out about it for Stone to know."

"One user on the blockchain found the glitch and went to the FBI. Nothing happened to his money, but he reported it to the FBI anyway instead of bringing it to Billy's attention."

Special Agents Sorensen and Bowden. The connection to Stone. Maybe not in the adversarial role that he claimed. Were they all working together? Could Stone have sent the Shadow Man to my room last night? To try and torture the information out of me that Stone thought I knew but hadn't given him? My lack of updates to him, quitting the case, lying to him about where I was. Did I really think I could get away with fooling Peter Stone about where I was?

Had he been playing me all along? Was he responsible for Claire Timmins's murder?

"Did Billy talk to someone at the FBI?" Find the connections.

"Yes."

"Do you remember the agents' names?"

"Not really. Something like Thorson and Bolles, maybe."

"Sorensen and Bowden?"

"Yes. I think that's it."

CHAPTER 49

RASKIN HAD BEEN interviewed by Sorensen and Bowden. They talked to him but didn't arrest him. Whatever the truth was about the keys, it never went public. Why not? It had the potential to be a huge scandal. The kind of thing the press would eat up. There was already a lot of publicity and press cynicism about cryptocurrency. This would be a headline grabber that perfectly fit the media's cryptocurrency corruption narrative.

The recently leaky FBI had suddenly clammed up. Why? Back to best practices, or was there another reason? Something darker involving two potentially rogue FBI agents. Sorensen and Bowden questioned Raskin about the key controversy brought to them by a lone BitChange user. Did they keep what they learned from Raskin to themselves? Did they see the loose keys and Raskin as their chance to hit the jackpot?

They already had some bent in them. Bowden had broken her vow under God to her spouse. A sign of the corruption within. And the more they each broke vows and oaths, the easier it would be to break the next one. The sacred oath they'd taken to protect the Constitution and the people of the United States of America.

But according to Special Agent John Mallon, Sorensen and Bowden were legitimately working the case through proper channels. As best as he could tell.

"When was the last time Raskin talked to the FBI agents?" I asked.

"I think it was about six weeks ago."

"How many times did they talk to him?"

"Three or four."

"Did Raskin tell you what they asked about?"

"They asked him about the keys and made him show them the transaction history of traders on the blockchain." Angela blew out some more vapor and set the nicotine delivery device down onto the coffee table.

"How did they make him show proprietary information and information that should have belonged, at least partially, to BitChange users?"

"He said they'd put him in federal prison for ten years if he didn't show them. But he doesn't have them anymore. He deleted them."

"What do you mean?"

"He deleted them from the cloud and all the copies."

"He must have one copy left."

No treasure island in Fiji without access to the keys to the kingdom. Someone who worked for Peter Stone and Sergei Volkov didn't suddenly go altruistic after a tough interrogation from two FBI agents.

There was another copy somewhere, whether Angela knew about it or not.

"Angela, we have to leave now. Too many people want Raskin and those keys, and they'll torture you to find him."

"I can't leave. Billy's coming for me tonight!"

Not if he was burned to death in a house on Cabrillo Avenue in La Jolla.

"When was the last time you talked to him?"

"On Tuesday."

"You mean you saw him when you were down in La Jolla visiting your daughter?"

"Yes." She blinked a few times rapidly.

"Where did you meet him?" The death house on Cabrillo Ave? Had he been in it talking to Special Agents Sorensen and Bowden while Moira and I sat on it?

"In Coronado at an Airbnb." She folded her arms across her chest and tilted her head to the right. "You're not going to find him there if you go looking though. He moves to a different location every night.

A digitized pong came from inside the front of the house.

"He's here!" Angela sprang from the sofa and ran toward the foyer.

"What?" I shot up and hobbled after her, jump-skipping with the cane to try to catch up. "What's going on?"

But I already thought I knew what it was.

Angela sped right from the foyer down the hall. I followed as quickly as my three legs would allow. She turned into a room on the right side of the hallway.

Another pong just as I hit the doorway. The room was no bigger than a small walk-in closet. The only thing in it was a table with a laptop and five computer monitors on it. The images on the monitors were in black and white and were of Cerro Noroeste Road and the driveway to the house. The laptop had smaller matching images on its screen. I caught a glimpse of the back end of a large, black SUV on the second monitor before it disappeared. Raskin must have hidden closed circuit cameras along the road after he bought the house.

"It's not Billy." Eyes wild, head on a swivel, panicked voice. "It's someone else!"

"Where's the camera that just showed the SUV?" I tried to say calm. Her panic was enough.

"A half a mile away. They'll be here in about a minute."

The only escape was back up the road the SUV was heading down right now or into the woods on foot. I wouldn't have a chance on my ankle. Angela wouldn't have time to get far enough away to outrun a bullet either.

Our only chance was to defend the castle and hope help would somehow be on the way. For that I needed weapons. My Ruger .357 was in the trunk of my car. At least twenty seconds to my car and back.

"Are there any guns in the house?" I asked Angela.

"What?" She shook her head. "No!"

"Open the garage door!" I sped back into the foyer toward the front door.

"What!" Angela's voice trailing behind me. "Wait."

"Open the garage door now!"

I went out the front door and scampered three-legged across the deck to my car. Whoever was coming down the road—Sergei Volkov and his men or Special Agents Sorensen and Bowden—would know my car. It could even be Peter Stone. If they saw it, I'd lose all element of surprise, and surprise would be the only advantage I'd have in a very disadvantaged game. A game that would end in death.

The garage door closest to the house rose up. I started my car and sped to the garage. I burst out of my car as the garage door was already descending, popped the trunk, and grabbed the holstered Ruger. Two seconds later, Angela opened the door into the house. I hustled inside and locked the door behind me.

"Make sure all the doors are locked and bolted," I said and followed her down the hall.

She ran into the family room. By the time I caught up, she was locking the sliding glass door that led out onto the deck. She slipped in the bolt near the top of the door, then turned back toward me.

"What now?" she asked.

"Is there a landline or a satellite phone in the house?"

"No. That's why I stayed with Claire most of the time. No phone or internet."

"How about a safe room? A room fortified with steel that has a steel door. Is there one in the house?" I put on the holster and unsnapped the leather strap around the trigger guard.

"No."

Shit.

"Do all the bedrooms upstairs have glass doors that open onto the deck?"

"Yes."

"Go lock yourself into the one that has the least exposure to the outside and pull the curtains."

"What?"

"Go! Now!"

She threw her hand up to her throat and grabbed her necklace. An inch-and-a-half-long black rectangular pendant hung from the end of a silver chain necklace. She opened the pendant and showed me a flash drive inside. "This is what they want. The private keys to the transactions. It's worth over $320,000,000!"

CHAPTER 50

ANGELA TOOK OFF the necklace and handed it to me.

Did whoever was in the SUV know that Angela had the keys, or were they just looking for her to find out where Raskin was? Didn't matter. Whatever they wanted, Angela was dead if they made it upstairs. And so was I.

"They won't let you live after you give it to them." The people after the keys didn't leave witnesses. They'd already killed once, possibly twice. I handed her back the necklace. "Upstairs!"

Angela looked at me, then the door, then back to me, then bolted up the staircase. Her feet thundering her retreat. I sped down the hall into the video surveillance room and grabbed the laptop, then gimped up the staircase to the landing, which looked down upon the front door.

I sat on the top step and set the laptop down next to me. I looked at the two little boxes on the computer screen that had views of the driveway and beyond. Nothing yet. No SUV pulling up or men marching on the house holding guns. It had been more than a minute since I saw the SUV from the camera on Cerro Noroeste Road. Longer than Angela thought for the SUV to get to the house.

Another minute, no SUV or any vehicles on the computer screen. There wasn't an outlet before they got to the house. Was the person driving the SUV lost and decided to try to make a very dangerous three-point turn to retrace their steps instead of following the road to its end? If so, I should have seen them going back the other way on one of the cameras. Unless they did it before I grabbed the computer.

Or . . . shit!

I hopped down the staircase on one leg, grabbing the handrail with my right hand and holding my cane in my left, and went back into the garage to my car and grabbed my binoculars. I slung the strap to the binos around my neck, went back inside the house, and hustled upstairs.

"What's going on?" Angela stood on the landing, eyes round with fear.

"Show me the room with the best view of the road." I edged past her.

"This way. The master." She ran past me to the last room at the end of the hall. I scampered after her.

The room I'd seen through the binoculars.

"Wait inside, away from the door and windows."

I opened the sliding glass door just wide enough to be able to slip through and army crawled on my belly to the edge of the deck. No SUV visible on the road through the two clearings I could see. I pulled the binoculars to my face and looked at the clearing farthest away. Nothing. I slowly moved the binos along to the right and caught glimpses of asphalt road between pine tree limbs. No SUV.

The binos hit the next clearing and, again, no vehicles on the road. This was where the road started tilting downhill as it twisted toward the house. I followed it through the pine trees and underbrush again. A hundred or so yards down, I caught a black glint.

The SUV. It sat, still parked on the road. Pine tree limbs blocked much of the vehicle so I couldn't get a clear make. But I had a bad feeling about what kind of SUV it was. I moved the binos ahead inch by inch and caught an opening that revealed the front passenger window and a profile in the driver's seat. I couldn't make out much of the person. Male, black combat jacket, black ball cap. Sunglasses in the dimming sunlight.

What was he waiting for?

I moved the binos past the SUV. Splotchy patches of the road came in and out of view. Then I saw them.

Three men dressed like the drivers of the SUV. Except these men were carrying rifles. Looked to be fully automatic. And wore tactical vests. Body armor.

Shit.

They walked slowly down the road. I could only see their profiles. They each looked like they had thin black microphone headsets on top of their ball caps. One had a small canvas bag strapped over his shoulder. Another moved his head slightly toward the right, and I caught sight of white lettering on his cap. Not long enough to make out what it read. Just white.

I estimated that they were at least a quarter mile away. Taking their time. Waiting for the sun to go down before they assaulted the house? And why not drive all the way to the house with a show of force? Because they didn't want to be seen by the security cameras on the front of the house? Did they know about those cameras? Thank God they didn't know about the ones Raskin had installed along the road.

I scanned to the right. Movement caught my eye. A rock and grainy dirt rolled down the sheared side of the hill above the road. I moved the binoculars up the path where the rock had come from. Thirty, forty, fifty feet. Nothing. Then a slash of black between the trees. And the butt of a rifle. The man was dressed like the rest. Black gear and cap, flak vest. Again, in profile. I started to move the binos off the man to look for others when he stumbled and turned his body in my direction to catch his balance. That's when I read the white lettering on his ball cap.

FBI.

CHAPTER 51

THE FBI? IN Pine Mountain Club? Why did they park their vehicle a quarter mile away and send armed agents out on foot? It would be much easier to just roll the SUV up in the driveway and knock on the front door and shout, "FBI." Who did they think was in the house? Theodore Raskin? Did they think he was armed? Is that why they were dressed in SWAT tactical gear? Were Sorensen and Bowden in another car trailing behind?

Whatever the case, I didn't need my gun anymore. I let out a long exhale, and my shoulders relaxed for the first time since I left the Pine Mountain Inn. We were safe. Angela would have to deal with whatever criminal conspiracy that Raskin had rubbed off on her, but I'd kept her safe, out of the grasp of Stone and Sergei Volkov's men. I did my job. Not the one I'd been paid to do, but the one I had to do. Ultimately, the thing my conscience compelled me to do.

My final case was over. Stone being Stone would learn the truth. That I'd found Angela, and so had the FBI. That I'd gone against his wishes. I'd give him back his money, but he'd want more. Maybe blood. Maybe not. He wasn't in a position to lift his head up above the ground. I'd deal with him as needed. And I'd do the same with Sergei Volkov.

Now I just had to go downstairs and wait for the Feds to arrive. Take off my gun and shoulder holster and stick them in the trunk of my car, then wait on the front porch. The Feds would probably grill me for a few hours, maybe the whole night, but I'd be driving home in the morning at the latest. My new life could start tomorrow when I began making minor repairs on my house in preparation to put it on the market.

Maybe Sterlingshire Inc. would make me an offer.

I hoped to be in Santa Barbara for good within the next few months.

I pushed up off the deck on my hands and knees and was about to stand all the way up when the FBI popped into my head. Why hadn't the Feds used a SWAT vehicle? They had agents in tactical gear but no tactical vehicles. Maybe they were using undercover vehicles.

I slid back down onto my stomach and brought the binoculars up to my eyes again. I found the closest clearing along the road and moved the binos down the hill until I came to the black SUV. Why come in SWAT gear but ride up undercover? Why not flash the powerful presence of the U.S. government in the form of the Federal Bureau of Investigation? The FBI. Those bold three letters were more intimidating than anything else the government could throw at you.

Why the secrecy?

Because they weren't really the FBI? Maybe the men in the SUV didn't want a neon sign on their vehicle that would risk catching the attention of the police who wouldn't be fooled by FBI hats bought online.

I swung the binoculars down the hill to try to find the armed men. Found them through the patched openings in the trees. Still in profile. Now only a couple hundred yards away from the house.

I tracked the binos up the hill above the road where I'd seen the one man almost head-on and read his hat. Gone. I slowly checked the underbrush and trees to the right of where I'd seen him, trying to judge the distance he could have traveled. I needed one more look at him. Straight on.

I kept slowly edging the binoculars to the right for forty to fifty yards. Nothing. I searched farther up the side of the hill. A flash of black. The man in the FBI hat. Angling away from me at forty-five degrees as he climbed the hill. I saw enough of his back to see that the flak jacket didn't have any writing on it. No FBI emblazoned on the material. The Feds were big about calling out their brand. They plastered FBI on almost every piece of tactical gear and vehicle available to them.

Anybody could buy an FBI hat or jacket online. But not body armor.

I could have been wrong about all the places the FBI branded their gear and equipment. Maybe they only stenciled FBI on the front of their flak jackets and not the back. I needed one more straight-on look before I decided to lay down my gun or use it.

The road leading to the house. It started to curve to the right on its descent. I should get a straight-on look when the armed men were about a hundred yards out. But could I afford to wait that long?

I had to take the chance.

I found the men on the road and followed along with them as they descended the hill and started to make the turn to the right. Still in profile through the tree limbs and underbrush. Then a bit more of a turn. There! I could see half on the front of the lead man's flak vest.

No FBI stenciling.

The heavily armed men coming for us weren't with the FBI. But they wanted us to think they were.

So we'd drop our defenses and be an easier kill.

CHAPTER 52

I ARMY CRAWLED backwards as fast as I could back into the house. I didn't bother to close the door. No extra movement for the fake FBI agents to pick up on if they got a glimpse of the house through the trees.

Angela stood next to the door out of sight from the road.

"What is it?" Her eyes as frantic as her voice. "What's going on?"

I stood up next to her away from the windows.

"There's an SUV and at least five men out there. One parked in the SUV, three coming down the road, and at least one up on the hill."

"Oh God!"

"They're pretending to be FBI agents. They're not." I hustled to the bedroom door. "Let's get out of here."

Angela followed me out. "How do you know they're pretending?"

I stopped in the hallway and turned toward her. "Not the correct gear." I held out my hand. "Give me your necklace."

"What?" Her eyes went big. "I thought you said they'd kill us even if we gave them the keys."

"I may be able to use it to give us time." Some sort of Hail Mary. I hadn't figured out what that could be yet, but I needed any advantage or delay tactic I could get.

Angela took off the necklace with the mini thumb drive and handed it to me.

"Give us time? Is someone coming to rescue us?" A flicker of hope in her eyes that ripped open a jagged wound in my stomach. No one was coming. No one knew we were in trouble. The irony was the only way to send out an SOS was to hope the sound of gunfire would carry far enough away to get someone's attention. But could I hold off five gunmen with automatic weapons with my Ruger .357 Magnum snub-nose revolver long enough for help to arrive?

The odds weren't good. If there were any odds at all.

I couldn't pick off assassins from a window shooting a handgun with a two-inch barrel. No one could. Maybe world champion target shooters, but they'd probably never had a live human between their sites.

"Someone will come. Now go get into the other bedroom!"

Angela ran past me and went into the first room above the staircase and slammed the door. I heard the click of a lock as I passed by it on the way to the landing and the laptop with the security camera images.

I left my cane on the landing, grabbed the laptop, used the handrail for support, and went down four steps on the staircase then sat down. Eight steps to the ground floor, four back up to the landing. Advance, retreat. I looked at the computer screen and tried to settle my heartbeat and my breath. All screens clear.

I'd never had a problem pulling the trigger of a gun pointed at a human being. The aftermath of the first time had been hard. The killing had been easy. Him or me. No thinking necessary. Contemplation would have been suicide. But that didn't stop the thoughts, doubts, and what-ifs that came later. Insomnia or drenched-sheeted nightmares followed. But only after the first one.

All but three had been split-second reactions in life-or-death situations. Them or me. Live or die. Shoot to kill. One was just thirty seconds past self-defense and the death sentence a monster deserved. For the other two, I'd laid in wait. Premeditated. First degree murder. The lying-in-wait had been difficult. The killing, easy.

A preemptive strike to save myself and Moira from murder attempts I was certain would come. My actions for what I deemed the greater good. I'd played God to defeat evil. Self-justification or evil in its own right? I would probably learn the answer to that question in the next half hour.

I pulled the Ruger out of the shoulder holster and checked the cylinder even though I knew it was full. Five bullets. I snapped open the two leather compartments in the holster one at a time and checked the two speed loaders. Five rounds in each. Fifteen rounds total to take on five men with automatic weapons.

Yes, barring a miracle from God, I'd get my answer from him very soon about the condition of my soul.

Last chance. A quick glance at the computer screen. Still clear. I whipped out my phone. No cell connection as I anticipated. I thumbed to the tape recorder app and hit RECORD.

"Leah and Krista, I love you both more than I've ever been able to express."—I blinked back tears gathering in my eyes and kept my voice steady. Strong.—"I've made some bad choices that have hurt you, and I'd do anything to take them back. But I can't. I could only try to never make them again. Leah, you tried as hard as you could to pull me back from the ledge, but I kept creeping farther and farther out onto it. You did all you could. And then you rightly decided you had to protect Krista and take her away from the danger that swirls around me. That is inside me. You did the right thing when I couldn't. Now that I've seen the light, I fear that it's too late. Maybe too late even if I manage to see you both again. I hope I'm wrong, but I'm afraid that I won't get the chance to find out. Know that I love you both with all my being. Please pray for my soul."

I stopped the recording, entitled it "Leah," attached it to an email to her, and pushed SEND. Nothing happened, but I hoped it would send to her if someone found my phone when they did my body and drove it through a live cell area.

As the seconds ticked down on my remaining time on earth, I was relegated to hope and prayers.

CHAPTER 53

I PUT MY phone away and glanced at the laptop. Two fake FBI agents walked up to the driveway with their automatic weapons across their chest. Where was the third? And how close was the one on the hillside?

The two stopped at the edge of the driveway thirty yards from the house. One of the men looked like he was talking, but he wasn't looking at the man next to him. He must have been talking to the rest of his team through his headset. Planning their assault on the house.

If the men breached the house, Angela and I were dead. Five, four, or three to one? It didn't matter. Two to one was enough. Even one to one, when one had an assault rifle and one didn't.

But getting inside wasn't going to be as easy as they thought. One of them may have been able to use a hook and a rake to pick the lock on my door at the Pine Mountain Inn, but he wouldn't be able to on the Sterlingshire house front door. No key opening. They'd need the right magnetized key card. Or a battering ram. A big one. Unfortunately, they had one. A 6,000 pound SUV.

They'd get inside eventually, but I had to delay that entry as long as possible. I needed a force multiplier, and I might just have one. If I could get creative and act quickly.

I picked up the computer and hobbled upstairs to the room that Angela locked herself into. I gently knocked on the door.

"Angela. It's Rick. Unlock the door."

A click and the door opened. Angela, eyes still wide, tight mouth, worry lines etched into her forehead. She looked like she'd aged ten years in the half hour I'd been at the house. I didn't know what I looked like. Just what I had to do. And what I had to ask Angela to do.

"What's happening?" Her voice, cracked glass. "Did they go away?"

I glanced down at the screen of the laptop I held in my right hand. The light in the security camera image was fading. Darkness would soon fall. The men in the boxed screen hadn't moved. Still outside the driveway on the right side. They probably thought they were out of sight of a security camera. They must not have known that there were two under the eaves on either side of the front façade of the house.

"No." I gently took her hand in mine. "But I need your help. I'm going to ask you to do something dangerous to give us a chance to survive this and make enough noise for someone to notice something's going on out here."

I prayed the Sheriff's Deputies had arrived at Claire Timmins's house. Or that there was a Deputy within range of the sound of gunfire.

"What do you want me to do?" Terror in her voice and eyes.

"I want you to stand out on the balcony and call to the men at the end of the driveway. Say, 'I have the keys right here. You can have them.'" I let go of her hand, pulled the necklace she gave me from my pocket, and gave it back to her. "Tell them they can have it if they promise to leave."

"I thought you said they'd kill us no matter what."

"They'll try. After they promise to leave once you give them the necklace. That's why I need you to distract them and to get them to come close to the house." My kill zone with the snub-nose Ruger was, at the most, twenty feet. Probably less because they all had to be head shots. The flak jackets. And I wouldn't have time to steady and take good aim. I'd have to be quick.

I checked the screen again. The man with the canvas bag opened it and handed the other two men at the end of the driveway long, cylindrical tubes and took out one for himself. They all screwed the tubes onto the barrels of their guns.

Shit. Suppressors. The cacophony of gunshots I hoped would echo around the mountain wouldn't come from their guns.

It would have to come from mine.

Any iota of fear that I might mistakenly kill an FBI agent evaporated. The FBI didn't use suppressors. At least not when breaching a house in the middle of nowhere. Assassins used suppressors. They were aware of the echo in the mountains, too, and they'd come prepared.

Survival just got more difficult, but certainty was mine.

"What is it?" Angela, urgent. She must have read something on my face when I looked at the killers screwing silent death onto their gun barrels. I'd lost my poker face.

"These men are coming to kill us. There is no doubt about that. So I need to kill as many of them as I can and make as much noise as possible doing it." I grabbed her hand again. This time firmly. "Will you help me do that?"

Terror in her eyes. She didn't say anything.

"Will you help me do that?" My voice firmer.

Angela nodded her head and whispered, "Yes."

"Good." I stepped into the room past Angela and looked around. No bed, no furniture at all. The windows and sliding glass doors to the deck didn't have curtains or any covering. No curtain rods either. "Is there a bathroom in the house that has shower curtains?"

"Yes. In the bathroom of the guest room next door."

"Show me."

Angela hurried out of the room and led me into the next bedroom and then its bathroom. There was a bathtub with a cheap vinyl shower curtain held up by an adjustable metal curtain rod. Must have been where Angela liked to bathe, and she bought the curtain at Target or Walmart in Bakersfield to use while she waited for Raskin to arrive.

I handed Angela the computer, then yanked down the rod and tilted it downward to let the rings holding the curtain fall onto the floor. I hustled out of the bedroom and caned myself down the hall toward the master bedroom where I'd gone out onto the deck with the binoculars.

"What are you doing?" Angela, right behind me.

"Making a surrender flag." I didn't want some hot-triggered fake FBI agent spinning and shooting at Angela's voice before he had a chance to understand what she was saying.

"What?"

I went into the master bedroom and over to the bed. The sheets were more taupe than white, but close enough. I yanked the comforter to the floor, grabbed the top sheet off the bed, and tied two ends of it a couple feet apart onto one end of the five-foot-long curtain rod.

"What are you going to do with that?" Angela, two inches from my hip.

I tossed the makeshift flag onto the bed and took the computer from Angela. The men were still at the end of the driveway. Dusk was falling fast.

"Do the security cameras under the eaves have lights that go on when it gets dark?" I asked.

"Yes, when there's some kind of movement outside."

That would give the night some visibility, but only briefly. The men outside would probably shoot out the lights when the firing started. I needed to engage them before the sun went down. You can't shoot out the sun. "Okay. Here's how we're going to play it." I kept my voice calm. "You're going to crawl out on the balcony of the room nearest the staircase and stick the flag through the slats on the railing and wave it up and down. Wait until they notice it and say something to you. Then—"

"I thought you wanted me to yell to them first."

"Changed my mind. We don't want one of those guys to jump at the noise and start shooting."

"Oh my God. You think they'd do that?"

"Doubt it, but don't want to take the chance." Still calm, like discussing sales strategy about how to keep a buyer on the hook. "Just stay back from the railing and keep moving the flag up and down. Eventually they'll see it and yell something up to the balcony."

"And then you want me to tell them I have the keys and I'll give them to them if they agree to leave?"

"Yes. Then toss the necklace over the balcony and go back inside the house."

"Then what happens?"

"You go into the other bedroom, lock the door, then go into the bathroom where I got the curtain rod and get into the bathtub. Keep as much of yourself below the edge of the tub as possible."

"Why?"

Because I didn't want her to get hit by a stray bullet that penetrated the walls of the house.

"It's safer. Just do it!" A little too gruff. "Please."

"Okay." She nodded her head, but a tear slipped out of her eye and rolled down her cheek.

I reached out and wiped the tear off her face and put my hand on her shoulder.

"You can do this. We just have to make some noise and hold them off for a little while. The road to the house is a dead end. They won't want to stay out here too long with the possibility of being cornered by the police." I wanted to believe my own words as much as I wanted Angela to. "Plus, they won't have too much of a reason to stay after you give them the keys. They're all wearing hats down over their eyes and are dressed the same. We wouldn't be able to pick them out of a lineup if given the chance. And, aside from their weapons, they haven't really broken any laws yet."

"Then why did you say they'd kill us even after we gave them the keys?"

"They're pragmatists. The keys will eventually be used for illegal purposes. Given the choice, they'll get rid of all witnesses. But, if it takes them longer than they planned and possibly puts them in danger or the chance of getting arrested, they'll bug out of here."

"I just want to see my daughter again." Tears double barreled out of her eyes.

A quick glance at the computer screen and the men in the darkening dusk. No movement. I set down the computer on the bed and put my other hand on Angela's other shoulder.

"You're going to." There was a possibility that the scenario I just laid out might happen. And that we'd both be able to see our daughters again. There was also the possibility that the men would let Angela live after they killed me and somehow she'd make it back to La Jolla to see Cassie again. "I promise."

If I was right, a promise kept. If not, then it really didn't matter. Angela believing me and doing her part was the only chance in hell we had of making it through the night alive.

I rubbed Angela's shoulders. "You can do this. Take a few deep breaths and let the air out slowly."

She wiped her eyes and took a couple deep breaths and long exhales. The tears stopped flowing. A few more breaths and then one very long exhale.

"Okay." Her eyes bloodshot, but dry. "I'm ready."

CHAPTER 54

I STOOD AT the bottom of the staircase on the left side of the front door. Angela looked down at me from the top of the stairs next to the mattress I'd pulled out of the master bedroom and dropped on the floor behind the railing on the landing. An aerie perch I hoped to be able to use if I could kill one of the invaders and grab his assault rifle.

Angela held the taupe surrender flagpole with both hands and stared down at me. Fear in her eyes, but her body read resolute. She was ready to fight through the fear. The definition of courage. She'd found faith in me that my Hail Mary scheme might work.

I had to make it so.

I checked the laptop, which now sat on a chair that I pulled out of the video room and pushed against the wall in the foyer. The two men still stood at the end of the driveway. I guessed the third man who I'd seen earlier was somewhere off to the left side of the house.

The sky had turned gray-brown. It would only be a few short minutes before the assault began.

I looked up at Angela and nodded my head. She took another deep breath and let it out, then disappeared from my sight as she walked toward the first room at the top of the stairs. I checked the computer. The men hadn't advanced any farther forward. Angela hadn't gotten to her post yet.

I pulled the Ruger out of my shoulder holster, checked the cylinder to make sure it was loaded for the second time, and held it with a crooked elbow, barrel pointed at the ceiling. My finger on the trigger guard. I had the sudden urge to peek through one of the high windows in the door to make real the images I'd looked at on a computer screen for the last twenty-minutes.

Not yet.

I continued to watch. Suddenly the leader swung his head up and to the right. His weapon followed. Shit! The man next to him did the same thing. Neither fired their guns but had them aimed and ready.

The two men split about fifteen feet apart then started advancing forward. The leader looked like he was moving his mouth. Maybe giving instructions to the rest of his men. The second man disappeared from the screen but suddenly appeared on the next one filmed by the other security camera.

The leader got closer, about thirty feet to the right of the front door, and kept looking up at the deck. Thirty feet was definitely out of my kill zone for a head shot. And too far away to be able to grab his assault rifle if I did kill him. I needed someone on the porch in front of the door. The man opened his mouth wide.

"You, on the balcony. Show yourself! FBI!" The sound of his shouted voice came out of the computer on the table. The microphone on the security camera. A somewhat familiar accent. Israeli? The Shadow Man?

If Angela replied, the mics on the cameras didn't pick it up.

Then, from upstairs and faintly through the computer speaker. "I have what you want!"

"And what is that?" The leader, his gun still pointed upward, his finger on the trigger guard.

"The keys to the exchanges on the BitChange blockchain."

"Show yourself."

I wanted to shout up to Angela not to move. Not to show herself to the men. But feared the two men might be close enough to hear my voice from inside the house if I had to yell.

"What's your name?" The leader again.

"Please don't shoot!" Angela in stereo upstairs and through the computer.

Shit. She must have been standing where they could see her.

"We don't want to hurt you. Just tell me your name."

"Angela Albright. I have the keys right here." She must have held up her necklace with the mini flash drive attached.

"Thank you, Angela." More of the accent slipped out in his now patronizing voice. "Is there anyone else with you inside the house?"

Moment of truth. Did Angela trust me, or would she give into her fear and the men with more and bigger guns?

"No. It's just me." We had a chance. "Now please, if I give you the keys, will you leave and not hurt me? I don't even know who you are. I can't hurt you. I just want to get back to San Diego and my daughter."

"We're FBI agents." He didn't even sound like he convinced himself and he didn't call himself a special agent which was the title used by every Fed I ever talked to.

"Yes. FBI. Just please don't hurt me."

"Of course, of course." The man lowered his gun. "Now go down-stairs and open the front door and let me in."

Having the man on the front porch would put him in my kill zone. Bettering our odds of somehow surviving.

"I can't do that. I'm sorry." A wobble in her voice. "Here's what you want."

Shit. My fault. We didn't go over that scenario.

The man's head moved down slightly like he was watching something descend. The necklace with the flash drive. The man snapped his rifle back up.

Shit. I should have had Angela tell them she'd give them the necklace at the front door so I could get the men in my kill zone. A costly, possible fatal, error by me.

"You stay right there." He looked to his right and I checked the other man in the other screen box. The second man walked toward the house and picked up something off the ground. The necklace. He put it in his pants pocket and aimed his rifle upward, finger on the trigger. The leader spoke again. "Max, you have her?"

"Yes." Russian accent.

The leader lowered his weapon and touched the side of the headset in his ear. He said the name Elan then something in Russian. He tapped the earpiece then looked back up toward Angela.

"We have to check to make sure what you gave Max is what you say it is." He smiled. "Then we'll leave, and everything will be fine."

I prayed he spoke the truth. But I hadn't had a prayer answered in a long time. I didn't blame God.

"How old is your daughter?" the leader asked.

"Sixteen. She's on the high school tennis team." Angela, either by instinct or choice, was showing the leader that she had a life, a family. That she deserved to live.

"Mine is fourteen. She plays Xbox and wears black all the time." He laughed. "I don't know what to do with her."

"Fourteen is a difficult age." Angela's voice, caring. "Could just be a phase she's going through."

"I hope so. My boy, Isaac, he's ten. He's a good boy."

A black Hummer appeared above the driveway. The leader looked at it as it slowly approached, then walked toward the man with the rifle aimed at Angela. He went out of the frame, and I picked him up on the other camera. He held out his hand to the man he called Max. The man dropped his right hand from his gun, put it in his pocket, and pulled out the necklace and handed it to the leader.

The leader walked over to the Hummer, which was now parked in front of the house. I picked him up on the other camera. The driver's door opened, and the leader handed the necklace to the driver, who had a laptop on his lap. The driver fiddled with the pendant and removed the mini flash drive from it. He attached it to a mini-USB port and typed rapidly on the computer keyboard. His hands stopped, and he appeared to be reading the laptop's screen. He then looked at the leader and said something in Russian. The leader frowned and waved his hand at the man.

The driver pounded the keyboard again and waited some more. He then pinched his lips together and shook his head. The leader spun from the car and glared up at Angela.

"We have a problem." His voice sharp and serrated.

CHAPTER 55

"WHAT?" TERROR IN Angela's voice.

The leader snapped his fingers to the driver of the SUV and held out his hand. The driver snatched the mini flash drive from the computer and gave it to the leader. He turned and faced Angela, then held up the drive between his thumb and index finger.

"This doesn't have the real keys. They are fake." He threw the flash drive down onto the driveway and yelled. "Why did you give me fake keys? You think I'm stupid?"

"No! No! Billy gave them to me." Her voice a shriek. "He told me they were the keys and to hold onto them! I swear!"

"Come downstairs and open the door right now!"

"I didn't know! I swear!"

"Open the door or we'll drive right through it. Your choice."

I scrambled up the staircase to the first room on the right. The door was open and I could see Angela's back as she stood out on the deck. I crept inside over to the open sliding glass door.

"What are you going to do? I didn't know!"

"We are going to search the house." The leader's voice now coming from below the deck outside.

"Angela." I whispered from just outside the door to the balcony. Her neck tensed. "Don't look at me."

"You have ten seconds." The leader below.

"Tell them okay, then come inside." I hissed a whisper.

"Okay. I'm coming downstairs. Please wait!"

She turned and dashed into the room.

"Lock the door after I leave, then get in the bathtub." Still whispering.

I hustled out of the room and down the stairs. I checked the video boxes on the computer screen on the chair. The leader stood fifteen feet away from the front door, slightly off to the right. He held his suppressed assault rifle across his chest, the barrel pointed in the direction of the front door. Max was approaching the door from the left, twenty feet away.

I limped over to the front door and crouched down a few inches to stay under the front door's windows. I unlocked the door and eased out the deadbolt. It made a slight squeak that neither man seemed to hear. Max stepped up onto the porch. His rifle raised to his shoulder and pointed at the door.

Shit.

Did he plan to shoot Angela as soon as she opened the door, or was he in a defensive posture? Or just a show of force to scare her? They wouldn't kill Angela right away. They'd torture her to see what she knew first. He was posturing.

I had one chance. He'd expect to see Angela right in the middle of the doorframe when she opened the door. She wouldn't be there.

One more check of the computer screen. The men hadn't moved.

Then, a miracle. A gift from God. Max took his finger off the trigger of his rifle and raised his right hand to knock on the door.

I stood to the left side of the door and reached my left hand across and rested it on the doorknob, my right arm and elbow at ninety degrees, gun pointed at the ceiling. A pounded knock from outside.

I whipped the door open with my left hand and aimed the Ruger at Max's face with my right. His eyes wide as he snapped his right hand back to his rifle. I pulled the trigger twice.

The house echoed the concussions and blood tattooed my glasses and right cheek. Max fell dead across the threshold of the door as I was already firing at the leader. He ran to the left and two explosions from my gun missed him. Max's body lay on the floor in front of me, half in and half out of the house. His assault rifle pinned underneath him.

I had to get the rifle and shut the door.

One more shot toward the leader who ran behind the garage. Empty. The Hummer's ignition cranked over and it burned rubber, spitting out of the driveway. I slammed the Ruger in my shoulder holster and bent over Max's body. Blood pooled around what was left of the back of his head and enveloped my shoes.

I grabbed his body under the shoulders and pulled him toward me. An inch at a time. The rifle strapped around his shoulder scraping along under him. A big man, in all his gear he had to weigh over two-fifty. I took a step back for leverage, slipped on blood, and my bad ankle collapsed under me, sending me on top of Max's body. My head broke the threshold of the door. Three muted snaps and three bullet holes in the door.

Someone was on the left shooting a suppressed assault rifle at me. I shimmied backwards off the body as fast as I could. Three more snaps as I cleared the door back inside the house.

Shouts in Russian outside. I grabbed the Ruger and a speed loader from my holster, snapped open the cylinder, and emptied the shells onto the marble floor. I slid the five bullets anchored by the speed loader into the slots in the cylinder, pressed the back of the loader to release them, and pushed the cylinder shut.

A quick look at the computer. The leader and the new gunman, rifles shouldered, were advancing from either side of the door, both about fifty feet away. I stayed back from the door and fired the Ruger toward the right where the leader was advancing. I couldn't see him from my post and wasn't worrying about trying to hit him. I was trying to slow him and the other assassin down and make as much noise as possible.

I snuck up to the door and stuck my hand out around to the right and fired off the last three rounds, then pulled my hand back inside. Empty. Five left in the other speed loader.

I grabbed the dead man's hands, pulled, and backpedaled as fast as I could, eating the pain from my ankle. Grunts from me and the scraping of the rifle under the body. I strained, backing up, and felt his feet clear the threshold. One more yank backwards to clear him from the path of the door. I dropped his arms, sped to the door, slammed it, and bolted it.

I rolled Max's body over onto its back, freeing the rifle underneath. A hole where his left eye used to be and another one just inside his hairline above his forehead. Him or me.

His M4 carbine had a smear of blood along it where it had slid along the floor. I wiped it off on my pants and cleaned the blood off my glasses with my shirt.

I checked the weapon. It was set on automatic with three round bursts with each pull of the trigger. That worked for what I needed. Rapid stopping power and death. The chamber held a cartridge. I released the magazine and looked inside. It looked to be full, probably less the cartridge in the chamber. Each cartridge spring loaded to the top of the magazine after the one above it is racked into the chamber of the rifle. So, to get a precise count, you'd have to unload the magazine and count the bullets. I didn't have time for that, but the weight of the magazine felt like it was full. The magazine looked standard and probably held thirty rounds. I clicked the magazine back into place.

I searched Max's cargo pants for more magazines but didn't find any. Thirty rounds in the M4 magazine and five more bullets for the Ruger. Thirty-five rounds might be enough. I said a prayer in my head that they would be.

CHAPTER 56

IN MY SEARCH through the dead man's clothes for more ammo, I found a wallet. I checked his driver's license. California. Maximillian Sascha Antonov. Thirty-seven years old. Resided in Los Feliz in Los Angeles. There was a plastic photo flap in the middle of the wallet. I didn't look at any of the pictures. I didn't want to know if the man I just killed had children waiting for him at home.

I'd done what I had to. It had been him instead of me. God rest the souls of his family, if he had one.

I unscrewed the six-inch-long steel cylinder off the end of the rifle's barrel. I wanted noise. A lot of it.

The roar of the SUV outside, coming fast. I broke away from the door toward the staircase. Two steps up, an explosion behind me. I turned and swiveled the rifle up to my shoulder. The front door flew all the way through the foyer into the living room, and the Hummer skidded to a stop three-quarters of the way inside the house.

The airbags in the front of the SUV had all blown. A ruffle behind one in the driver's seat. I fired a burst of three rounds through the passenger-side window. The booms echoed inside the house and my head. Missed. The driver had already escaped out his door on the other side of the vehicle.

I backed up the staircase with the rifle shouldered and pointed at the SUV, readying for an all-out assault. My ankle making the backward climb wobbly and painful.

Suddenly, a cannister tumbled through the hole where the door used to be along the floor. I spun and hopped up the last two steps of the staircase, closed my eyes, and dove behind the mattress. An atomic bomb and a flash so bright I could see it with my eyes closed.

A flashbang.

Ringing in my ears against a vacuum of numbed silence. No sound at all but the ringing. Movement behind the SUV. A gun barrel appeared at the front bumper. Thump-thump-thump into the side of the mattress. Only vibration, no sound.

I rolled my body over to the other side of the mattress, came set, and pulled the trigger of the M4, letting loose three rounds at the figure next to the bumper of the SUV, then ducked behind the flat mattress. Three, four more thumps in return into the mattress.

Four men left with at least four times the ammunition I had. Even with the high ground, I couldn't last forever.

A barrage of thumps into the mattress. A dozen. More. They were coming. I had to hold my position. If I retreated, I'd lose my advantage, and Angela and I would die.

I snapped the rifle around the left side of the mattress and saw another assassin charging up the stairs. His gun aimed at me. We fired at the same time. Three from me. Thump, thump from him. I hit him in the upper chest of his flak jacket. He staggered backwards and tumbled down the stairs. Spits from the Hummer's hood sizzled past me. I fired at the shooter and lunged to my left. He ducked down behind the Hummer.

The man on the staircase raised his head as he tried to get up. I pulled the trigger and sent three more missiles. A cry that penetrated the silence ringing in my ears.

Neck shot. He'd be out of action, even if he survived.

A singe along the left side of my forehead. I rolled back behind the mattress, then popped up and fired at the SUV and dropped back down. I caught a glimpse of a man crouched behind the hood of the SUV before I ducked down. The leader.

If I could take him out, I might be able to end the firefight. I still had the high ground. They had to come to me, but I was running out of bullets. They didn't know that. I hoped.

First, assess the damage to my body.

The side of my head stung, but I was pretty sure the bullet had only grazed me. No penetration of my skull. I touched my head above my ear. Blood, warm and thick. I ran my left index finger along the furrow in my hair. Bloody, painful, but not fatal or too debilitating. Head wounds bled a lot, but I wasn't in danger of bleeding out or passing out from blood loss. The blood would soon start to clot.

I wiped the blood from my wound on my pants and waited for the next assault. The longer they waited, the dicier it got for them. Hopefully, someone had heard the echo of my unsuppressed gunshots and alerted the Sheriff's Office. Maybe squad cars were coming from Claire Timmins's house. The men below had to fear that the police might be on the way down the dead-end street.

Two more quick thumps into the mattress and a hole in the wall of the landing. This time I could hear the suppressed clap of the assault rifle discharging the rounds. My hearing was coming back.

From my prone position, I lifted the M4 above the mattress and let go another three rounds to try to force the killers to cover. The kick from the weapon, without my shoulder behind it, almost knocked the M4 out of my hands.

"Hey. Cahill." The leader's voice from below. The same voice I'd heard outside my room last night. "You're bleeding, aren't you? How long can you last? No help is on the way. We've got a first aid kit in the

Hummer. We can stitch you up and make sure you live to see your family again."

He knew who I was and enough about me to try to leverage what he knew.

I stayed silent, listening with my improving hearing for the sound of advancement. Nothing yet.

"Don't be greedy, Cahill. Two hundred thirty million is enough to split among all of us. We'll even cut the girl in if you want. Is she your mistress? You have nice taste."

No sound of advancement.

"Maybe you don't have the keys, huh? Is that it? Just came up here as the night in shining armor to save the woman in the high castle? If that's the case, let's talk. We'll get you stitched up and send you on your way. We only want to talk to the girl and search the house. That's all we were ever going to do until you killed Max."

No emotion in his voice. He was lying. And he probably knew that I knew. I listened for movement during his silence. No advancement.

"That was pretty cold-blooded, Rick. In fact, cold-blooded murder. But we can keep it to ourselves. Max's death was the price of doing business. He'd understand. We just want to finish the job and go home. No one else gets hurt. So why don't you put your hands on top of your head, stand up, and leave your guns there, then walk down the stairs so we can move forward?"

I strained to hear movement from below. Nothing.

Was he stalling or rushing? Worried about the police coming and desperate to end this quickly or talking to distract me? Was the cavalry coming? His or mine? Where was the man I'd seen on the hillside?

Maybe I was the one who was running out of time. I was definitely running out of bullets. The ratio of the bullets I had left to bad guys would only get worse if more fake FBI agents arrived.

"Sheriff's deputies will be here any minute. They were already at Claire Timmins's house when I discovered her body. My shots outside echoed all over the mountain." I stayed behind the mattress. "Once they turn down Cerro Noroeste Road, you're blocked in. There's nothing here for you. Apparently Raskin gave Angela dummy keys to throw everyone off. Unless you or someone else killed him in the house on Cabrillo Avenue in La Jolla and burned his body, he killed someone else and did everything he could to make it look like he was the dead man. Angela was a dupe, just like the dead body in the house at La Jolla. We've all been duped. I'm good walking away. Right now."

"Almost a deal. We just want to talk to the girl and search the house." Fake joy in his voice. "Let's start with you leaving your guns on the mattress, putting your hands on your head, and walking down the stairs. Then we can all do what we have to and avoid the police."

"There's nothing here. You'd be wasting your time. But I'll make you the same deal. You both put your weapons down, walk to the middle of the room with your hands on your heads and kneel on the floor,, and Angela and I will leave. Then you can search the house all you want. You can start right now by helping your injured man at the bottom of the stairs."

"Petrov." The leader said something in Russian to the driver, who I couldn't see. A discussion ensued. By the tone, it sounded like the driver didn't want to do whatever the leader told him to. Finally, "Rick, Petrov is going to walk out with his hands up and kneel on the floor. Then I will."

"What about your injured man?"

"He's already dead. That's two for you."

"And the man on the hillside?"

"Artem? He'll come in after me. We have to be careful with you, Rick. You're a killer." A sick laugh.

"Send him out," I said from behind the mattress, then quietly pushed myself on my stomach to the other end of it.

The driver was the decoy. As soon as I popped my head up to confirm that he was on his knees in the middle of the floor, the leader would put a bullet in it. I had to be a moving target. And a target that was loaded. The leader was probably on the move, too. My guess was that he'd circle back outside around the Hummer and shoot at me from the left side of it, just inside from where the front door used to be. He'd probably be ten to fifteen feet to the right from where I'd last seen him. The instant it took for me to search for him would be enough time for him to pull the trigger.

The location of the man I'd seen on the hillside was unknown.

I'd lost count of my ammunition. I had maybe six bullets left in the M4. They had to find their target.

I popped my head and rifle over the mattress from my new position, saw the driver walking with his hands on his head to the middle of the foyer, then caught the barrel of a rifle peeking into the house on the left side of the hole in the wall.

The leader's rifle swung toward me, and I fired at him until my weapon clicked dry. The leader staggered back against the Hummer then stumbled out of the house. I dropped the M4, grabbed my Ruger from the shoulder holster, and skipped over to the staircase then hopped down it on one leg. Past the dead assassin, his eyes open, lying upside down off the bottom of the stairs. I snatched his M4 off the marble floor and hustled into the foyer.

"Don't shoot! Don't shoot!" The driver, now huddled on the floor in a ball with his head in his hands.

I shuffled over to the hole in the wall. A quick step and I swung the carbine around the corner. No leader. No fifth man. Only a small puddle of blood on the porch and a few drops beyond it. I must have hit the

Israeli in the shoulder above his flak vest or in the arm. Too bad I missed my target. His head.

He couldn't have gotten far. The sun had already disappeared behind the mountains and night was falling like a curtain. I retreated back into the house.

The driver's eyes slid from the massive window that looked out over the deck to me. Eyes wide. The window exploded, and I dove under the SUV. The fifth man. He must have used a rope to climb up onto the deck. The window deflected his shot just enough to save my life.

He sprayed the front of the Hummer. The right front tire burst, and the Hummer dropped lower. I spat three rounds out from underneath the SUV and shimmied out from under it on the left side.

Movement behind the sofa straight ahead in the living room. The driver sprang up from behind the sofa and fired his rifle. I fired mine first. Another burst of three rounds. The top of his head split open, and he collapsed onto the floor.

I crouched down and tried to listen beyond the ringing in my ears. The fifth man was missing. I peeked under the Hummer and saw the flash of one boot moving toward the back of the vehicle.

I spun around and fired right as the man broke toward me from behind the Hummer. Three rounds to his armored chest and the gun emptied just as hot searing pain punched my left shoulder. The jolt almost knocked me down. I dropped the rifle and pulled my Ruger from my shoulder holster as the man staggered from the shots to his body armor. He righted himself and brought the rifle back up to his shoulder. Ten feet away, one chance. I pulled the trigger of the Ruger. The last bullet in the gun hit the man below his right eye. He crumbled to the floor.

Blood rolled down my left arm. The pain in my shoulder clenched my teeth together in a tight grimace. I looked down at the fifth man.

Eyes wide. His mouth puckered like a fish out of water. Blood collected underneath his head and started to spread.

Him or me.

Gunsmoke hung in the air like an acrid fog.

I stumbled over to the Hummer and searched for the first aid kit the leader claimed was inside it. A camo backpack in the back seat. I grabbed it and opened it. A blue plastic first aid kit inside. I pulled it out and staggered to the staircase. The room grew dark, and the walls closed in on me.

"Angela!" I yelled and tripped over the dead man at the bottom of the stairs and fell onto the staircase. "You can come out now! It's safe. I need your help."

My voice faded on the last few words. I rolled over onto my back on the stairs. The ceiling pressed in on me. The room dimmed to darkness.

Krista looked down at me. Her baby blue eyes impossibly big. "Dadda?"

CHAPTER 57

THE FACE I woke up to wasn't Krista's. It belonged to FBI Special Agent Dennis Sorensen. He stared down at me from the foyer of the Sterlingshire house. He was crouched like a catcher behind home plate. The chandelier overhead was on. I didn't know what time it was or how long I'd been lying on the floor. Or how I'd gotten from the staircase to the floor next to the chair with the laptop on it and next to my putter cane.

Sorensen ran his eyes over my shirtless torso.

Had the calvary really come?

"Jesus, your body looks like a scarred battlefield," Sorensen said. "We've got an ambulance on the way."

I didn't say anything. My shoulder still burned. I glanced at it and was surprised. It had been wrapped with gauze and some type of bandage underneath. Blood had seeped through, but it looked tacky, like it was starting to clot. My shirt, sliced in half, was on the floor next to me. Somebody had patched me up.

"Did you bandage me?" I asked.

"No. You were like this when we found you."

Angela? But, where was she now? I shifted my head to my right and saw another head looking down at me. Special Agent Charlene Bowden, bent over at the waist.

"Where's Angela Albright?" Bowden asked.

"I don't know where she is." For once, I was being 100 percent honest with law enforcement. I glanced at my shoulder. "I assume she bandaged me up, but I don't remember her doing it."

I thought of the ambulance on the way. Then thought again. How could they call an ambulance when there was no cell phone service at the house or within a mile of it?

"There's a lot of dead people here, Rick." Sorensen staring down at me. Some grit in his voice. "Must be a hell of a story, but without Angela to give your side, things may not go that well for you with the local police or with us if we have to get involved."

"I honestly don't know where Angela is." I studied the faces of the two FBI Special Agents. Flat expressions except for their eyes. Malice, staring to get free. "When do you think that ambulance is going to get here?"

Sorensen and Bowden side glanced each other.

"Could take a long time, Rick. A long time." Bowden, play acting over. "Now why don't you make it easy on yourself and tell us where Angela is?"

Bowden and Sorensen had fooled John Mallon and apparently the Special Agent in Charge at FBI Headquarters in Sorrento Valley, but now the game was up. They were who I feared they were. Malignant and still trying to steal the pot of gold.

"I don't know where she is. I got shot, passed out, and woke up like this. But if you're looking for the keys to the BitChange transactions, she doesn't have them. The ones she had were fake."

"What do you mean?" Sorensen, raw anger. His face clenched into a fist.

"Raskin gave her a necklace with a mini flash drive in it with fake keys. The dead guy over by the sofa checked it in his computer for the crew's leader, and they didn't work."

"It's too late for lies, Rick. That ambulance might never get here." Bowden.

"I'm telling you the truth." Desperation leaked out in my voice. "Go out onto the driveway and look for the flash drive. The leader threw it down when he found out the keys were fake. The evidence is out there. Raskin gave her the fake keys in a necklace. My guess is whoever burned up in the house in La Jolla without teeth or fingertips wasn't Theodore Raskin. He duped everyone, including Angela."

Another shared side glance from the two heads above me. Something malevolent passed between them. I could see it in their eyes.

Sorensen put a blue nitrile–gloved hand on his thigh and glared down at me. I hadn't noticed he'd been wearing gloves before. A quick glance at Bowden. Gloves. Shit.

Gloves because they didn't want to contaminate a crime scene? Or for some other reason. They were already in the middle of a crime scene. There weren't any EMTs hovering over me. And there wouldn't be.

I was the reason for the gloves.

Sorensen thrust his right hand down onto my bandaged shoulder and squeezed. A shock of lightning exploded throughout my torso. I yelled and grabbed his arm with my right hand. He took hold of my arm with his free hand and Bowden teamed up. They pulled my hand off him and he continued to squeeze.

"Where's Angela?" His eyes went darker still and he squeezed harder.

The pain in my shoulder vibrated throughout my entire body. I screamed through clenched teeth. Sorensen and Bowden stared down at me, the corners of their mouths edged upward.

Movement behind the two bent special agents. Sergei Volkov's enormous head appeared as Sorensen continued to squeeze my shoulder. I screamed louder as Volkov watched, unnoticed by my torturers. His eyes blank, lips in a straight line. He watched me scream for another ten seconds.

"That's enough," Sergei spoke, and the special agents stepped back from me. Unsurprised. Unworried. They were working together. From the start.

A wall of pain opened up inside me worse than anything Sorensen and Bowden had done to me. Worse than anything anyone could ever do to me.

My email recording to Leah and Krista would never arrive. My phone would be buried in the same hole that I was. No cell reception from three feet underground up in the hidden mountains of Pine Mountain Club. Leah and Krista would never know my last thoughts before I died were about them. And they'd never know what happened to me.

I'd just be erased.

"He's telling the truth." Sergei walked to within three feet of the special agents, revealing a man behind him. One of the men who'd been with him inside my house. The one who'd checked my phone. "He would have already told you if he did. He is American. He doesn't know real pain."

Sergei turned his head and nodded at his bodyguard.

The man made a quick sidestep, whipped up his hand. A silenced handgun was in it. The gun spit four shots out in a second. Sorensen and Bowden dropped straight down like weighted ragdolls.

Four headshots. Dead before they hit the floor.

"They failed." Sergei's oil barrel baritone.

"But they got you out of prison early," I said. The pain in my shoulder and the pain of my anonymous fate crashed into each other. I was still prone on the floor in the foyer. Twenty feet from the Hummer that made its own carport out of the Sterlingshire house entrance. The driver with the key fob lay dead fifteen feet from the Hummer. I'd never be able to get to him, grab the fob, and start the Hummer before the assassin shot me in the head.

I'd have to make my stand right there in the foyer. Unarmed and severely injured. The wound in my left shoulder was bleeding again. Shock was already closing in from the pain.

I wanted to live, but that looked impossible. I prayed to God, not for my life. He'd given me that back when he gave me Leah and Krista. I prayed for their lives. And that I'd die within range of a cell phone tower so that they would know I was thinking of them right to the end.

The only chance I had was time. That somehow Angela had gotten far enough away to get cell service and called 911. Maybe she'd taken my car and driven away. I slowly slid my right hand down along my pants to the outside of my pocket.

And felt the outline of my key chain. Shit. Maybe she'd fled on foot.

Sergei pointed his head to the door, then looked back at me. The bodyguard yelled out the front door in Russian.

My life's clock ticked down.

"Was the body in the house on Cabrillo Avenue Raskin?" Talk was all I had left. And pain. "He didn't give Angela the real keys. If he's not the dead guy, he took off with 230 million dollars and is in the wind. If he is dead, who knows where the money is? All I know is that it's not here."

I pushed my body up to a sitting position against the wall with my good leg. Away from the bodies of FBI Special Agents Sorensen and Bowden. Disgraced and dead. A long way from when they'd probably joined the FBI with stars and stripes in their eyes. Something turned sour inside them, and now they'd end up in the same hole in the ground as me. Or maybe we'd all be left to rot inside Theodore Raskin's mountainside mansion.

"You killed four of my men." No inflection. A simple statement.

Four. That must mean the Israeli leader of the fake FBI SWAT team wasn't dead outside on the driveway. The count didn't matter to Sergei. The fact that I'd killed them did.

"It wasn't personal. It was them or me."

Sergei took a couple steps forward and loomed over me. His body-guard, just outside his left shoulder. His gun down at his side.

"Da. Business is not personal." A flicker in Sergei's coal black eyes that scared me more than the assassin with the silencer next to him. "Family is personal."

Another step too quick for a man his size and he kicked me in my testicles. All the air shot out of me, and my body twisted into a knot. I rolled over onto my side in vice-squeezing pain and vomited up my last meal.

My last meal ever.

I heard a whimper over my closed-eyed hyperventilation. I opened my eyes and saw Angela crying next to the Hummer. The man who'd put a gun to my head in my house three nights ago held her by the arm. She hadn't escaped. No call to the police.

No rescue on the way. No email to Leah and Krista. Only hidden, anonymous death.

Sergei bent down over me. My hands clamped against my crotch, too late for the first assault.

"I talked to Peter Stone today." Sergei sliced off the words.

Stone dead. One less cavalryman on the way. Not that he'd be riding to my rescue. Unless he knew I'd found Angela and, in his mind, the keys to the BitChange exchange transactions.

I didn't say anything. My ploy for time was futile. I didn't know the exact time, but I figured it had to be over an hour since I shot my Ruger .357 out the door. If anyone reported the gunshots, Kern County Sher-iff's Deputies would have arrived by now. Even way up in the moun-tains, an hour was enough time.

Stone was dead. No one reported the gunshots. The cops weren't coming.

No one was.

CHAPTER 58

SERGEI'S BALD, CONCRETE brick of a head pushed down at me. His black eyebrows pointed at my face.

"Stone traded me something for his life."

I didn't know whether to believe him. It didn't matter. I had nothing to trade. All I had was one last Hail Mary to try to get a message out to my family before I died.

"I've got copies of keys to batches of transactions in my room at the Pine Mountain Inn. Not all of them, but they're worth thirty million dollars." Still trapped. Still in pain. But still alive. And my putter-cane just within reach. "That's what I have to trade for my and Angela's lives."

If I could get them to drive me to Pine Mountain Inn, my email to my family would be set free.

"Stop the games." Sergei's face now just eighteen inches from mine. "I know about Tatiana."

All the blood whooshed out of my face. Vertigo spiraled in my head. Shock was closing down my body.

More pain would start up. Soon.

"What?" I tried to form words. "What do you mean?"

"Don't play games. Stone told me. You killed my daughter." His voice, still devoid of emotion, but his eyes shone revenge. And cruelty.

"You will die tonight. In agony. But know that I will kill your family. Your wife. And your little girl in Santa Barbara. It's not business, it's personal."

He straightened back up and turned toward his bodyguard, who handed him the silenced Kimber Aegis 9mm. Sergei turned back to me and pointed the weapon at my face. I said the Lord's Prayer. There was no negotiating with Sergei. And God had already made his decision. Before I was born.

Sergei snapped the gun down at my left knee and pulled the trigger.

Searing pain exploded through my leg. A guttural howl burst from my lungs, and I grabbed what was left of my kneecap. Viscera and blood. I barely heard Sergei's voice over my own screams.

"Before you die, you will crawl across this floor and beg for your family's life." He aimed the Kimber at my other knee. "Did you make my daughter beg for her life?"

An explosion concussed the inside of the house. A geyser of blood sprayed Angela face. The man who'd been holding her collapsed. The remaining half of his head still gushing blood.

Angela screamed.

"Down!" Peter Stone emerged next to the Hummer and Angela dropped to her knees.

The bodyguard dove to his right and rolled. Sergei swung the Kimber at Stone just as Stone leveled his automatic shotgun at him. Sergei fired first. Three rapid pffts.

Stone fired a round that hit the ceiling as he stumbled backwards but stayed upright. The bodyguard sprang to his feet with a hidden gun in his hand and fired as Stone retreated backwards toward the hole in the entrance. Sergei kept firing.

I grabbed the putter and adrenalin-sprang on my good leg off the floor at Sergei. I swung the putter at his head. It connected above his temple and the putter head broke off the shaft and clattered along the floor. Sergei staggered but stayed up and turned toward me, still holding the gun.

Gunfire between Stone and the bodyguard echoed behind me.

Sergei fired as I hopped and dove at him with the jagged end of the broken putter shaft. His shot missed. The shaft didn't. It punched a hole in his tree trunk neck. Blood shot out at me. I hopped at him and thrust harder. His black eyes bulged, but he brought the gun up again.

I yanked the shaft from his neck and whipped it down on his wrist. The Kimber tumbled to the floor. I dropped down, grabbed the gun, and pulled the trigger until the pfft sounds stopped. There were only two, but both shots hit Sergei in the chest. The life drained out of his hollow black eyes.

He staggered. One hand on his neck. Blood oozing between his fingers. The other hand, red with blood against his chest. He fell to the floor. His head hitting it like a bowling ball on concrete.

The gunshots between Stone and the bodyguard had stopped. Both men lay prone on the floor. Angela screaming from under the Hummer. I rolled over to Special Agent Sorensen's body, worked his gun out of the pancake holster on his hip, and struggled up to vertical on my one good leg and the putter shaft.

The adrenalin ebbing from my body opened the door for the excruciating pain of my shattered kneecap. I fought it and dragged myself over to the bodyguard lying on the floor twenty feet away. He groaned and blinked and held the hole in his stomach. His Kimber K6s snub-nose conceal gun three feet from him on the floor. I picked it up. Its six-round cylinder empty. I put it in my pocket and limped away from the dying man.

By the time I got to Stone, Angela was pressing on his chest with a bandage from the first aid kit and crying. Her hands couldn't hold back the pumping blood. His face pale-gray. A trace of life left in his dead shark eyes.

I collapsed down next to him. Blood seeping from the mess of my kneecap.

"I had to draw him out." Stone's voice, a weak rattle. No hint of his once confident baritone. "Had to get him where I could find him and kill him. That's why I told him about Tatiana."

"Angela," I said. I looked at her crying over her father. The man who had saved us both. Or, at least her. I needed medical care soon. "You have to drive down where you can get reception and call 911."

She kept pressing her hands down on the blood-soaked bandage.

"Now!" I yelled. "It's the only chance he's got."

Stone was bleeding out. He couldn't move on his own, and I didn't have the strength to move him. Even with Angela's help. He'd die on the marble floor in a mountain mansion off the grid.

Angela getting help was the only chance I had. But I couldn't go with her and quicken my chances of getting help.

I wasn't going to let the man who saved my life three times die alone.

Angela shot up and started for the opening in the front of the house.

"Wait." I pulled out my phone and handed it to her. "Use this."

She took it and ran to her car.

Now, if I didn't make it, my family would know that I was thinking of them until the very end.

CHAPTER 59

"DID SHE HAVE the keys?" Stone, his voice a wet rasp.

A dying man's last wish. One last lie to tell Peter Stone.

"Yeah. She has the keys. All 230 million worth."

"Well, then she's going to be okay." A cough full of blood sprang out of his mouth. "I really did need that kidney. I guess not anymore."

He coughed some more blood. And some more. Then went still. Forever.

* * *

Eight hours later I woke up in Bakersfield's Mercy Hospital's recovery room. The surgeons there went through a gallon of B+ blood putting me back together. As best they could. The hope was that I'd be able to walk without a cane after months of rehabilitation.

The next time I woke up was in a private hospital room. Tubes sticking out of me and machines beeping next to me. And Leah staring down at me. Her mouth quivered and her sunrise ocean blue eyes shimmered with liquid. Her beauty in grief was stunning. And it made me ashamed.

"I can't keep standing over you in hospital rooms waiting for you to wake up." The liquid in her eyes broke free and ran down her cheeks.

"Because one of these times I'm standing over you, it won't be in a hospital. It will be in a morgue."

I raised my arm—the one that didn't have an IV sticking out of it—and tried to wipe the tears from her cheeks, but she turned her head away.

"I deleted your message." She roughly wiped the tears off her face. "I don't want Krista to ever hear a message like that. How could you do that to her. It's not fair to her . . . It's not fair to me."

"I didn't want either of you to think I'd abandoned you." Tears filled my own eyes. Not because of what happened to me. Because I'd failed the two most important people in my life and almost left them wondering what happened to me. "I didn't know if anyone would ever . . ."

"Find your body?" A sharp stab. "That you were afraid we'd never know what happened to you? Never have a gravesite to mourn you?"

I dropped my eyes. I couldn't look at her. "Yeah."

Neither of us said anything for a solid minute. Finally, Leah gently put her hand on top of mine. Barely touching. Still, it felt like a warm, snug, full body hug. I wanted to feel that touch again. Every day for the rest of my life.

"It hasn't been easy." A slight squeeze of her hand. "Krista talks about you the whole two weeks she's with me after she comes home from San Diego. In her little chirpy baby language. I don't know what she's saying but I sure hear 'Dada' a lot."

"She talks about you, too." I twisted my hand around to couple with hers. "I'm done. I'm selling the house as soon as I get back to San Diego. Then I'm moving up to Santa Barbara to be closer to Krista." Fear strangled my voice. The fear that I might never get back what I'd lost. "And closer to you. The only reason I'm still alive is that I had to see you and Krista one last time. The last week has changed me. Forever. I can't live without you and Krista in my life. And I can't die that way, either.

I need to see you both every day. Not every two weeks. I want to make our family whole again."

Leah brought her other hand up and gently squeezed mine with both of hers. "I'll be back in the morning. We'll talk some more then."

*   *   *

Moira came in after Leah left.

"I talked to a realtor friend of mine. She's ready to list your house as soon as you get back." She tugged a tear away from her eye. "You better invite me to Santa Barbara at least once a month."

"Twice." I touched her cheek.

Moira leaned down and kissed me on the forehead, then left.

*   *   *

The DNA from the body at Cabrillo Avenue was never identified. It wasn't in any known databases. However, Sterlingshire Inc.'s Keith Barent Johnson was reported missing soon after the body in the house on Cabrillo Avenue in La Jolla was found.

The FBI bust of a major Russian Mob ring in Los Angeles splashed across the headlines a month after I killed Sergei Volkov. His early release from prison benefited the Feds more than it did him. The FBI investigated BitChange and would have charged Theodore Raskin with fraud and embezzlement if he hadn't disappeared. He was never heard from again. However, rumors started circulating online about an American who was building a compound on a remote Fijian island.

EPILOGUE

A KNOCK ON the front door of our new house in Santa Barbara. Leah was in the kitchen making pancakes, Krista's favorite breakfast. And mine. I'd passed down the sweet tooth gene to my daughter. She was in the backyard playing with Midnight. With Moira playing referee. Just the fourth week in our new house and Moira's first visit.

We were a family. Whole again.

I started my own security consulting business in Santa Barbara, catering mostly to the uber wealthy in Montecito and a few businesses downtown. I hired independent contractors—mostly private investigators, some I knew from San Diego—as security for events and stayed out of the action myself. Not that there was much action. The pace in Santa Barbara was a lot slower than in San Diego. I was okay with that.

After months of physical therapy, my knee was workable, but I'd walk with a limp that would never go away. All in all, aside from occasional CTE complications, my life had settled down nicely.

The life I'd finally earned.

I limped to the door and looked through the peephole. A bearded FedEx driver wearing a company ball cap stood on the porch, looking down at a clipboard in his left hand. There was a large package on the ground near his feet. Leah must have ordered something online that needed to be signed for. Probably material for her interior design business. There were often packages arriving at the house.

"You expecting a package?" I said over my shoulder to Leah in the kitchen.

"Yes."

"It's a big one."

"It shouldn't be," Leah said as I turned and opened the door. Pots rattled in the kitchen behind me. "Rick, wait!"

The FedEx driver looked up and raised his right hand and pointed a gun in my face. The Israeli.

"This is for Tatiana and Sergei Volkov."

An explosion in my ear. Another.

The Israeli dropped, and I spun around and saw Leah. Tears in her eyes. My Colt Python in her hand. The one I kept hidden in a kitchen cabinet. Six other loaded handguns were hidden throughout the house, outside of Krista's reach. Waiting for a day like today.

The guns would still be hidden in place tomorrow. And all the tomorrows.

There might be more days just like today.

BOOK CLUB
DISCUSSION QUESTIONS

1. The title *Odyssey's End* sets readers up with the expectation that a long journey is coming to a close. What journeys, whether literal or metaphorical, have the characters taken during *Odyssey's End* or throughout the Rick Cahill series?

2. Rick was previously diagnosed with Chronic Traumatic Encephalopathy—CTE—in *Doomed Legacy* (Rick Cahill #9). Given what we know about Rick's personality, how are the symptoms of CTE—flashes of uncontrollable anger, memory problems—particularly difficult for Rick?

3. Father-daughter relationships are a recurring theme in *Odyssey's End*. What similarities and differences do you see in the relationships between Rick and Leah, Peter Stone and Angela Albright, Sergei Volkov and Tatiana, and Spence Landingham and Leah?

4. Peter Stone approaches Rick for help in part due to a terminal illness. How does Stone's condition mirror that of Rick himself?

Do you see irony in the fact that both men share this common bond?

5. Rick has proven himself a "lone wolf" throughout the entire Rick Cahill series, though he has created a small network of friends including Moira MacFarlane. What role does her friendship play for Rick? And what role do you think Rick may satisfy in Moira's own life?

6. We have seen Rick's loyal companion Midnight age over the course of the Rick Cahill series. What role has Midnight played in Rick's life? What significance do you give to the fact that Rick is a "dog person"?

7. *Odyssey's End* closes with a shocking act of violence from an unexpected source—Rick's wife, Leah. How do you think her actions will impact their family unit going forward, and how will Leah herself be altered?

8. Rick often ponders his decades-long battle against evil and sometimes questions his own morality. He has killed people in what he's considered preemptive self-defense. Do you think such actions are inherently evil? Or can you justify them as Rick does?

9. Do you think Rick will be happy in his new domesticated stage of life, or will the urge for another righteous quest threaten its longevity?

For more information about Matt Coyle and the Rick Cahill Series, visit his website at: mattcoylebooks.com.

PUBLISHER'S NOTE

We hope that you enjoyed *Odyssey's End*, the tenth novel in Matt Coyle's Rick Cahill PI Crime Series.

While the other nine novels stand on their own and can be read in any order, the publication sequence is as follows:

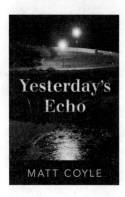

Yesterday's Echo (Book 1)

A dishonored ex-cop's desperate chance for redemption

"Coyle knows the secret: digging into a crime means digging into the past. Sometimes it's messy, sometimes it's dangerous—always it's entertaining."

—Michael Connelly,
New York Times best-selling author

Night Tremors (Book 2)
Powerful forces on each side of the law have Rick Cahill in the crosshairs

"Following an Anthony Award-winning debut isn't easy, but Matt Coyle slammed a homer. Hard, tough, humane—*Night Tremors* is outstanding"   —Robert Crais,
New York Times best-selling author

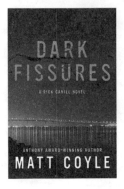

Dark Fissures (Book 3)

Hard-edged suspense with a heart for fans of
Robert Crais and Michael Connelly

"*Dark Fissures* is a roller coaster ride through the streets of
San Diego. Tightly plotted with memorable characters. An
outstanding read!"

—C. J. Box,
New York Times best-selling author

Blood Truth (Book 4)

Rick Cahill can't escape his past—or his father's

"Matt Coyle's protagonist, Rick Cahill, is haunted both by
the sins of his father and by his own mistakes—but he's
driven to find the truth, no matter where it takes him, and
that's what makes this story so compelling. Coyle is the real
deal, and [*Blood Truth*] is the best PI novel I've read in years,
period."

—Steve Hamilton,
New York Times best-selling author

Wrong Light (Book 5)

Rick Cahill defies all limits in his quest for truth

"With *Wrong Light* Matt Coyle is on top of his game and
Rick Cahill ascends to the top ranks of the classic private
eyes. Coyle knows the secret: digging into a crime means
digging into the past. Sometimes it's messy, sometimes it's
dangerous—always it's entertaining. You'll find all of that
and more in this great read."

—Michael Connelly,
New York Times best-selling author

Lost Tomorrows (Book 6)
Perfect for hard-boiled PI fans who like a tainted hero living by his own code

"Sharp, suspenseful, and poignant, *Lost Tomorrows* hits like a breaking wave and pulls readers into its relentless undertow. Matt Coyle is at the top of his game."

—Meg Gardiner,
Edgar Award–winning author

Blind Vigil (Book 7)
Rick Cahill defies all limits in his quest for truth

"Southern California has turned out its fair share of thriller and noir superstars—some of them transplants, of course, before making their names on the west coast—such as Michael Connelly, Robert Crais, T. Jefferson Parker, James Ellroy, Raymond Chandler, and Ross Macdonald. Matt Coyle is quickly writing himself onto that list."

—*New York Journal of Books*

Last Redemption (Book 8)
Rick Cahill's chance to finally be a father is threatened by an insidious disease and trained killers as he races to save his best friend's son

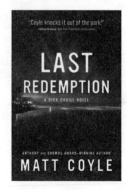

"Rick Cahill is on another thrill ride of a twisty mystery, but this time it's far more personal—he's looking for his best friend's son amid a backdrop of murder and high-stakes medical research. Just when you think Coyle has reached the top of his game—he does one better."

—Allison Brennan,
New York Times best-selling author

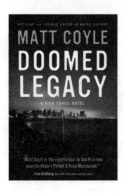

Doomed Legacy (Book 9)

A sinister private detective agency, a shady shell corporation, and a dead friend—Rick Cahill is on his most dangerous mission yet

"Matt Coyle is the rightful heir to the PI crown worn by Robert Parker & Ross Macdonald."

—Lee Goldberg,
New York Times best-selling author

We hope that you will read the entire Rick Cahill PI Crime Series and will look forward to more to come.

If you liked *Odyssey's End*, we would be very appreciative if you would consider leaving a review. As you probably already know, book reviews are important to authors and they are very grateful when a reader makes the special effort to write a review, however brief.

For more information, please visit the author's website:
mattcoylebooks.com

Happy Reading,
Oceanview Publishing